The Ashen Knight™

By Robert Barrett, Bruce Baugh, Richard E. Dansky
and Wendy L. Gash

And does all this frighten religious terror
In panic from your heart? Does the great fear
Of death depart, and leave you comforted?
What vanity, what nonsense! If men's fears,
Anxieties, pursuing horrors, move,
Indifferent to any clash of arms,
Untroubled among lords and monarchs, bow
Before no gleam of gold, no crimson robe,
Why do you hesitate, why doubt that reason
Alone has absolute power? Our life is spent
In shadows, and it suffers in the dark.

– Lucretius, *De rerum natura*
(trans. by Rolfe Humphries)

Credits

Authors: Robert Barrett (The Chivalrous World, Knights Famous and Infamous), Bruce Baugh (Cainite Knights, Templars, The Order of the Bitter Ashes, Road of Chivalry, Arms, Templates), Richard E. Dansky (Introduction, The Chivalrous World), Wendy L. Gash (Knightly Orders, Knightly Things)

Additional Material: Philippe R. Boulle

Developers: Philippe R. Boulle and Richard E. Dansky

Editor: John Chambers

Art Director: Richard Thomas

Layout & Typesetting: Pauline Benney

Intern: Abby Woodward

Interior Art: Guy Davis, Charles Dougherty, Patrick Lambert, Vince Locke

Front Cover Art: William O'Connor

Front & Back Cover Design: Pauline Benney

Special Thanks

The developer wishes to thank Pierre H. Boulle and Wendy L. Gash for last-minute help and quote-hunting and Richard E. Dansky for many questions answered.

735 PARK NORTH BLVD.
SUITE 128
CLARKSTON, GA 30021
USA

For a free White Wolf catalog call 1-800-454-WOLF.

Check out White Wolf online at

http://www.white-wolf.com; alt.games.whitewolf and rec.games.frp.storyteller

PRINTED IN THE UNITED STATES.

Contents

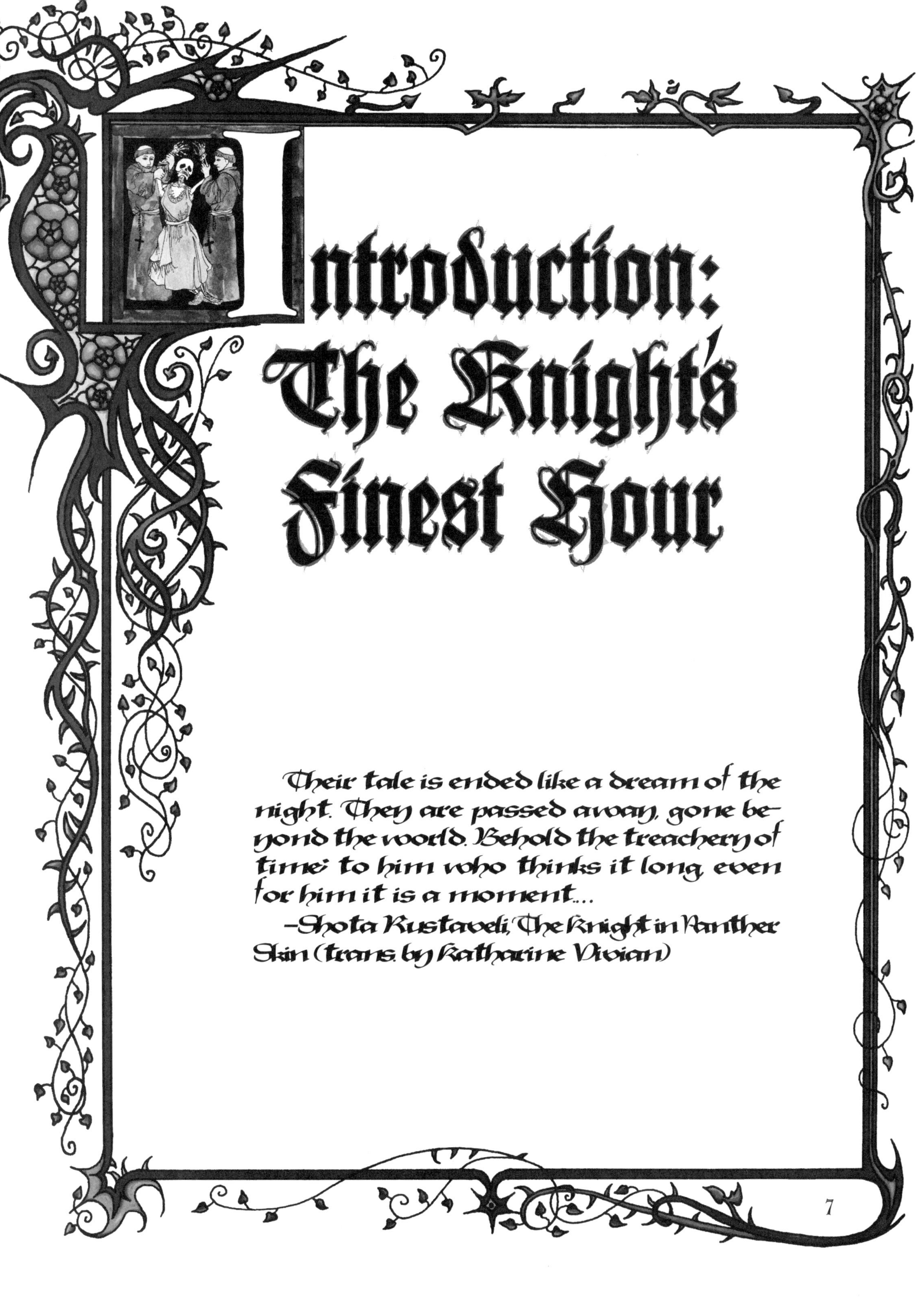

Introduction: The Knight's Finest Hour

Their tale is ended like a dream of the night. They are passed away, gone beyond the world. Behold the treachery of time: to him who thinks it long, even for him it is a moment...

—Shota Rustaveli, The Knight in Panther Skin (trans. by Katharine Vivian)

Few figures stride forth from the pages of history with more majesty, more presence and more power than that of the knight at arms. For centuries, the image of the lone knight clad in shining armor, riding forth to joust or battle, has fired the imagination of millions. Indeed, to many, that image personifies the so-called Dark Ages and is a symbol of hope in a dark and lawless time.

The truth of the matter, of course, is somewhat messier. From the British Isles to wind-swept Outremer, knighthood is a chancy, expensive and dangerous thing. It's not all plate mail and damsels' favors — as a matter of fact, it isn't about plate mail at all in 1197. Still, in most cases, it's better to be a knight than not to be one. It's just a very different experience than what a modern reader might expect.

That brings us to the heart of **The Ashen Knight**. This is a guide to chivalry and knightly characters for **Vampire: The Dark Ages**. It is a guide to working things knightly and chivalric into a chronicle, a reference for creating characters with knightly background or influences and a resource for the Storyteller. It is not the be-all and end-all of information on knighthood, but it has everything you need to use knights in your chronicle, either as characters or antagonists.

How To Use This Book

This book is both a Storyteller and a player resource. While some Storytellers may wish to restrict players' access to some of the material (particularly the chapter about the Order of the Bitter Ashes), most of the book is intended for wide use. Hopefully, players will take the historical and cultural information into account when creating knightly characters (or characters who control or oppose knights), while Storytellers will find it a useful resource for creating believable and enjoyable chronicles.

How Not To Use This Book

The Ashen Knight is not a history textbook. While the information on knighthood's history and culture is accurate, this book is about creating characters and telling stories about those characters. With that in mind, the book does on occasion tip its hat to knightly romance, the chansons de geste and other fictions that have shaped our thoughts on what a story about knights ought to be. Certainly, the material provided allows a Storyteller to do as grim and gritty a chronicle of hardscrabble knighthood as one would wish, but at the same time, the book is intended to allow Storytellers and players to ascend into the realms of knightly romance and chivalric epic, should they so chose. **The Ashen Knight** is a resource for creating chronicles about knights for the sake, not of recreating history, but rather of creating interesting chronicles. Hewing to absolute historical accuracy tends to leave the vampires out, after all.

Vampires

The point of **The Ashen Knight** is, after all, vampires. However, it is not just a book about "how to play a vampire who is also a knight." Rather, its purview is the interaction between Cainites and chivalry. That certainly includes characters who are vampire knights (Embraced before or after earning their spurs), but it also covers Cainites who sponsor or otherwise control knights, the Road of Chivalry, the ways in which vampiric knights can still carry out their duties and maintain their reputations, the history of knighthood (and vampires' effects on it) and more. The book is about vampires *and* chivalry, not just vampires who follow chivalry. The difference is all-important.

Cainites and Chivalry

As far as most Cainites are concerned, chivalry is a babe in the philosophical woods — a barely nascent system of belief about the proper relationship between faith and war. Many elders look down upon it as human clap-trap and look back to their own days of fighting with or against Rome for a more viable example. These princes and warlords of the night often disdain dealing with kine as more than prey and scoff at their pretense of divine favor. Chivalry is only a concern in that it encourages some mortals to seek out "devil-spawn" to hunt in quest of righteous glory.

Some more resourceful princes and ancillae see this new development in human thought as potentially useful. Bonds of fealty might well be helpful in reining in younger neonates and maintaining some influence in mortal courts. Knowing what qualities mortals now prize is essential if one wishes to move among them unseen, after all. These Cainites move in chivalrous circles as many others do in the church, paying lip service to mortal belief and using mortals institutions to their own ends.

Chapters One and Three, which detail mortal chivalry and knightly orders, along with Cainite doings around them, deal most directly with these Cainites.

Ashen Knights

Cainites who consider themselves knights are a special and still-rare lot. They are not just vampires who wear armor and ride horses; there have been night warriors of that ilk for centuries. No, these Cainites believe in the newly developed (and still evolving) chivalrous ideals and spend much of their existence trying to reconcile them with the Curse of Caine. This is a hard road indeed, but some have found it to be an effective way to suppress the Beast and give meaning to an eternity of darkness. Almost all these knights are neonates who came to admire knights and knighthood in their breathing days. Many were even knights in life and now struggle to maintain their duties. Others never had a chance to attain knighthood in life and have translated some of the Curse's benefits into a new opportunity. Rarer still are those who have come to know chivalry after death, finding in it a way to deal with their immortality.

All these "ashen knights" share some attraction to and longing for humanity. Chivalry is a human development, born of the kine's amazing ability to spawn vibrant beliefs out of contradictions like righteous warfare. Often despite themselves, chivalrous Cainites keep going back to human tournaments, courts and battlefields in order to be close to the truly chivalrous. They see chivalry as a way to hold on to their humanity, and to them, it depends on remaining part of the human chain of fealty. Elders scoff at this, knowing that the centuries will grind down such idealism in the young, just as it has in them.

The difficulties of being a Cainite knight in mortal company have led to efforts to bring chivalrous models into more vampiric settings. Often, this just leads to princes who manipulate fealty to their advantage, but the proponents of chivalry have carved out some space of their own. Philosophically, the Via Equitum — the Road of Chivalry — is spreading and evolving, becoming a belief in reciprocal fealty rather than simple lordship. Proponents of chivalry have also established several small knightly orders — modeled on mortal counterparts — to allow Cainites to be knights in full measure, at least among their own kind. It remains to be seen whether this route will lead to a distancing from the human ideals of chivalry.

Chapter Two deals explicitly with chivalrous Cainites, while Cainite knightly orders appear in Chapters Three and Four.

Organization

Chapter One: The Chivalrous World presents an overview of the state of chivalry in 1197. This mortal movement is still very much in evolution, but holds sway in large parts of Western Europe and has spread with the Crusades. Although the chapter deals with human affairs, it also traces Cainite interactions with knights and knightly matters.

Chapter Two: Cainite Knights addresses the unique constraints and concerns of those vampires who wish to continue as or become knights. It explores how they can circumvent the limitations of the Curse, what roles they can play at court, and what motivates them to undertake such a difficult path.

Chapter Three: Knightly Orders details several of the prominent orders of knights in the Dark Medieval world. The Knights Templar, the Hospitalers and many other orders appear in these pages. The chapter also deals with some of the emergent Cainite orders.

Chapter Four: The Order of the Bitter Ashes details the most mysterious of the Cainite orders. With roots in antiquity, the Grail Knights move silently across Europe, searching for relics and helping the worthy. Some say they are blessed by God, but the truth — as in all things — is more complicated.

Chapter Five: Knightly Things provides additional advice and game mechanics for dealing with knights and

chivalrous matters in a **Vampire: The Dark Ages** chronicle. The process of creating a Cainite knight forms a large part of the chapter, but it also expands upon the Road of Chivalry, provides rules for weapon quality and several new Traits.

Appendix: Ill-Made Knights includes a roster of vampiric knights and ladies, including both ready-to-play templates and prominent Cainites.

Recommended Reading and Resources

Fortunately, there is a wealth of material available for the student of chivalry. Below are some of the most useful sources on knighthood, which may be helpful in conjunction with **The Ashen Knight**. Bear in mind that history, like any other human endeavor, is an imperfect exercise and that both the passage of centuries and the wishes of what might have been have dimmed our knowledge of knighthood. Take the sources below for what they're worth; in many cases the fictions will be at least as useful in creating a chronicle as the drier histories.

Chansons de Geste

Chanson de Roland and *Cantar del mio Cid* are both excellent examples. They're superb examples of knighthood in action before romance takes off and courtly love begins to influence the historical narrative. Both of these tell tales of the *Reconquista* and feature heroes of that historical process (Roland and El Cid, respectively). *Chanson de Roland* is more mythic in its style and portrays Saracens like unto hideous beasts. *Cantar del mio Cid*, on the other hand, is more realistic and much more even-handed in its treatment of Muslims.

French Romances

The French Romances are where the true legend of knighthood begins. Chrétien de Troyes' five romances put the Arthurian court into play and might well have had a great deal of influence on the needs and dreams of young French knights and barons. Indeed, in many ways de Troyes' romances are the wellspring of the Arthurian myth, and much of the Western popular imagination of knighthood flows from these texts. *Yvain* (also known as *The Knight with the Lion*) is probably the most central of the five, while *Erec and Enide* builds on the same narrative model but adds a great deal of information about marriage relations and what women do in knightly culture. *Lancelot* (or *The Knight in the Cart*) and *Perceval* (or *The Story of the Grail*) introduce more narrowly Arthurian stories. *Cliges* is Chrétien's "anti-Tristan" (a recurring motif in romances) and is useful for getting a sense of women's predicaments in this society.

A good follow-up to Chrétien are the lais of Marie de France. The lais are short, lovely narratives, most of which depict situations in which knights find themselves and their values put to the test. *Guigemar*, *Equitan*, *Yonec* and *Lanval* are perhaps the most useful, but the others are exceedingly brief and also well worth a look. One, entitled *Bisclavret*, is even about a werewolf.

German Romances

Gottfried von Strassburg's *Tristan* is probably the greatest version of the story of Tristan and Isolde. His retelling is also quite useful to the Storyteller looking for information on knightly behavior, as the text covers everything from displays of knightly skills in non-combat arenas to the problem of how to romance one's liege's wife while remaining loyal to one's liege.

Wolfram von Eschenbach's *Parzival* brings the Grail into play, along with questions of race (Parzival has a half-brother, Fierifiz, who's white with black spots). The text also touches on the Templars and the myth of the Fisher King, both of which can easily be woven into a Dark Ages chronicle.

Finally, there is the *Nibelungenlied*, better known to some in its operatic incarnation as Wagner's Ring Cycle. The work can best be described as what happens when the world of Teutonic epic (the poetry of clan and vendetta) runs headlong into the world of chivalric romance.

History and Culture

Among the best sources for medieval life in general are the books by Frances Gies. Of particular interest to fans of all things knightly (and presumably readers of this book) are *The Knight in History*, *Life in a Medieval Village* and *Life in a Medieval Castle*. The trio more or less covers every aspect of knightly existence, both glamorous and not.

Also highly recommended are Colin McEvedy's *The Penguin Atlas of Medieval History* and Maurice Keen's *Chivalry*, both of which are excellent, accessible and readily available sources. Finally, Storytellers may wish to consider *The Knight and Chivalry* by Richard Barber.

Knightly Orders

Books on the Crusades and the military orders have exploded in number over the last decade or so, making information on Outremer easy to find but harder to judge in quality. Monty Python alumnus Terry Jones's video series *The Crusades* is the most enjoyable introduction available, if only for the sight of Jones in full 11-century armor hiking past a great many bemused modern Turks (there's also a companion book for those unable to rent the videos). The names to reckon with in the field are Steven Runciman and Jonathan Riley-Smith, both of whom have a variety of histories and introductions to the Crusades available. Amin Maalouf's *The Crusades through Arab Eyes* is filled with anecdotes from the other side of the conflict, most of which register amazement at the inexplicable behavior of the iron-clad Franks. Templar fans will want to look at the work of Malcolm Barber (*The New Knighthood*, *The Trial of the*

Templars) and John Robinson (*Dungeon, Fire and Sword: The Knights Templar in the Crusades*).

Modern Fictions

There has been a positive flood of literature dealing with knights and matters of chivalry in recent years, and many players and Storytellers no doubt already have some sitting on their shelves. Some of the best include Guy Gavriel Kay's *Lions of al-Rassan* and *A Song for Arbonne*, Robert Shea's *All Things Are Lights* (which also deals with the Cathars) and John M. Ford's *The Dragon Waiting*. Fans of Arthuriana may get a surprising amount of inspiration from T.H. White's *The Once and Future King* (though avoid the Disney film of *The Sword in the Stone*, at least for these purposes).

Film also has its uses in portraying chivalry. Four of the best renditions are:

• **Henry V:** The version directed by Kenneth Branagh is much more useful than the Olivier version. While set well after the heyday of **The Ashen Knight**, the film's depiction of medieval warfare is excellent. The dialogue is, of course, Shakespearean, but the siege of Harfleur, the battle of Agincourt and the discussions in the French camp before the battle should prove inspirational to a Storyteller.

• **Flesh and Blood:** Directed by Paul Verhoeven, this is a grim, gritty, nasty, filthy and extremely useful look at, among other things, siege warfare and the Black Death. The film stars Rutger Hauer and Jennifer Jason Leigh and is not recommended for viewers of delicate sensibilities.

• **Ladyhawke:** Entirely fanciful, this other Rutger Hauer period piece nevertheless manages to convey a sense of chivalric romance. While there's precious little that's accurate about the film, it does set its mood and feel up very well.

• **Excalibur:** Directed by John Boorman, this film is a phantasmagoria of Arthurian legend and psychosexual imagery. Storytellers may want to check it out for its skillful weaving of myth, legend and bloody reality, or they may just want to kick back and enjoy the spectacularly staged battle scenes.

Chapter One: The Chivalrous World

He who achieves more is the more worthy.

– Geoffrey de Charny, the Livre de chevalrie

In 1197, the European knight is at the apogee of his career as a military and political force. Behind him lie the formative years of the 10th and 11th centuries, the time when he first rode against pagan invaders and threatened the Church with his unrestrained violence. In the more recent past is the newly mature period of the 12th century, an era in which all of chivalry's tenets finally come together. The golden age will not, cannot last forever, but at the moment, the knight is at the peak of his power, prestige and influence. **Vampire: The Dark Ages** and **The Ashen Knight** thus take place at a moment of transition for knighthood. Nothing is set in stone, and acts of courage, foolhardy or otherwise, echo throughout Christendom. It is chivalry's finest hour, a time of power and glory for the knighted class.

And where one finds power, one finds Caine's childer.

The Cainite Perspective

Cainites are naturally interested in and attracted to knights. Knights are both warriors and lords, wielding martial and political might. Such nexuses of power draw ambitious vampires like flies to honey, and the high courts and great tournament have their fair share of pale manipulators. This is not to say that Cainites *control* human knights and human courts. They traffic more in influence, carefully directing these potentially dangerous warriors away from their own schemes and toward their rivals. Used to the demands of battle and kingship, knights make excellent candidates for the Embrace, especially among the Ventrue and Lasombra.

Basic (and Flawed) Definitions

Concepts of chivalry and knighthood are very much in evolution in the 1197. The modern perception of cultural homogeneity across medieval Europe is seriously flawed, and the role of the knight changes from region to region (as the gazetteer later in this chapter will amply demonstrate). Only in the past century have the fires of the Crusades and the songs of the troubadours created any real sense of an overall ideal of chivalry. Because of all this, the basic definitions that follow are — at best — stereotypes. They exist only to give some basic context to the details in the rest of this and later chapters.

The Knight

The simplest definition of a knight is a mounted warrior, but in the Dark Medieval context, he is something more. A knight is not just a soldier who happens to be on horseback, but a member of the nobility (sometimes tenuously) tied into the pyramid of feudal relationships that make up his society. He is a lord or has his eyes on lordship but is also a vassal, serving his betters both on the battlefield (generally 40 days a year) and at court. He is wealthy enough to afford the trappings of knighthood — a fine horse, weapons and armor — but is not yet in the upper tiers of power on a national scale. The knight's wealth comes from holding a fief (sometimes very small, sometimes quite large) and so owing fealty to the lord who granted it.

Training and Background

Knights become so after *dubbing*, a ceremony in which a monarch or other powerful lord recognizes the candidate as a knight and grants him that title. Dubbing is almost always the culmination of long and arduous effort. Generally, this comes in the form of 15 years of training, during which the prospective knight (usually the eldest son of a noble family) serves in the house of a powerful lord, first as a page and then as a squire. As a page (from age 7 to 14) the lad gets to know the workings of a noble castle or manor and serves the lord in menial ways. As a squire (age 14 to 21) the young man trains at martial skills, assists and learns from knights and may even go on campaign to learn in the field. He must also — and increasingly so in this period — acquire the skills and graces of courtly behavior and etiquette. A knight not only serves his lord as a skilled warrior, but also honors him with appropriate manners.

The exact form of the dubbing itself varies from region to region and lord to lord, but it generally involves a night-time vigil in a church, during which the soon-to-be knight prays for guidance. The lord then ceremoniously strikes the new knight with the flat of a sword, which is to be the last blow the knight receives without answering in kind. Some lords may require the newly dubbed knight to swear an oath to them, but this is more properly done when the lord grants a fief, and it is quite possible that the knight at this time has not yet inherited lands from his father. Once the knight inherits, he takes on the duties of estate management and renews the bond of vassalage between himself and the lord who granted the fief in the first place. The lord will demand that the knight swear a formal oath of fealty, making clear to all that he has accepted his father's responsibilities along with his lands.

For more on feudal relationships (as well as some additional insight into the lot of a page) see **Three Pillars**.

Chivalry

Chivalry is the largely unwritten code of behavior and expectations that governs knights. Enhancing the feudal relationships of vassal and lord, it adds expectations of religious piety and (increasingly) courtly love. The truly chivalrous knight is fierce in battle, respectful to his lord, chastely loving of a fine lady and burning with his faith. Even those who do not feel these yearnings quite so keenly behave as if they do because their social standing depends upon it.

Chivalry flirts with the status of a philosophy. The songs of the troubadours set up the models of Roland, Arthur and Galahad as ideals of human existence, not just models for effective knighthood. In 1197, chivalry remains the exclusive domain of the knights who practice it, but they already judge the worth of the rest of the world by the strictures they follow.

The practice and tenets of chivalry form the meat of this chapter.

Cainite Perspective

Many Cainites deride chivalry, others fear it and still others thrill at it. The concept of pure and virtuous warriors is laughable when set against centuries of experience with bloody conflict and the equally horrific acts of some of these supposed paragons of virtue. Elders especially see this young movement as a ludicrous joke, yet another case of human self-delusion. Virtue and the sword do not go hand in hand.

To some of Caine's childer, chivalry is a grave concern. For vampires accustomed to ruling the night through fear, the concept of well-trained warrior-lords actively seeking some righteous conflict to justify their martial ways before their God is chilling. Thank Caine for the "chivalrous" tendency to battle other knights for feudal standing and female attention; without it, this class of soldiers might actually pose a serious threat.

A smaller number of Cainites, mostly neonates who knew of chivalry in life, takes this new movement to be a ray of hope in the Long Night. These vampires see a parallel between Cainites and knights: Both struggle to reconcile the bloody necessities of their condition (battle and the Beast) with the desire to be moral and, ultimately, human. The ongoing development of the Via Equitum, the so-called Road of Chivalry, is the hallmark of these vampires.

Origin Theories

Scholars in the Dark Medieval world have their own theories regarding the beginning of chivalry. In 1133, Honorius of Autun traced knighthood back to the aftermath of the Great Flood and the efforts of Noah's children to be fruitful and multiply. He noted that this moment in history marked the division of humanity into three estates: freemen, knights and serfs. Freemen were descended from Shem, knights from Japhet, and serfs from Ham, the son who laughed at Noah's drunkenness and received his father's curse (Ham, Honorius declared, belonged to the race of Caine). Honorius's ideas altered a great many family genealogies, as knights and nobles rushed to work Japhet and Noah into their family trees (usually several generations before Woden and other pagan deities and heroes — an ancestor's prestige was more important than his faith).

A later theory about the origins of knighthood came from Ramon Lull, a 13th-century knight-turned-theologian and author of an extremely popular guide to chivalry. Lull seized upon the similarity of the Latin terms for "knight" (*miles*) and "a thousand" (*mille*) and proposed the following narrative: Early in human history, when men lived in peace and plenty, there was no need for rulers or guardians. But the advent of sin and crime threatened life and property, and the people cried out for protection. Inspired by God, they found one noble man (the *miles*) for every 1,000 (*mille*) normal men and provided

Cainite Interest

The popularization of a genealogy that included Caine was of immediate interest to Cainites, particularly those whose favorite pawns had suddenly begun playing around with the same lineage as their unliving masters. Cainite reactions to this sudden rush to include, indirectly, near relatives of Caine — and the close examination of Biblical genealogy that it entailed — were mixed. Some encouraged the habit among their mortal pawns for amusement's sake; others were less sanguine about having kine mucking about so near the roots of their ancestral line. These Cainites worked to discredit Honorious, to promote competing theories of knightly origins and to confuse the issue as much as possible.

Unfortunately, in some cases the cure proved as much a problem as the putative disease, and Lull's theory of knighthood (see below) got itself conflated with tales of the Second City by many younger vampires. The fact that Lull himself was sponsored by a rather crusty Toreador with an interest in decimating the entire chivalric tradition is one of history's little ironies.

him with the weapons and horse he would need to keep them safe. These virtuous warriors, Lull claims, were the founders of the honorable and ancient order of knighthood.

A Chivalrous Gazetteer

At the end of the 12th century, chivalry is a pan-European phenomenon, with influence throughout Christendom and beyond. It owes its international prominence to the diaspora of French knighthood. Thanks in large part to the Norman conquests of the 11th century and three Crusades, French knights have fought their way across much of the known world, bringing their values and beliefs with them. The result is that knighthood is known and made manifest in almost any given Western medieval setting. Local conditions do matter, however, and chivalric institutions vary from region to region.

France and the Low Countries

Birthplace of knighthood and spiritual homeland of chivalry, France is the standard to which all knights worthy of their title look for inspiration. Frenchmen first established feudal relations, and Frenchmen were pioneers in the use of the lance from horseback. Everywhere in Europe, knights and aristocrats copy French fashions, read French books, seek out French singers and ape French manners. Only the omnipresent Romans ever had more of a cultural universality in Europe.

French politics lies somewhere between the constant warring of the seemingly infinite number of tiny German principalities and the staid parochialism of the English. The great French territorial lords are princes in their own right, more often than not treating the French king as a poor cousin without the troops to enforce his wishes. Periodically, they go to war, and their struggles disrupt the otherwise peaceful French countryside. Needless to say, the magnates spend the time between battles competing for the service of hardy knights who can serve them in the next round of inevitable conflict. Men of skill, military or otherwise (not all conflicts are physical in nature), routinely find themselves courted by powerful dukes and counts, men known throughout Christendom for their wealth and might. Indeed, this relentless bidding for knights' services is uprooting families of decades' or centuries' standing, as knights abandon their ancestral fiefs and manor houses to assume new titles and new homes in the keeps and castles going up everywhere across France. There is a dark underside to this perceived prosperity, however. As they acquire lands and titles, knights often find that they have increased responsibilities and duties as well. These responsibilities force them into greater expenditures, debts only their lords can pay. In 1197 France, moving on up drives a man down, deeper into debt and service.

For many knights, however, the benefits of increased rank exceed the limitations duty places on their autonomy. The courts of France are the envy of all Christendom, dazzling in their opulence and overwhelming in their scope. In the north and in the Low Countries, men seek out Champagne, Flanders, Hainault and Brabant. Here commerce and chivalry come together, the great fairs providing knights and nobles with luxuries for the buying and money for the borrowing. Tournaments offer tests of strength, and erudite clerks stand ready to answer the questions of those knights of a philosophical bent. The south of France beckons as well, summoning knights with an interest in the mysteries of *amor de lonh*, "love from afar," and a taste for wine and warm nights. Provence, Languedoc, Toulouse, Poitou, Gascony, even Spanish Barcelona — the newfound proving grounds of the heart — achieve a level of cultural sophistication missing from Christian Europe for centuries.

A Gathering of Blades

Sites like Champagne are very useful to Cainites, whose nature limits them from traveling too far along Lupine-infested roads. The great gatherings of the flower of chivalry are beacons to Cainites looking for potential vassals or ghouls. Here, all of the mortals' talents are on display, from their skill in the lists to their wit and courtesy. Here, a vampire can assess a potential ghoul — or childe — in competition against the very best.

Indeed, the fairs are their own peculiar sort of Elysium, where all are free to mingle as long as none are too greedy and proper respect is shown to the resident Cainites. Some fairs have complicated systems of permissions and tithes in place, but the general rules are "Don't be greedy" and "Don't be sloppy."

The British Isles

England occupies an important position in the annals of European chivalry: William the Conqueror's victory over Anglo-Saxon infantry at Hastings in 1066 "settled" the question of cavalry's military superiority and ushered in the era of mounted shock combat. The conquest also provided William with a chance to build a completely centralized feudal society. In England, all fiefs — from the smallest knight's fee to the largest county palatinate — are held from the king, and all nobles, no matter their specific rank, are his vassals. As his barons make clear from time to time (most notably during the civil war between Stephen and Matilda from 1135 to 1153 and the upcoming Magna Carta crisis involving John Lackland in 1215), the monarch's control is not total, but the machinery of justice and taxation is in place, sending sheriffs out to the counties and funds back to the Crown at Westminster. The turmoil endemic in fragmented realms like France and the Holy Roman Empire only serves to emphasize the unity of English politics and military organization.

Landed knights play key roles in the functioning of the English state. The king keeps his court relatively small, preferring that his vassals remain on the lands granted to their ancestors during the era of the *Domesday Book*. There, they help to manage the bulk of the population and oversee the collection of revenues. Approximately 20 years ago, Henry II set his knights to serving on juries appointed by his royal sheriffs and designed to settle property disputes. During the 13th century, these "knights of the shire" will take part in the emergent Parliament, helping to govern England directly. English knights also fill a variety of royal offices, working as coroners, forest officials and even sheriffs.

Despite England's legendary reputation as the home of King Arthur, there's precious little adventure to be found. Young men with little chance of taking their father's place tend to leave the island and seek their fortunes elsewhere. One local option for these restless sons is to join the ongoing pacification campaigns in Wales and Ireland. England's Celtic opponents continue to thwart the Normans' best efforts to subjugate them, but new properties await those knights strong enough to wrest territory away from the rebellious foes. The Scottish border is also a hot spot with rewards for men willing to hold the line against England's fractious northern neighbors (or for ambitious Lowlanders interested in heading south).

Germany

The German heirs of Charlemagne's Holy Roman Empire took their developing feudal system in an entirely different direction from that of their Frankish cousins. The strong, centralized rule of the Ottonian emperors of the 10th and early 11th centuries didn't leave the same room for the creation of a free knightly class that the weak French kings did, and the result was the German *ministerialis* , a legally unfree warrior. Originally, the *ministeriales* were essentially serf-knights, bound to their lords by an ideal of hereditary service. Like French villeins, they could only marry or sell property with their lord's consent, were prohibited from pleading in open court and paid taxes similar to those required of peasants. In some cases, *ministeriales* were actually bought and sold at their lord's discretion. They were accounted quasi-nobles, however, and they often received a small fief to support their families and keep themselves in arms. Most of their time was spent working elsewhere as officials in one of the great households, managing estates or tutoring heirs.

Over the course of the last 150 years or so, the *ministeriales* have been slowly working to improve their condition in order to gain the same rights and privileges as the *Edelfreie*, the lower ranks of the free German aristocracy. The long struggle between magnate families over the right to occupy the imperial throne has aided their cause: The emperor's identity may have changed, but the *ministerialis* administrators remain the same. After all, they are truly indispensable servants with the know-

Plenty of Room for an Ambitious Man

With the Ventrue holding the tightest grip on the mortal institutions of Germany, it comes as no surprise that there is a tremendous vampiric interest in the *ministeriales*, their rights and their status. Hard-line elder Cainites speak loudly about putting the arrogant peasants back where they belong and reminisce fondly about the days when one could buy and sell *ministeriales* like livestock. Those same Cainites, however, are more than happy to play the nobles of the realm off against particularly talented *ministeriales*. While the status of these half-nobles is still a hot-button issue for more traditionalist vampires, Caine's childer are a pragmatic breed, and most are more than willing to put aside their prejudices in order to use a *ministerialis* to smite a rival's pawn at court. Still, old habits die hard, and if a Cainite of more than a century's vintage takes a *ministerialis* to ghoul, he most likely takes one of the palace administrators. After all, they know their place and the value of their silence.

The younger generations make the most effective use of and express the most interest in the pseudo-knights of the empire, seeing in the *ministeriales*' disenfranchisement a mirror of their own. Younger, more aggressive Cainites have served as patrons (known or unknown) for some of the most outstanding examples of the class, particularly those who have wrung concessions from the crown. That is not to say that every advantage gained by the *ministeriales* has come through vampiric assistance, but rather that many Cainites of ninth and higher generation have a vested interest in seeing these mortals succeed — and seeing them displace the tools of the elders in the process. The reward for ousting a mortal or ghoul who serves an elder Cainite, even unwittingly, can be immense. Many of the vampires who watch over the ascendant *ministeriales* were once among their ranks and received the Embrace for services rendered.

how to make things work, and without them, the empire crumbles. The current imperial dynasty, the Hohenstaufens, has a well-established policy of pitting their household *ministeriales* against the fractious upper ranks of the nobility. The rewards for such loyal service are great: the right to hold multiple fiefs, the designation of those fiefs as hereditary in nature, the ability to make one's own marriage arrangements and the right to testify in the courts. These days, most *ministeriales* are free-born nobles in everything but name.

The *ministeriales* are also the center of chivalric culture in the empire. Arthurian romance and troubadour verse reach Germany via these pseudo-nobles, and their ranks currently hold such luminaries as Gottfried von Strassbourg (*Tristan*), Wolfram von Eschebach (*Parzival*) and Vienna's renowned minnesinger Walther von der Vogelweide (*Minne* being the German equivalent of France's *fin amor*). The French epitomize chivalry and all it represents, but the Germans appear to be taking knighthood to new levels of refinement… if only they could stop fighting amongst themselves.

Iberia

Mobilized for warfare against what is, theoretically, a common foe, the Christian kingdoms of the Iberian peninsula continue to invent new ways of training and acquiring knights for their armies. The ongoing success of the *Reconquista* means that acres and acres of what were formerly border zones are now open for settlement. Of course, "settlement" really means "settlement by those strong enough to hold the land." After all, it does the cause of the *Reconquista* no good to wrest lands from the Saracen by force, only to give them back when some weak-willed farmer flees at the first sight of a naked scimitar.

As a result, the King of Castile encourages immigration to these newly conquered regions, offering not only land to be owned outright, but knighthood to any freemen capable of footing the bill. Frontier towns easily receive royal authorization to establish urban militias (*pedones*) and civic cavalries. In many settlements, horses and arms are town property issued to families on loan for purposes of defending the town. Elsewhere, possession of a knight's most basic equipment is compulsory for all inhabitants of a certain rank (and, given the continuing threat of Saracen raids, few men shirk this particular duty). The high quality and low cost of Spanish horses makes the burden of knighthood easier to bear here than, say, in France, and as such, the institution has evolved differently.

Spanish chivalry lacks a certain mystique as a result of such accommodations to the requirements of the *Reconquista*. The chivalric hierarchy in Castile, for example, is based less on birth and more on wealth and political acumen. *Ricos hombres* (royal advisors) and *infanzones* or *caballeros hidalgos* (magnates) surround the king at court, while the *caballeros villanos* (literally, "villein knights," though many are no man's vassal) fill the countryside, governing their small estates and ranches. Songs celebrating Spain's greatest hero, El Cid Campeador, chart his climb from small landowner's son to royal champion and father-in-law to the Kings of Aragon and Navarre, and many *caballeros* hope to follow his example.

For some time now, Spanish knights have been joined in battle, if not in their specific aspirations, by French knights crossing the Pyrenees to fight the infidel. These French knights, as well as their peers from more distant lands, testify to the chivalric ability to reconcile pious duty and fiscal practicality. God wants the Saracen driven back, and these holy warriors reason that He doesn't mind if you line your pockets in the process. The Frenchmen also carry out a sort of cultural exchange: Through their agency, Arabic fashions and verse forms move north to be transformed into troubadour poetry and love songs aimed at an audience of appreciative European nobles.

The war in Iberia has settled into a regular rhythm. Yearly raids across the uninhabited frontiers between Toledo and the remnants of al-Andalus are the most frequent form of conflict; large-scale, aggressive campaigns designed to seize and hold territory occur at a rate closer to the generational. One of those great pushes will be underway in another decade, climaxing in the Christian victory of Las Navas de Tolosa in 1212. Islamic Spain will be reduced to the southern kingdom of Granada, and another period of stasis will set in, this one lasting right up

El Cid

As has been noted elsewhere (most prominently in **Libellus Sanguinis I: Masters of the State**), El Cid is the object of special veneration to many Christian Lasombra. Young would-be knights of the clan of shadows earn their spurs by keeping a nightlong vigil at the slain hero's tomb, and Lasombra instructors in the ways of war (both Christian and Muslim, as El Cid fought on both sides) hold up his campaigns as object lessons for their students.

In truth, the status of El Cid among the Lasombra is something of a conundrum. After all, he was but a mortal, resolute in his refusal of the Embrace, and of relatively low birth. On the other hand, his deeds and life so expressed many of the clan's ideals and tenets that, unwittingly, he has evolved into something of an icon. "By growing into that which we feared, he became that which we think we are," said the Islamic (and Lasombra) poet Yusuf ibn Rasheed. In that statement Yusuf crystallizes the appeal and power of this figure, now safely dead, to capture the imagination of an entire clan.

Wise Cainites know that the fastest way to incite the ire of Christian Lasombra in Iberia is to mock El Cid and warn their childer accordingly. Among Muslim members of the clan, the reaction to this paragon of knightly virtue is less clear-cut. Some Cainites admire his skill and achievements, while others see him as a turncoat and the author of the current state of affairs on the peninsula. The vast majority of the younger Muslim Lasombra hew to the latter viewpoint, and they often attempt to disrupt the affairs and vigils conducted at "El Sayyid's" tomb. These Cainites are perhaps the greatest danger to chivalrous vampires in Spain.

until the *Reconquista*'s successful conclusion in 1492. At present, though, the armies of Spain, Christian and Muslim, content themselves with harrying one another across the border, burning and looting as they go.

Italy

Knightly visitors to Northern Italy find themselves in a world turned upside-down. Instead of gratefully receiving charters from royal or magnate masters, the Italian city-states presume to negotiate with the noble families of the rural *contado* regions as equals. That the two sides work together at all is due to the city fathers' need for trained warriors to fight their interminable wars and the aristocracy's desire for luxury goods and urban financing. Northern Italy is one of Europe's bloodiest, most chaotic battlefields (only Germany and Spain are in the same league), and the great cities go to tremendous lengths to acquire trained, competent soldiers. Mercenaries are increasingly common (the economic prosperity of the region, despite the constant strife, is more than enough to ensure that sellswords do very well for themselves), and companies swallow up landless younger sons almost as soon as they cross the Alps. By the 14th century, these *condottiere* will dictate policy to urban dictators and oligarchs alike. Cities concerned with the loyalty of their armies have taken to knighting any man of low birth who can provide his own equipment. For the indigent knight, the scene is ripe with opportunity.

Southern Italy is a more familiar landscape. The Kingdom of Sicily is a thoroughly feudal realm, established by Norman adventurers who brought their systems of ownership with them. The hot Mediterranean sun shines down on fiefs and estates similar to those of northern France — provided one overlooks the lingering architectural influences of the Byzantines and Muslims the Normans drove out in the first place. The peasants are darker-complected, to be sure, but they're no less obedient than those in Normandy. Courts at Naples and Palermo rival those of Languedoc, Champagne and Flanders for chivalric accomplishments. They're also a center of intrigue, caught between the secular ambitions of the German Emperor (who has inherited the throne of the kingdom) and His Holiness the Pope. Knights with a knack for courtesy and the finer things in life do well here, as there are many nobles with largesse to bestow who can appreciate a well-mannered knight.

Lands and Power

The lands settled by freshly minted knights under Castilian edict are a great prize to young, landless Cainites. After all, the entirety of civilized Christendom is under the thumb of one powerful elder or another, leaving only scraps for the younger generations. The settling of conquered lands by Christian knights, however, opens up vast opportunities for Cainites without domain. Suddenly, there are hundreds of square miles that have been forcibly vacated by those who once held them, and the humans moving are, for the most part, without supernatural allegiance.

The result, to no one's surprise, is a bloody free-for-all. The situation is not quite as appealing as it seems — for one thing, the population density of the newly resettled regions is nowhere near sufficient to support Cainites in proper fashion. That means there are relatively few domains worth having but many fortune-seeking Cainites who have decided to stake their claims. Furthermore, many of the Lasombra whose mortal pawns were driven off are less than sanguine about giving up their possessions and have no love for these self-proclaimed lords of the realm. As a result, most of the vampires flocking to Castile vanish abruptly, victims of either their rivals or those they are seeking to dispossess.

Those few lucky Cainites who survive their peers, their predecessors and the 1,000 other perils of the peninsula quickly realize, however, that their safety lies not in the land, but in those who dwell upon it.

Scandinavia and the Slavic Lands

Chivalry has yet to really take hold along Christendom's northern and eastern boundaries. While a group of Frenchified Vikings (better known as the Normans) are responsible for the spread of much of what we recognize as knighthood, their relatives who remained behind in Scandinavia tend to rely on home-grown, Nordic systems of property and military organization. Skilled infantry remains popular this far north, in part because mounted armies fare poorly at best in wintry climes. The Scandinavian courts and trading centers nevertheless remain in regular contact with their southern neighbors (mostly via England and Germany), and chivalric ideas have already begun to work their spell on the Norse elites. Tristan and Isolde are current favorites on the literary scene, as are Arthur and all his knights, taken straight from the pages of well-traveled and well-translated copies of Chrétien de Troyes and his fellow writers.

Knighthood is essentially non-existent east of the Danube, both in socio-economic and cultural terms. The quasi-feudal levies there are largely foot soldiers, many of whom use spears and axes in the old Frankish style. Fortifications in these lands are still primarily log stockades (a decision which makes economical use of local resources). Unfortunately for Eastern Europe and Russia, the Mongols are arriving a few decades hence and these defenses are wholly inadequate in the face of the threat from the Central Asian steppes. Timber fortresses are easy prey for horsemen shooting flaming arrows, and heavy infantry is almost always vulnerable to a swifter, more maneuverable foe. The one consolation for the Slavs and their neighbors is that mounted shock cavalry will also prove to be equally ineffective against the invaders. Christendom will catch a huge break when the death of the Great Khan in 1227 causes the Mongols to withdraw from Europe proper (although the Russians will have to wait a few more centuries for their liberation to occur).

Byzantium and Outremer

Europe's southeastern frontier is extremely familiar with Christian chivalry, thanks to the Crusades and a constant stream of armored pilgrims and adventurers. The practice of knighthood as the West understands it is largely limited to the remaining crusader enclaves in the Holy Land and elsewhere, although the Byzantine Emperor Manuel Comnenus did take part in a tournament held in Antioch in 1159. The historical continuity of the Eastern Empire means that Byzantine armies are organized, however inefficiently, along Roman lines. The French cavalry charge certainly made an impression on Constantinople's elite during the First Crusade's stopover there: The emperor's daughter Anna Comnena noted in her *Alexiad* that the mounted Franks seemed powerful enough to smash right through the fabled city walls. Contemporary Byzantium will soon find out just how right she was, courtesy of the Doge of Venice and the upcoming Fourth Crusade (1202-1204). As payment for Venetian transport to the Holy Land, Christian chivalry will sack and loot the imperial capital in 1204, an act which will establish the Latin Empire (1204-1261) and earn the knights the dubious honor of being the first group of crusaders directly excommunicated by the Pope.

Outremer, the set of crusader kingdoms "beyond the sea," is much reduced in size a century after the glorious victories of the First Crusade. Only the Kingdoms of Acre and Cyprus and the Principality of Antioch-Tripoli remain in Christian hands, along with the seemingly impregnable castles of the military orders. The crusaders continue to control the eastern Mediterranean, aided by Venetian and Genoese fleets; naval power guarantees Christian supply lines and insures that military access to the coast is available whenever it's needed. Religious knights will find the pilgrimage routes to Jerusalem open to all Christians, armed or otherwise. The main challenge here is having the wherewithal to pay the modest fee the Muslim authorities require of all pilgrims who wish to enter the Holy City. Violence is never distant in the Holy Land, but the crusaders' defensive posture allows for a great deal of peaceful interaction and trade between adherents of the two hostile faiths.

Chivalry and the Infidel

Knighthood is largely a Western European phenomenon, due to its affiliation with feudal polities, Germanic warrior values and Christian rituals. Two centuries of Crusades and ghetto massacres have left non-Christians less than impressed with the ideals of chivalry as practiced. Civil and canon law prevent Jews from bearing arms, owning land and accepting the homage of Christian vassals, the hallmarks of the successful *chevalier*. Muslims live, for the most part, beyond the boundaries of Christendom, occupied by their own complex systems of politics, property and warfare. The Baltic pagans have better ways of killing Germans than dressing up in metal and dashing at them.

The extent to which European knights see chivalry everywhere they look is, therefore, surprising. Much of it can certainly be chalked up to a chauvinism capable of understanding the world only in its own terms, but a substantial amount stems from honest attempts to give credit where credit is due. Crusaders have always expressed clear admiration for the martial skills of their Muslim opponents. "If only such warriors fought for Christ," they sigh and turn back to their wine. The Third Crusade (1189-1192) witnessed an explosion in this attitude, thanks to the dashing figure cut by the Saracen leader, Saladin. His encounters with Richard the Lion-Hearted are already the stuff of legend, and the English king is quite open about the respect they shared. In fact, the first notable manual of chivalry, the *Ordene de chevalerie*, conveys its information in the form of lessons a captured knight gives an eager Saladin to avoid paying a heavy ransom.

Knights also read chivalry into history, looking to the ancient struggles of Israel and the campaigns of Rome for inspiration and edification. Certain historical figures, Jewish and pagan, are increasingly recognized as paragons of chivalry. Joshua, King David and Judas Maccabaeus are singled out from the pages of the Bible, soldiers of God during the reign of the Old Law of the Israelites. The Latin texts of pagan Rome present knights with the noble examples of Hector of Troy, Alexander the Great and Julius Caesar. By the 14th century, these six figures will be teamed up with three Christian heroes (King Arthur, Charlemagne and Godefroy de Bouillon, conqueror of Jerusalem in the First Crusade) to compose the ranks of the Nine Worthies, models whose examples all knights are urged to follow.

The Virtues of Chivalry

Medieval scholars devote much time to classifying and codifying just about anything they can get their hands on or heads around, and knights are no exception. Manuals of chivalry started to appear 50 years ago and are growing in popularity and number. These commentaries all put forward different schemes and systems of knighthood, and each individual definition says more about the specific interests of the writer involved than about knights per se. There is no single universally accepted, itemized code of chivalry. But in the numerous, overlapping ones that do exist, there arises a sense of which knightly values are essential to chivalric identity. These values are the ideals to which knights aspire, even if they don't always live up to them.

The Problem With Examples

It is not uncommon for a young vampire, all aflame with the ideals of knighthood, to wax endlessly rhapsodic about the virtues of a supposedly chivalrous historical figure. Such naïve souls will go on for hours, if allowed, about the courtesy, nobility and other fine qualities of these figures, usually to the amused laughter of whatever elders are present.

Only when the inexperienced vampire has finished making a complete fool of himself will one of the older vampires mention that he knew the worthy in question and that he wasn't like that at all....

• ***Prouesse* (prowess, *Manheit, Pretz*).** At the core of chivalry lies *prouesse*, the combination of strength, martial skill, bravery and experience that makes knights the supreme military force within Christendom. A knight must be able to wield his weapons effectively, wear his armor without complaining and guide his steed through the chaos of battle. He must never flee from the enemy or display fear; these are the marks of the coward. The test must be met. Prowess demands hard work, requiring men to spend much of their time practicing at war, both at home and at tournaments. A lazy (or uxorious or decadent) knight sooner or later finds himself paying a deadly and inevitable price for his neglect of arms. If he's lucky, he'll die in battle, ineffectual, but ending as all true knights should. If he's unlucky, he'll survive and face ignominy and shame, a fate he can escape only by seeking *aventure* and, thereby, once more proving his skill.

Even knights with sound reputations feel the constant call to arms, the tempting lure of action. Prowess depends on the attempting of great and notable deeds, which no one has ever managed to achieve while managing fief or tilting at the quintain. The enemy of prowess is idleness; knights who stay too long at rest give up the glory which could be theirs. At the same time, the responsibilities of maturity and age demand stability. Knights who seek to hone their prowess, therefore, devote their youth to errantry, hoping to build their skills and make their names in the years between their dubbing and their assumption of their fathers' duties. Younger sons lack the benefit of inheritance and, therefore, devote themselves all the more to the cultivation of their prowess.

• ***Loyauté* (loyalty, *Trowve*).** *Loyauté* is the chivalric virtue that binds knights together as men in arms and that justifies all designations of knighthood as an order directly established by God. *Loyauté* is fidelity to one's self, one's betters and even one's inferiors, the reciprocal force that empowers all oaths and all feudal relationships.

The Cainite Perspective

Prowess is something to encourage in knights. It makes them more useful tools and better prepared for the demands of unliving existence, should they be deemed worthy thereof. Furthermore, knights who are off performing gallant deeds are also in a position to advance others' agendas by those deeds and not at home poking into matters that don't concern them.

As for Cainites who wish to take up the mantle of chivalry themselves, they walk a fine line. Prowess is all well and good, and certainly, skill at arms is useful in settling vampiric affairs of state. (Hacking a vampire into bits is one of the few ways to slow an opponent down, in truth; the heavy weapons of the 12th century are remarkably effective against Cainites, especially when wielded by Cainites.) The real difficulty comes when it's time to perform deeds proving their prowess, especially after losing face. Then the virtue becomes much more of a hindrance and, occasionally, a fatal one.

It has cosmic implications as well. Many knights understand their relationship to the divine in explicitly feudal terms. They see no difference between their political fidelities and their Christian *fides*; here, God is simply the ultimate seigneur. Indeed, it's not surprising that medieval English speakers used the same word to mean both "troth" (as in "to plight one's troth," to swear a solemn oath of allegiance) and "truth." A knight who breaks his vows, who betrays his faith to his lord or comrades, is an oathbreaker, kin of outlaws and all of those who live beyond the boundaries of society. Knights who wish to change allegiances had best do so carefully and in public, as no shame adheres to a knight leaving a lord openly recognized as tyrannical and arbitrary. The knight who switches allegiances in secret, however, faces censure and calumny.

The ceremony of homage makes loyalty material; during this ritual the suppliant vassal places his hand between those of his lord, symbolizing his obedience and his lord's protection. More elaborate homage rituals have emerged; in these, bareheaded and weaponless vassals kneel before their lord and verbally affirm their loyalty, often swearing on a relic to become their sire's man. The bond established in either rite is understood to be an exclusive, personal one. Unfortunately, the patchwork nature of medieval property ownership (and its vexed relationship with the equally scattered nature of medieval politics) often means that knights end up swearing *homage* to multiple lords. Ingenious solutions are applied to these conflicts of interest, one of the more interesting appearing during the 14th century and the Hundred Years' War. A Flemish knight living in a border area and thus owing fealty to both the English and French kings worked out an arrangement in which he changed service based on the geopolitical location of whichever army he happened to be attached to at the moment.

• **Largesse (generosity, *Milte*, *Larcs*).** Generosity on a grand scale, largesse is the just reward knights receive for their deeds of prowess and oaths of loyalty. The wise lord showers his men with unasked-for gifts that reveal his love for his faithful vassals and his pride in their great achievements. Indeed, what many in the Church consider prodigality, knights consider extreme virtue. The lord who hoards his wealth sooner or later finds his hall empty and his levies unanswered, but the lord who lives on the edge of destitution and poverty due to his generous gift-giving has his praises sung to the four corners of the world. The etymology of "lord" contains its essence: The Anglo-Saxon *hlaford* was the bread-giver, the ring-man or lord of the rings. He gave warriors shelter and support, honoring them with riches and sustenance itself.

The Cainite Perspective

Loyalty is something Caine's childer value very highly in their vassals and something they constantly seek to subvert in others' servants. Most, if not all, Cainites pay at least lip service to this ideal, though some of the more idealistic vampires hew to it to such an extent that they trust their retainers without the added impetus of the blood oath. Other Cainites have a word for these noble souls. It's "fool."

Today, the varied structures and systems of feudalism result in a more abstract sense of largesse: property. Combining Roman, German and ecclesiastical practices, the modern lord grants his vassals units of land (known as fiefs, benefices or knight's fees) in exchange for their willingness to fight on his behalf. He may also distribute fiefs under his control to recognize acts of extreme valor and loyalty. The ongoing economic boom allows many knights to either "sublet" their fiefs to lesser knights in exchange for cash or receive direct monetary payments from their lord. Vestiges of the old epic way do survive, even if they are more or less retained to counteract the increasing cost of knighthood. Upon being dubbed, indigent young men of noble birth often receive their first arms and horses from their lord. Gifts of clothing, usually expensive mantles or cloaks, and splendid feasts are also common.

• ***Courtoisie* (courtesy, *Zuht*).** Originally, *courtoisie* simply meant a knight's command of the etiquette and ritual practiced at his lord's court (the *curialis*). If the knight could get by without insulting anyone directly or shedding unprovoked blood, he was usually considered courteous. As aristocratic lifestyles have become more refined over the course of the last century (due in part to the great kings and lords' increasing reliance on educated clerks and scholars), the idea of courtesy has expanded, and knights must take much more care to observe proper courtly manners. Nowadays, a man must learn to dress well and follow changing styles lest he appear the rube ("Sir Baldwin, pointed shoes with bells were all the rage — *last* winter!"). He must also work at mastering the intricacies of polite speech without appearing too much the flatterer or lapsing into obsequiousness. Knights with a reputation for courteous behavior find themselves welcome at

The Cainite Perspective

Largesse is certainly worth encouraging, as far as vampires are concerned. Creatures who may not be able to hold lands directly are always anxious for their pawns and cat's-paws to acquire it for them. Knights who expect largesse from their mortal seigneurs can also thus enter easily into similar relationships with vampiric benefactors, though the gifts a Cainite can bestow are somewhat different than those a mere man can. Common tokens of vampiric largesse include lands, riches, ghoul animals (especially steeds), weapons, vitae and the lives or humiliations of enemies. What is important is that these things are offered properly, as just reward for service, and not as unsubtle, ignoble bribes. The Embrace is not often given as largesse, but rather, is saved for truly spectacular deeds — at least, if the vampire in question has any sense of propriety.

Vampire knights expect and give largesse as part of the natural order of things. Cainite knights who do not receive what they perceive as their just due, however, are less likely to abandon their lieges and more likely to seek vengeance. Such knights are fond of leaving gruesome reminders as their own "largesse" to stingy lords who take the service of talented vassals for granted.

all of the more cosmopolitan *curiales*. Men seek them out, if only to catch a glimpse of how they carry themselves at dinner.

Courtesy is also one of the few areas in which old-style chivalry has taken notice of the existence of women as anything more than markers of alliance or investments in fertility. The courteous knight knows his romances backward and forward. He can sing, dance and play most instruments. He pays the ladies at court assiduous attention, entertaining them with exchanges of wit, logic and double-entendres (a quick glance at modern collections of troubadour lyrics demonstrates beyond a shadow of a doubt that proper knights and ladies of the Middle Ages had a taste for material even "sophisticated modern audiences" might think twice about mentioning in polite company). The old-style rules about aristocratic women's chastity are still in effect, however, so most exemplars of courtesy practice their art in order to gain social, political and economic favors — not sexual ones — from highly-placed women.

• **Franchise (free status, free birth).** Perhaps the most alien (to modern ways of thinking) of all chivalric values, franchise is best understood as the relaxed, open bearing that publicly demonstrates a knight's good birth and legally-free status. It distinguishes knights from the peasants and villeins they protect and lead, manifesting in a quasi-physical sense. A man with franchise knows he's free and (more often than not these days) noble; he stands tall and enjoys the freedoms his position brings. He never acts in a cringing, servile manner (lords and vassals of free birth interact as greater and lesser equals), and he never shirks the responsibilities of power. Franchise lacks a direct German equivalent at present, due to the prevalence of the *ministeriales* in the Empire. There *Dienst*, the ideal of service nobility (i.e. a man can achieve nobility through the practice of virtuous service), is central to many knights' identities. A sense of this ideal survives in English; the Old English word for "retainer" (*cnecht*) became our modern term, "knight."

• ***Honeur* (honor, *Ere*, *Valors*).** *Honeur* is the social marker of a knight's virtue, the metaphorical currency that drives the chivalric economy. Knights earn honor for openly exhibiting all of the virtues described above, and they guard it jealously, swiftly responding to any attempt to question or diminish their reputation and good name. They do so because honor is the only evidence of a man's identity other knights care to recognize at this time. Internal virtues and a private sense of self are fine for monks and priests, but men of valor measure worth in terms of actions undertaken (said actions need not be successful to generate honor). Moreover, a great deed means nothing if it goes unknown. For this reason, many knights are notorious braggarts, either handling their own publicity or turning it over to well-supported minstrels and poets. Few knights look askance at such boasting: If you don't blow your own horn, no one else is going to do it for you.

The Cainite Perspective

Courtesy and vampiric existence go hand in hand. Down through the centuries, courtesy and strictly enforced codes of behavior have been the thing that has allowed Cainite society to endure with some measure of continuity. More erudite vampires draw parallels between the traditions of vampiric society and the demands of chivalric courtesy and encourage the mortal practice when they can.

Vampires who subscribe to the chivalric model take very easily to displays of courtesy. After all, the expressions of this virtue among mortals can be only pale shadows of the forms it takes among ancient and puissant Cainites. Cainite knights are well aware that the expression of courtesy among mortals is a substitute for aggressive action and that as many battles can be won through well-placed bons mots as through sword strokes. They've also been trained in this art by their sires and their sires' sires and have seen up close precisely why courtesy is used to head off bloody constraint. Two lords going at it over a perceived insult have nothing on two vampires who remember Carthage tearing into one another with seven centuries' worth of pent-up hatred.

The Cainite Perspective

Cainites are as ineluctably above humans as knights are above villeins — if not more so. It comes as no surprise that vampires support the notion of franchise wholeheartedly. It prepares mortals for dealing with them with suitable humility.

The Cainite Perspective

Honor is perhaps the most problematic chivalric virtue for a Cainite knight to uphold. Most deeds of renown must be performed, perforce, by day. A vampire knight thus misses most of the opportunities to establish his reputation.

For more on this matter, see Chapter Two.

Money and Management

Chivalry is an expensive undertaking. Medieval Europe's preference for local economies makes it difficult to determine exact prices, but it's clear that knights pay dearly for the tools of their trade and that inflation is everywhere. In the early years of the Crusades, a knight's steed cost five times the price of a good cow. Now, ordinary riding horses on sale in Spain set knights back some 40 cows, and the price of a well-trained destrier is even greater. The going rate for a new suit of mail is an entire fief; future improvements in armor technology, such as the great helms and iron plating of the next century, will only add to the expense. Three separate generations of crusaders have sold their patrimonies to finance their Holy Land journeys, and local Jews (the only merchants allowed by religious canon to loan money) do a lively business in loans both before and after tournaments. In the near future, the

average knight and his retinue will possess equipment and mounts equal in value to six to eight months' wages.

Added to these military expenses are those of the court and great hall. The first knights were content to inhabit dark and drafty manors, eating plain meals and entertaining the odd minstrel. These days, polite society considers men who live under such conditions either unfortunate paupers or boorish thugs. For good or ill, a solid century of cosmopolitan crusading and a general rise in European trade and prosperity have heightened sensibilities and transformed would-be *milites Christi* into excited consumers. Eastern silks and spices, Iberian stallions and Toledan steel, Flemish tapestries and all-stone construction — for the sake of luxuries such as these, many knights will risk their family's future, motivated by anxieties about their status within the aristocracy. Other knights simply want to live like the kings and counts they serve.

The rising cost of arms and luxury goods coincides with the relatively static nature of feudal revenues. At the time of the First Crusade, the average fief was only a few square acres in size, and the annual requirements of knightly service swiftly consumed most of the income it produced. The situation is little different a century later. Many knights still live close to the land, distinguished from their peasant vassals only by their feudal duty to answer their lord's summons to war. Wealthier men avoid such costly calls to arms by refusing knighthood altogether and remaining esquires and valets. The lingering separation of knighthood and nobility helps them here. Ancestry and bloodline are still more important in establishing a man's aristocratic credentials than any oaths he might swear at his dubbing. Anticipating corporate sponsorship by nearly eight centuries, many local associations of knights pool their resources to fund and equip one of their number for battle. It's not enough to halt the tide, however. Feudal levies grow smaller every year, forcing lords to curtail their military operations. Today's crisis in finance is tomorrow's defeat on the field of honor.

To cope with the Western European shortage of landed knights, the English crown relies on creative accounting and innovative fiscal schemes. The most important of these is the practice of *scutage*, the shield tax (*scutum* is the Latin word for shield). First instituted by Henry II during the 1160s, scutage allows vassal knights to substitute cash payments (or approximations thereof) for their annual knightly service. English knights pay six pennies for every day of service they forego and have the option of forking over one pound to cover the traditional 40-day term of service. The money thus collected goes to finance the hire of professional mercenaries, an important part of any contemporary army.

In 1180, Henry also introduced *distraint of knighthood*, which English and French monarchs will rely upon most heavily after 1220. While scutage permits knights to pay for someone else to fight in their stead, distraint focuses on the larger problem of supply and demand. It requires all males of a certain annual income level or higher to take on knightly status and outlines legal penalties for those who fail to do so. Distraint thus attempts to close the esquire loophole (which allowed some to attain minor noble rank without military service) and place more knights in the field. The English supplement it by requiring men to carry weapons appropriate to their social station. From a chivalric viewpoint, the policy does have the unfortunate side effect of allowing wealthy peasants and merchants to ennoble their bloodline as a matter of administrative policy. Cash-hungry kings may love distraint for the boost it provides to their coffers and military ambitions, but most knights find it distasteful. Situated precariously at the bottom of the aristocracy, they argue for increased barriers between the classes.

Knightly Course to Wealth

According to class-conscious knights, chivalry is its own solution to economic woes. Knight hire is one alternative. Cash-poor knights may give up their fief and join a great lord's *familia* or household, demonstrating loyalty even as they achieve security. Stout service under another man's roof allows a knight to escape the depredations of scribbling clerks and greedy crown agents. There is also something to be said for maintaining ancestral estates, however, even past the point of financial ruin. In the Middle Ages, property is an effective synonym for gentility; indeed, estates are often referred to as "honors" (i.e. "Sir Stanley holds the honor of Lathom"). A man who too readily relinquishes his birthright gives up his nobility in the eyes of many, and land cannot be easily reclaimed once a man has moved off it.

Land-proud knights, therefore, take up their swords and become "entrepreneurs" of violence. They may initiate a private conflict with their neighbors over a disputed boundary line, hoping to increase their square acreage (these small-scale wars often begin with the "discovery" of a hitherto unknown charter granting the property in question to the aggressor). This option, with its propensity for drawing superiors and vassals into the fighting, runs the risk of irking the local bishop. The Church likes things to be peaceful for any number of reasons and tends to look unkindly on nobles who start tearing up the crops, scattering or killing the peasantry and occasionally looting churches. (Sir Thomas Malory, just to name one famous example, was imprisoned for precisely this offense. For the knight

Distraint Dodgers

The knights fighting against the leveling effects of distraint are not alone in their struggle. Aiding their efforts are the very commoners the policy targets. These yeoman farmers and urban merchants view distraint as nothing more than a tax in disguise, levied by kings desperate for the chance to get their hands on hard-earned fortunes. They also see knighthood as a dubious honor at best. Where's the advantage in dying on some distant battlefield alongside or at the hands of men who despise your churlish origins?

short on cash and scruples, the rich vestments and sometimes remarkable treasuries of churches can offer an irresistible target.) Excommunication is always an option.

For that reason, many knights opt instead to take part in foreign wars, seizing whatever booty they can get their hands on in the field. Medieval custom permits them to retain their hard-won gains, and military strategy positively encourages looting. Even mercy increases a knight's earning potential: Defeated knights and soldiers command substantial ransoms, and their arms and horses go to their captor. Those men who fail to find a enemy village ripe for the picking can trust to their lord's largesse. After all, campaign booty is one of the least painful ways for a great seigneur to acquire a reputation for generosity (and keep the loyalty of his troops). Lords are also more than happy to reward valiant acts with seized treasure and outright gifts of land. A knight who leads the vanguard or cleverly outflanks the foe may find himself a baron on the morrow.

Dealing with Serfs

It's popularly held that medieval masters have power of life and death over their peasant vassals, especially those bound to the estate as serfs. To a great extent, and in a great many locations throughout medieval Europe, that statement is true. Lords at all levels, even the relatively lowly knightly class, can compel their tenants both to pay a variety of fees and request permission to carry out certain actions. Their legal right to mete out extreme, even fatal, forms of punishment is nevertheless, a limited one. A man who maims or kills one of his own peasants is, effectively reducing his own income and acting against his self-interest. If he kills another noble's serf, he can be ordered to pay a compensatory fee or even face armed reprisal. In England, knights sitting as justices are restricted to property disputes and arbitration. Peasants accused of capital crimes can only be judged by crown courts.

Overshadowing these more practical concerns are the moral demands of chivalry and the Church. One of the most common clauses in any knight's oath requires him to defend the weak and the poor against aggression. Christian doctrine is partially responsible for getting that clause in the oath in the first place, and clerics constantly exhort knights to practice charity and mercy. Sermons dwell on the numerous defeats of biblical tyrants and urge men to follow Christ's example instead. Few knights live up to such standards, but no knight in Christendom can claim to be ignorant of them or publicly dismiss them out of hand. Those who do so risk accusations of heresy or even excommunication, and knights at such a disadvantage are easy prey for their enemies.

Errantry

Yet, even the poorest farmer-knights have a firm claim to nobility. After all, as landowners, they actually receive an income, albeit a slight one. Their younger brothers and cousins are not so lucky, however. These unlucky souls are left to their own devices and denied their share of their fathers' patrimonies by primogeniture, the now-dominant system of undivided inheritance by the eldest son. The numbers of these landless knights grow with every passing year.

Of Wenches and Wedding Nights

In *Braveheart*, Mel Gibson has William Wallace's revolt against English rule begin with a sadistic English lord's decision to exercise the droit du seigneur, the right of the first night, on Wallace's new bride. Notorious throughout Europe, this right supposedly gives a lord the privilege of bedding his vassals' wives on their wedding nights.

While the droit du seigneur certainly would be enough to incite the ire of any red-blooded Scotsman, evidence for its actual practice is impossible to find. Documentation for the droit only goes back as far as the anti-aristocratic propagandists of the 18th century. It seems almost certain that the droit, like so many other cherished stories of the Middle Ages, is just a myth — one propagated by pamphleteers who had a vested interest in making the aristocracy look monstrous.

Even a little thought demonstrates the patent difficulty in reconciling the droit with the demands of everyday existence. Medieval knights have numerous reasons to avoid insulting their vassals in this way. Peasant tenants and villeins are the average knight's main source of income and food; keeping them happy — or at least indifferent — lets a man concentrate on the important things in life: tournaments, battles, hawking, etc. In addition, those poor knights who still have to manage their fields in person prefer to keep a woman's husband, father, brothers and sons — all of whom undoubtedly know how to handle a scythe, if not implements of war — on their good sides. Finally, the socially-conscious knight knows that a peasant wench is a peasant wench, good for a roll in the hay and not much else. Wealthy heiresses of ancient and noble lineage, on the other hand, demand a man's utmost attention and are unlikely to tolerate being set aside (even for a night) and having some dung-heeled peasant set in their place.

On the other hand, the droit du seigneur may be a popular myth, but so is the vampire. If you want to use the legend in conjunction with your chronicle, you're perfectly welcome to do so. After all, there's no reason an enterprising Ventrue couldn't anticipate the French propagandists by a few centuries, and the very nature of the droit serves certain of the baser needs of the vampiric condition astonishingly well. After all, if the droit du seigneur is commonly accepted in the lands your chronicle is set in, a villein isn't going to find too much that's suspicious about his wife being returned to him pale and weak after a night in the castle. By the same token, forward-thinking peasants could very well use the tyranny of the custom as a reason to revolt, only to find they'd gotten much more than they'd bargained for.

The landless younger sons of nobles are a particular problem, one that must be dealt with delicately. After all, they are noble-born and expect some degree of gentility — and presumably have received useful training in arms and the like as a hedge against the deaths of their elder brothers. On the other hand, having large numbers of dissatisfied, disenfranchised men who know how to use swords wandering about the kingdom is a sure recipe for disaster.

Foreign adventure and the Church are the two most profitable ways to drain off this pool of potentially restive, would-be knights. Sending them off to fight foreign wars serves multiple purposes: It provides a decent fighting force that has extra incentive to perform well (after all, a knight who makes a name for himself may get some land in the bargain). It puts those dissatisfied men far from home, in a situation where the hotheads can conveniently get themselves killed off. And if all goes well, it provides a built-in occupation force for conquered territories, men who will fight tooth and nail to hold onto their freshly minted fiefs. After all, if they lose their new lands, these men are right back where they started from, figuratively, and much farther from home.

Excluded heirs are fresh meat for the Cainites of the world as well. While the ancient and powerful may try to sink their claws into the sons who inherit, the younger and more daring find sufficient material to work with in the dispossessed and errant. After all, these men can travel more freely than their Cainite masters, and they can certainly be used to call inheritances into dispute. The latter tactic is an especial favorite of some of the French Toreador, who've used it to do everything from cut the revenues of rivals by detaching their estates to sponsoring any number of minor civil wars. An heir, even one who clearly should inherit nothing, is always useful for stirring up the rabble.

Blazoning Saddles

At the turn of the 13th century, the art of heraldry offers only hints of the complexity to come. It emerges in response to a number of shifts in military technology and familial identity. The most prosaic reason for the development of armorial bearings is the widespread adoption of the enclosed or visored helm over the last several decades. In the heat of battle, soldiers must be able to identify their commanders swiftly, and unique heraldic devices allow them to do so swiftly and beyond a shadow of a doubt. Clear markers of identity and affiliation are also crucial in more recreational contexts. After all, great deeds on the tourney field count for nothing if potential patrons and noble ladies are unable to recognize the knight striking such puissant blows.

The shield was the most convenient and effective means of conveying identity. Knights have always been able to buy or acquire shields displaying decorative patterns and abstract de-

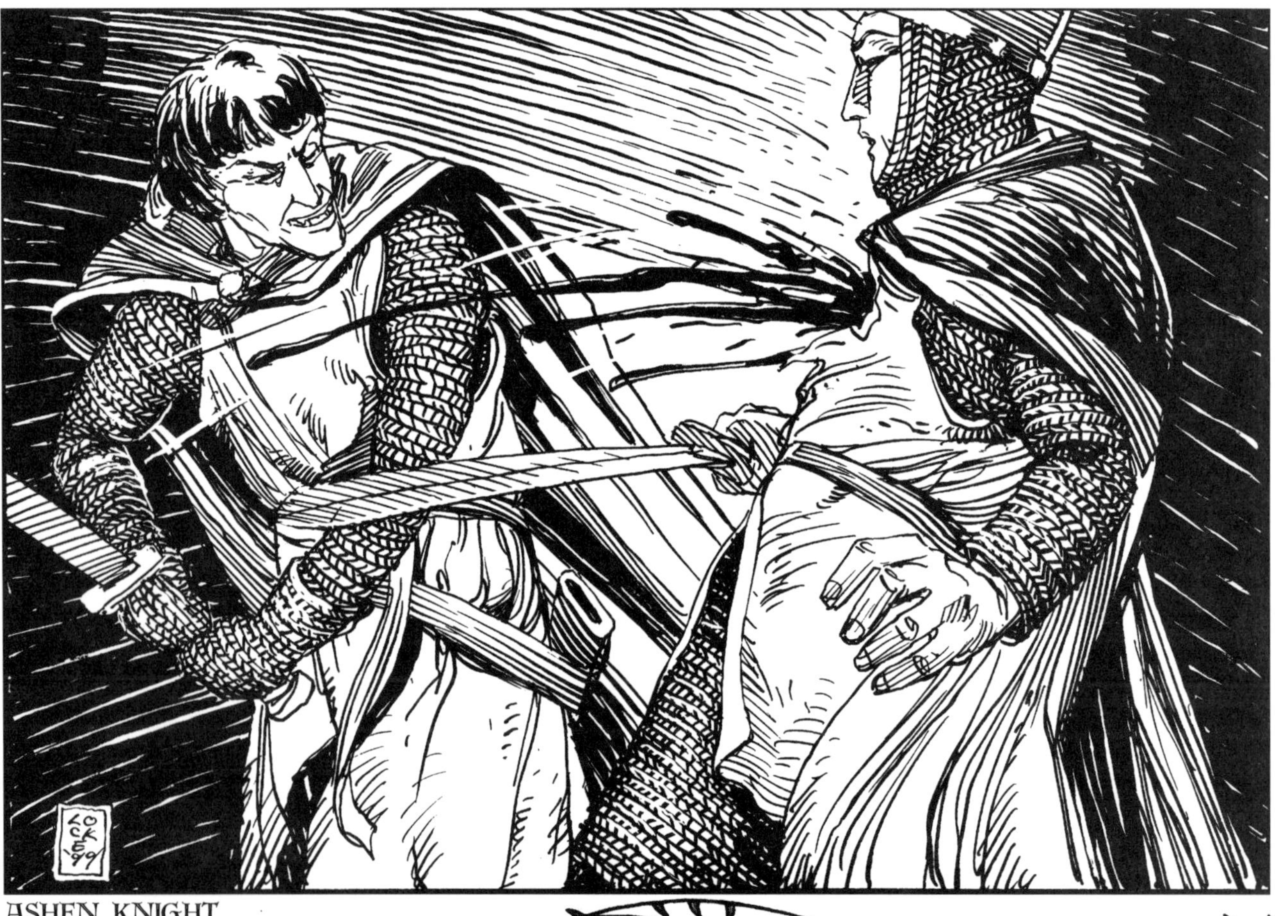

Ashen Knight

Ulrich von Lichtenstein, Queen of the Desert

The first "reenactors" in Western history were the men and women who introduced Round Table tournaments to Europe in the 1220s. In these contests, knights would pose as various characters from Arthurian romance and perform deeds of legend, rescuing damsels from "wild men" and "black knights." The fashion remained popular throughout the Middle Ages and encouraged a vogue for the *pas d'armes*, a tourney or jousting tour with elaborate trappings and highly literary scenarios. No *pas d'armes* was more bizarre than one of the first, Ulrich von Lichtenstein's 1227 *Venusfahrt*. To honor the goddess of love, Frau Venus, Ulrich spent a month traveling from Bohemia to Italy dressed in magnificent women's clothing and sporting long, blond braids. The Styrian cross-dresser (known to his peers as an honorable man and a stout warrior) challenged all comers to a joust, offering gold rings to those worthy of withstanding his dints and requiring obsequies on Frau Venus's behalf of anyone he managed to unhorse. He subsequently claimed to have shattered 300 spears during his journey.

The Round Table tournaments, to no one's surprise, stir up quite a bit of debate among Cainites old enough to remember the period the reenactors are so rosily re-creating. There is a constant hum of threats from hot-headed elders (most often Brujah) who have to been talked out of "showing those mortal children what their idols were *really* like," and unleashing the fury of centuries past on these rosy-visored romantics. There are also any number of vampires who claim to have know the "real" Arthur, and of late, they've taken to gathering at these tourneys for purposes of critiquing.

Round Table tournaments do serve another purpose for Cainites, of course. The outrageous dress and mannerisms serve as wonderful camouflage for Cainites and their deeds, and it's not surprising to find a shadow court of vampires meeting even as the faux-knights of the Round Table pound their flagons on the table and play their roles to the hilt.

signs, and the Bayeux Tapestry shows such shields in use during the Norman invasion of England. Sometime during the first half of the 12th century, the symbols depicted on shields began to consistently mark specific individuals: The Angevin Geoffrey the Fair bore a blue shield painted with golden lioncels at his knighting in 1128, and a similar device (six similar lioncels on a blue field) was hung over his tomb in 1152. Moreover, aspects of these designs became hereditary, if not entirely stable: Geoffrey's son and grandson both carried variations of his lion device, which clearly had become the family emblem.

In 1197, heraldry is still a largely fluid practice. Family members may display several different devices, and they often alter their arms both at will and from one generation to the next. In many instances, devices don't indicate family membership at all: The arms of a good many German *ministeriales* actually signify the identity of the lord who retains them. A common heraldic practice is the use of "canting arms," devices in which the charge humorously puns on the bearer's family name. Sir John le Botiler thus bears a butler's wine cups on his shield; Affenstein, an image of an ape breaking a stone. In the 1190s, only the greatest and richest lords and knights possess armorial bearings, but the custom will move down the ranks throughout the 13th century. The use of arms signifies a knight's commitment to gentle status.

Late 12th-century heraldry does make wide use of a set of rules known as the *blazon*. Developed in France, these simple guidelines regulate the appearance of devices, designating the nine acceptable tinctures that families and knights may use in their arms: *azur*, *gules*, *vert*, *sable*, and *purpur* (the five colors); *or* and *argent* (the two metals) and *ermine* and *vair* (the two furs). The blazon specifies that color must not be laid upon color, nor should metal be laid upon metal. It sets limits on the ordinaries (geometric patterns), birds, beasts and ornaments available for inclusion, and it establishes a sequence for presenting arms in conversation or in writing: (1) the color of the field; (2) the principal charge; (3) any additional charges; (4) such differences as marks of cadency (used to mark the bearer's position within the family). Saint George's arms offer a simple example of such blazoning, the red cross on a white field referred to as argent, a cross, gules.

The art of the blazon does not yet carry the weight of something akin to law, however. Elaborate and exclusive rules for determining precisely who deserves arms will only appear in the 14th and 15th centuries, triggered by a substantial increase in the number of merchant families acquiring knighthood. At present, most knights voluntarily assume arms. The heralds who will one day organize into national colleges and assign devices are currently a disheveled group of messengers and minor staff officials socially akin to minstrels and *jongleurs*, low-status entertainers. To supplement their meager incomes, they've studied blazon and

Hey, That's *My* Dragon, Rampant?

In the 1380s and 1390s, two English knights named Scrope and Grosvenor throw the nation into a tizzy when they take their argument over their identical coats of arms to the Court of Chivalry. Richard II and his most powerful supporters have their hands full keeping the two men from launching into a private war, and even Geoffrey Chaucer gets into the act, providing a deposition to the court on Scrope's behalf. The bitterness of the dispute testifies to the utter seriousness with which heraldry was taken, especially in an age that saw radical shifts in the class composition of knighthood. When family honor and tradition are at stake, quarter is neither taken nor given. Storytellers whose **Ashen Knight** chronicles make it into the later Middle Ages can have fun presenting their players with similar quandaries: What happens when Cainite elders clash over the competing heraldic claims of their mortal descendants?

taken to noisily promoting specific knights before, during and after tournaments. At this point, a knight's possession of a particular device can often come down to mere lung power.

Knightly Saints and Saintly Knights

...running his sword into the blasphemer's bowels as far as it would go.

— St. Louis IX of France, discussing the best way in which a layman might argue with a blasphemer

Faith is something of a sliding scale in the mortal world, and every grouping of men has its range, from the devout to the blasphemous. Why, then, should chivalry be any different? Certainly, love of profit or slaughter drives many knights, but others see a religious component or even calling to their work. The ultimate manifestation of the combination of martialry and faith is the establishment of the Knights Templar, whose very rule is scripted by Bernard of Clairvaux, a future saint canonized in 1174. But even outside the formal orders, many knights consider themselves *milites Christi*, soldiers of Christ, and strive to act accordingly. Of course, "acting accordingly" covers a wide range of behaviors indeed.

The Templars and some of the other crusader orders remain the epitomes (at least in theory) of pious knighthood, a unique melding of monks and knights (for more on the Templars, see Chapter Three). For more secular knights, the veneration and perceived emulation of saints provides a connection to things holy.

Knights are no strangers to matters saintly: They swear by the saints, venerate the saints and even wield them on occasion, acquiring swords with relics placed inside the hilt and pommel. The saints they honor most were usually soldiers in mortal life, in many cases martyred Roman centurions like Maurice. Still there is a trio of saints who stand out in particular, their cults comprised of knights from all over Christendom:

Michael

Michael is not a historical saint. Rather, he is described as one of the archangels and chief princes of the heavenly host. His name, meaning "Who is like unto God?" in Hebrew, is often written on shields as the Latin motto, "Quis ut Deus?" The Book of Revelations depicts Michael as the chief fighter against a serpentine Devil, and it is as dragonslayer that Michael appears most frequently in iconography. His most famous shrine in Western Europe is the coastal monastery of Mont-Saint-Michel in Normandy; in Germany, his shrines tend to be located in sites previously dedicated to the worship of Woden. His feast day, September 29, is known as Michaelmas in England and signals the end of the harvest.

James the Greater

The first of Christ's Apostles to die a martyr (he was slain by Herod Agrippa in 44 CE), James was also one of the Lord's most

beloved disciples. He witnessed both Christ's transfiguration on the mountain top and His agony in the Garden of Gethsemane. James's status as a warrior saint is based on the accounts of his evangelical work in ancient Iberia. His shrine at Santiago de Compostela is the third most important destination for Christian pilgrims during the Middle Ages (Jerusalem and Rome being the first two), and it is also the spiritual center of the ongoing *Reconquista*. The Christian struggle to reclaim Spain began in the area surrounding James's shrine; Iberian knights pray to him as the Moorslayer, defender of the faith against the infidel. Other crusaders venerate him as well, and the 12th century sees the founding of a Spanish military order in his name, the Knights of Saint James of Compostela. His feast day is July 25, and his symbols are the banner, the pilgrim's hat and the scallop shell.

George

He is the most popular of the military saints and a famous Christian dragonslayer. In a single day, George killed a hideous Libyan dragon, saved the dragon's beautiful virgin sacrifice (subsequently turning down her father's marriage offer) and caused the baptism of hundreds, if not thousands, of pagans. George was martyred around 300 CE by a despotic Eastern emperor (either Diocletian or Maximian; the saints' lives are unclear on this point), and it is in Byzantium and the East that his cult first took hold. Returning mercenaries made his name known in the West, but it took the Crusades to put his name on every knight's lips. The fall of Antioch in 1099 was signaled, not only by the discovery of the Spear of Destiny (the weapon that pierced Christ's side at Golgotha), but by a heavenly vision of George and Saint Demetrius as well. More recently, England's Richard Lion-Heart placed both his army and his own person under George's protection for the duration of the Third Crusade. As the personification of Christian chivalry and chivalrous ideals, George is usually depicted as a knight riding a white stallion, his mail gleaming and his sword ready to strike. His feast day is April 23, and his symbols are the banner and, not surprisingly, the dragon.

The Saint and the Patriarch

Michael is also the name of a powerful Toreador Methuselah who rules Constantinople's Cainites as their patriarch. The equally powerful Greek Orthodox veneration of the Archangel Michael is, at least in part, a form of tribute to the ancient and puissant Cainite. Michael, now in delusional semi-torpor, seems convinced that he is indeed the archangel himself.

Michael and his entourage are highly dismissive of "Latin" Western Europe, the lands where chivalry holds sway. The mortal veneration of the archangel in these lands seems untouched by Cainite manipulations (or at least manipulations by these particular Cainites). A Western European knight who becomes a vampire in lands closer to Byzantium (such as Outremer) may be in for a rude surprise when his veneration of an archangel becomes worship of a Methuselah who looks upon him as a barbarian.

For more on Michael the Patriarch, see **Constantinople by Night**.

Chivalrous Women

The world of knights is largely one of men. Knighthood is the province and prerogative of a small, increasingly elite group of men; indeed, most European men are legally and philosophically barred from membership. Women as a group fare even worse, as knighthood is primarily a very exclusive boys' club. Moreover, few medieval women have the opportunity to gain the extensive training required of mounted warriors. Such training takes years and involves a closely-knit company of pages and squires under constant supervision. Girls' education, while similarly rigorous and supervised, goes in entirely different directions and prepares young women for non-martial careers as wives, mothers, prizes and (in medieval romance at least) damsels in distress and secret lovers.

Women in Armor?

This does not mean that women are entirely absent from the chivalrous world, however. Indeed, the world of myth and legend does provide some examples for actual female knights. Western European cultures are not strangers to the archetype of the woman warrior, and she is well known to medieval audiences in a variety of guises. She might appear as one of the Germanic *Wälkure* or the Greek Amazons, led by their Queen, Hippolyta. The brave Camilla slays a great many of Aeneas's Trojans in Virgil's *Aeneid*, a poem known to every educated European, and even Homer's Penthesilea, slain by Achilles, is not wholly unknown to a readership largely unable to comprehend Greek. The same could be said for the infamous Queen Semiramis, conqueror of Babylon and her son's incestuous lover. The Matter of France gives romancers the character of Charlemagne's lady knight, Bradamante, and medieval scribes copy down the Irish tales of Medbh and Scathach. There are even historical examples: the Celtic queen Boadicea and her revolt against the Romans and Eleanor of Aquitaine's decision to ride with her husband to the Second Crusade. These examples rarely, if ever, translate into an actual common acceptance of a female knight, but they can serve as the basis for an exceptional individual to make space for herself — especially on the fringes of chivalry or in dire times. (Chapter Five discusses several viable ways to portray such an exceptional woman within a chivalric context.)

Other Roles

Of course, both knighthood and medieval warfare are more than galumphing about whacking off heads, and this creates other options for women to be actively and intrinsically involved in the world of chivalry. For example, knighthood's increasingly hereditary nature can, in some cases, combine with the extreme variability of local inheritance law to give women possession of a knight's fief or two (or even more, in some cases). A woman who becomes a knight in this fashion may not need to learn the arts of war to

Women and the Future of Chivalry

When the secular orders of chivalry — orders based on ideals taken straight from the pages of romance literature — begin forming in the mid-14th century, women will be among their first members. For example, 68 ladies, including consorts, will become Knights of the Garter between 1358 and 1488.

perform her duties as vassal. Instead, she can use her income to arm others and send them to her lord's summons in her place. After all, more and more men fight by proxy these days as well, as members of the nobility grow tired of risking their own necks. Possession of land brings certain privileges, rights and freedoms with it, regardless of the gender of the vassal holding the fief.

Surprisingly enough, a woman with an interest in things knightly can also rely upon the institution of marriage. While a woman's husband may be titular master of the castle, keep or manor house, the duties of chivalry often require him to be elsewhere. Wars, Crusades, garrison duty, pilgrimages, councils — all of these can drag male knights away from home, leaving their wives in charge of the estate in their absence. The right to command does not lapse with the outbreak of hostilities, either. The ubiquity of private warfare and feuds in medieval Europe means that sooner or later most knights' wives (and most women holding their own *demesnes* as well) find themselves the object of a siege. In these situations, neither extensive training with sword and lance nor male genitals are prerequisites for pushing ladders off of parapets, dropping large stones or pouring boiling oil through murder holes onto one's hated enemies. Defensive strategy and tactics are highly complex military skills, but they are hardly sex-linked, and women can be just as competent at them as their male counterparts. Among other examples, one such woman was Julienne, the illegitimate child of King Henry I of England, who stood side-by-side with her husband Eustache de Breteuil in their battle with her father in 1119 and led the defense of their home, the Château d'Ivry. Unsung but just as valiant, women who've had to do the same on similar or lesser scales are actually quite common.

The Cainite Perspective

Sexism is not unknown among the childer of Caine, but it usually takes a backseat to personal rivalries and biases of clan and sire. Any differences between men and women in physical capabilities vanish almost entirely with the Embrace, and eroding humanity also does away with much of the sexist social baggage of gender roles. Cainites are vampires first and women or men second (or third or fourth, even). Because of this, Cainite women have a far easier time adopting the mantle of chivalry than their mortal counterparts. All but the youngest of their Cainite fellows will accept a woman-at-arms, although usually not without some comment. The example of the fearsome Lamia (see the **Dark Ages Companion**) and many other martial women of the night also reduces sexist tendencies.

Unfortunately, chivalry remains primarily the domain of young neonates and the living. As such, the biases of life are still a concern to Embraced women. Nothing prevents them from embarking on the Road of Chivalry, swearing fealty to a vampiric prince or donning armor, but moving among mortal tournaments as such is very difficult. Most women in this situation adopt a double life, moving through mortal situations in the guise of courtly ladies and dawning martial gear when the only human eyes to see are those of their prey. Chapter Three has further details on Cainite ladies and knights.

The Heart Consumed

Not all the romantic tales of knights and fair ladies end happily, nor are they all innocent stories. The old rules of bloodshed and revenge often conflict with the new rules of courtly, amorous deception, with disastrous results. Before a knight makes eyes at his lord's wife, he had better be sure everyone involved understands that it's just a game....

Jakemon Sakesep's *Roman du châtelain de Couci* tells of la Dame de Fayel and her beloved knight, Raoul de Couci. Before Couci leaves to fight in the Holy Land, she cuts off her braids and gives them to him — saying that if she could cut out her heart without dying, she would give him that instead. Couci carries with him always her shorn braids in a jeweled box. On being struck by a poisoned arrow in battle, he orders his servant to cut out his heart, place it in the box and return the box to the lady.

Unfortunately, the lady's husband finds the servant before the lady does. Breaking open the box and discovering the heart, he becomes enraged beyond reason, bidding the cook to bake the heart into a fine delicacy and to make sure that it is fed to his wife that night. At the dinner table the husband watches her eat, then boasts of his triumph. The noble lady promises him she will never take another mouthful of food; keeping her word, she dies, and her husband is hounded into exile by her family.

Boccaccio tells another version of the tale: The two knights are best friends, until Sir Guillaume de Roussilon learns of his wife's affair with Sir Guillaume de Gaurdestaing. After Roussilon has slaughtered his former friend and torn out his heart, he instructs his cook to prepare the heart. She eats and he makes his declaration, to which the lady responds, "You have done the deed of a disloyal and base knight, which you are; for, if I, unforced by him, made him lord of my love and therein offended against you, not he, but I should have borne the penalty thereof. But God forfend that ever other victual should follow upon such noble meat as the heart of so valiant and so courteous a gentleman as was Sir Guillaume de Gaurdestaing!"

She then throws herself from the tower window; her broken body is eventually reunited with that of her lover in the sepulcher.

Even more legitimately (in the eyes of male knights), noble women are also some of the chief patrons and sponsors of chivalric poetry and treatises. Eleanor of Aquitaine was well known for her largesse toward the troubadours of her native country. Eleanor's daughter, Marie de Champagne, commanded Chrétien de Troyes to write his amazingly popular romance, *Le Chevalier de la Charette* (known to modern audiences as *The Knight of the Cart* or *Lancelot*). Andreas Capellanus also produced his satire *The Art of Courtly Love* as a member of Marie's court. In a sense, most of the recent changes in chivalric culture can be traced back to a handful of powerful aristocratic women, most of whom are related in one way or another to the Angevin dynasty established by Henry II of England.

The new ideals of courtesy and *amor* are female-influenced, and young men all over Europe have eagerly incorporated them into chivalric ideology alongside the more traditional, male-oriented values of prowess, loyalty and largesse. This impetus for courtly love among knights puts them at the service of women. As a rule, these women are neither foolish nor ignorant. Having lords and warriors vying for their affections and occasionally at their beck and call gives them a new level of authority. Of course, they must be cautious not to publicly undermine their husbands, but subtlety is not a rarity in these circumstances.

Finally, women with an interest in devout Christian service join several of the military orders operating along Christendom's frontiers (see Chapter Three). The Teutonic Order, currently negotiating for papal recognition, accepts *consoreres*, woman who assume the Teutonic habit and live under its rule. Other orders have actually gone so far as to establish "military" convents. The Hospitalers have numerous sister houses in England, Aragon and France, with each convent governed by a female *commendatrix*. Spain's Order of Santiago, known for accepting married members, has recently set up a group of convents headed by prioresses known as *commendadoras*. In 1233, Bolognese nobleman Loderigo d'Andalo will found the Order of the Glorious Saint Mary, the first order of its kind to grant women the rank of *militissa*. While the majority of the sisters in these orders function primarily as menial support staff and as hospitalers, they are nonetheless closer to combat than any of their counterparts under the rule of the more established conventual orders.

Chivalry without Christianity?

Knight, you are most fortunate,
For God has set before you His complaint
Against the Turks and the Almoravids,
Who have done Him such dishonor.

— Rallying cry of the Second Crusade, 1147 (trans. by Judith Tarr)

European knightly culture is solidly Christian, and there is little room for knights who do not swear fealty to Christ. Members of all the mortal knightly orders must at least appear devout in their faith, and knights at court are held to the same standard. It is nonetheless possible (if historically dubious) for a non-Christian knight to walk among his fellows in spurs. Such a knight would have to conceal his true beliefs, and such a charade may be difficult to maintain for extended periods of time. Alternatively, the indiscriminate slaughter of the Crusades and other conflicts may cause nominally Christian knights to find themselves disillusioned with the Church. There are certainly knights who call themselves Christian but are so in name only.

There are also those considered "knightly," yet completely outside of the Christian tradition. Saladin, the noble Saracen, is admired throughout Europe to the point of becoming a romantic literary figure. His courtesy, generosity, hospitality and selfless devotion to his faith are as legendary as Galahad's.

The concept of the Nine Worthies can also be useful to non-Christians seeking chivalrous recognition (see p. 20). Indeed, of the nine, three are pagans (Hector of Troy, Alexander the Great and Julius Caesar), three are Jews (Joshua, David and Judas Maccabaeus) and three are Christians (Arthur, Charlemagne and Godefroy of Bouillon). There is a parallel list for women, consisting of Lucretia, Veturia, Virginia, Esther, Judith, Jahel, St. Helena, St. Brigita of Sweden, and St. Elisabeth of Hungary. The latter list is not as clearly defined as the former: Some variants rely more or less on the model of woman as virginal victim, and some include such women as Deborah, Boadicea, St. Clotilde (who saved Paris from Attila's invasion), Semiramis, Tamyris, Melanippa, Hippolyta and Tanaquil. All these provide examples one can follow.

On a less admirable level, there are those who choose to present a public façade of chivalry. Some, having no internal moral compass, adopt the ways of a much-loved figure in order to mask their own failings. A very few particularly single-minded beings have even been known to pursue such chivalrous verisimilitude in order to better understand the thought and behavior of their enemies.

Devices and Their Uses

During the Middle Ages, all of the Worthies — male and female — are assigned coats of arms. Although these are at best of dubious authenticity, they are available for use and adaptation and are often proudly incorporated into cloaks, belt buckles and such as well as blazoned on banners and in tapestries.

Chapter Two: Cainite Knights

After good weather comes rain and storm,
Lamentation, tears, sighs come after great rejoicing...
When one man sinks, then the other rises,
We are wretched unless God helps us,
for our nature is prompt to all evil.
—Jean Meschinot, Les lunettes des princes (trans. by Leonard W. Johnson)

A Treatise on The Chivalrous Childer of Caine

Those of us who labor long centuries in the shadows, tending the glories of the past, often lose sight of what happens in the bright lights of the contemporary world. In the usual course of events, travelers come to me and bring their tales. From time to time, I distill their stories down into what I hope is a potent brew of narrative enlightenment, a stimulus for the mind as strong drink once was for our bodies.

It seems, as the world spins on its way toward the time of final wrath, that events press about us ever closer and faster. Quite recently, I completed an extensive compilation of the lore available to me about those unfortunate souls, the Salubri, and anticipated a time of returning to my regular chores. Alas, rest does not come so readily. Even as I worked on my chronicle of the Salubri, I found myself beset by ever more numerous accounts of a new movement among the warriors of Europe's western lands. In the normal course of events, I would prefer to let the latest fad play itself out for more centuries before regarding it seriously, but the accounts suggested that the matter warranted my attention.

Accordingly, I stirred myself and made such an excursion as I have not taken since the days of the Merovingians, may they find peace. My old friend Olivere, count of what I am told is an important castle in the Frankish province of Provence, renewed his invitation to stay with him, and I accepted. I spent half a year as his guest, observing the mode of existence of those who style themselves "knights" and who partake of our father's curse of the blood. Here I set down my own observations and the words of some Cainite knights.

This is not a general discourse on chivalry as such. You may read any of several fine accounts by mortal knights and their mortal observers. Here I turn my attention to what the phenomenon of knighthood means for our own kind.

What Is Chivalry?

The essence of chivalry is that the profession of arms as performed by mounted warriors is, or at least can be, not merely a career but a sacred calling. Knights regard themselves as protectors of those who cannot protect themselves, upholders of justice in a corrupt world. One can see at once how such a notion would appeal to those of us under Caine's curse. We *are* stronger than mortals, and many of us make most satisfactory warriors, and yet, too often, our existence seems to lack any moral purpose. While to the best of my knowledge there is no firm evidence for the proposition that chivalric deeds may earn redemption for Cainite souls, even the possibility of such redemption must inevitably draw seekers.

My older readers will recognize old themes in this account. In old Greece and Rome, similar notions of noble warriors held sway. The court of Charlemagne included some such sense, though in a far less developed form. On the religious side, Augustine of Hippo laid the foundations for the notion of a warrior caste apart from but allied with the priesthood in his discussion of the City of God and the City of Man. Later, Aquinas sanctified the role of secular leadership as one of God's institutions for justice. Chivalry nonetheless combines these elements with fresh thought about how best to promote justice and distinguish merit in this modern environment, so very unlike the courts of old.

The Siren Song of Humanitas

One of the greatest bonds those of Caine's childer who call themselves chivalrous share is an attraction to mortals and mortal circles. I will withhold from judgment at this point as to whether such an attraction is ennobling or degrading for our ilk. Whichever it is, it is true and strong. Despite the heavy limits the Curse imposes, these Cainites not only move in human circles but go to incredible lengths to pass as mortals and act as mortal knights. They invent reasons they cannot appear during the day, swear fealty to human lords and partake in mortal tournaments and courts. The concessions most of us make to the Sixth Tradition are as nothing compared to the fantastic masquerade these knights undertake.

This effort must seem ludicrous to some. It certainly did to me at first. Could not these knights serve the princes who rule our courts, who are of our blood? Of course they may, and many, in fact, do. Some wise princes have adopted more and more of the trappings of human fealty in order to ensconce neonates in a system they can recognize. Others have founded whole orders of knights of the blood.

And yet, many, perhaps most, still trickle back to human tourneys and human company again and again. It seems that the moral light they seek in chivalry, the key to their Via Equitum, must be replenished by human contact. Much as Artisans sponsor human artists and craftsmen, these knights look to human lieges and fellow knights as their model.

There are those who shun the human world of chivalry altogether while still manifesting the bearing of knights, of course. Most of these believe in chivalry in the way a Magister believes in Christendom: a convenient set of expectations to use for his own ends. They serve vampiric lords and their own ambitions, often not in that order. A minority do follow the model of human chivalry but cannot bear to be close to the kine they emulate, so great is the urge to feed or corrupt. These martyrs are prone to far-off quests.

Light in the Darkened Soul

This calling of arms seems to take on different meanings in the minds of Cainites of varying ages. I include here the self-descriptions provided by some of Count Olivere's guests, in addition to my own observations.

Some Cainites take up knightly duties in hope, others in fear, still others with nothing more noble than ambition or greed. Regardless of their initial impulses, they all face some common challenges. Most fundamentally, they must account for their absence during the day, while occupying prominent social niches. Every aspect of their expected duties changes because of the Curse.

The Chivalrous Neonates

Many of us spend our first few centuries pursuing the same tasks that occupied us in life or those tasks to which we aspired but could not attain in life. So it was in the beginning, and so it is tonight. Many men (and I suppose some women) who were knights in life remain so in death. Judging by the stories told to me, and told by one knight to another while I listened, some locales make it very easy to continue the practice of chivalry, while others make it very hard.

The city-states of Italy, locked in an endless succession of petty wars, scramble for the service of mercenaries. The basest villains of every kind ply their craft on that unhappy peninsula, ravaging without qualm or mitigation. So do would-be champions of the chivalric virtues, warriors who seek to protect the innocent, punish the guilty and restore the peace they claim their God commands. The turbulent circumstances make it possible for a Cainite to move from one identity to another with little difficulty.

All around the fringes of Christendom, lords lead their fellow knights and common soldiers into battle against kingdoms whose lords and people reject Christianity. I have no particular love for holy wars, but I must confess that the world as I've come to know it is strange enough that I do not care to say for sure that the Lord of Caine's father definitely does not command the bloody Crusades. In the Holy Land, in Moorish Iberia, in the wilds of eastern Germany and the dark plains of Hungary, Bulgaria and Romania, mixed lots of idealists and simple slayers muster. Some come to the edges of the world as they know it in search of wealth, others pursue fame and title, and still others seek to liberate the oppressed souls (real or imaginary) who groan beneath tyrants' heels.

Only a handful of knights the warrior orders like the Templars or Hospitalers fight the heathen year in and year out. Most knights who take part in holy wars gather for a few years, whether in response to papal summons or individual inspiration, and then return home. A careful Cainite can easily establish a new role for himself in the midst of the perpetual change in the ranks.

The Norman and Frankish kingdoms are the celestial center of chivalric inspiration. The knights of other kingdoms orbit them as the planets orbit in their spheres, drawing vitality from the Earth. Alas for the Cainite who seeks to practice chivalry, its heartland is rather too stable for quick changes of identity. Wars do sometimes break out in England and France, and the duchies of Brittany and Aquitaine keep many warriors busy (as witnesses one of the tales I record below). Even their wars proceed with a certain northern orderliness, however: These dynastic battles provide fine opportunities for improving one's standing through heroic deeds but few opportunities for disappearing and reappearing in another guise. An English or French knight under Caine's curse does well to travel and arrange a staged death far from home, then return as a traveler from another land.

Finally, chivalry draws a few knights from more remote lands. Troubadours and travelers bring new stories to still-pagan Scandinavia, the vast Russian plains beyond the reach of the northern crusades, Byzantine territories and even beyond. A young Cainite feeling detached from his old existence and looking for a new cause can hear the siren song of being one of God's chosen protectors. Popular songs glorify the noble spirit that sometimes rises in schismatic, pagan and infidel souls. A knight from outside the countries where chivalry enjoys popularity necessarily becomes the object of attention and must be prepared to carry himself carefully. Being exotic grants him some leeway, since almost anything can be excused as "a foreign custom" so long as it's not directly blasphemous or similarly drastic.

Chilperic of Brittany Speaks:

"I lived a miserable life and died a miserable death. I grew up in Brittany and spent a lot of my time keeping out of the way of English and French armies fighting for damned if I knew what, most of the time. Boasting rights, I guess. My family had the bad luck to hold some pretty nice land on the coast, so every few years some grand thinker in a castle way off somewhere got the bright idea of marching his armies through us as part of a great sneak attack. I was 13 when Father died in one of those stunts. He was trying to keep the soldiers from tearing up all of the vines, instead of just most, and some simpkin cut him down for his troubles.

"I finally gave up on it when I was 27 and ran away. I spent 20 years or so making my way as best I could. Then some half-senile thing with fangs that couldn't even remember its own name or what sex God had made it decided to Embrace me. It sure knew that it was a Ventrue, though, yes indeed. I'm not sure to this night whether it wanted me for a bum-boy, hired fists without the hiring or what. Doesn't matter, really, as I killed it and decided to try doing something for myself.

"That's when things started looking up. Now I'm strong, stronger than any of the dung heads that used to ruin my home, and I can make people do things for me. It wasn't very hard to get the money to buy myself a good horse and armor, and then, it was just a matter of practicing until I earned the attention of one of those desperate Brittany dukes. Naturally, he wanted to know why I couldn't go out in the daytime, so I spun him a story about a witch's curse and pushed some weak-minded priest into backing the story up with a lot of holy tripe.

Ennobling After Death

I write here primarily of Cainites who were knights in life, but of course, by no means all took up the calling before their Embrace. Many of Count Olivere's younger guests had been of the common classes in life, who took advantage of the gifts bestowed in the Embrace to better their circumstances.

"You know, though, once I was settled in, I started listening to the stories the troubadours told. I realized that they were onto something. I've got no more use for God than I think he has for me. But someone's got to protect the people like I used to be. It's got to be someone with the strength to fight off the destroyers and the spoilers, and that's me. I do for others now what nobody did for me."

Grazide of Provence Speaks:

"Little did I suspect, when I married Sir Renier, that I would end up a leader of warriors. My family had trained me in the maiden's arts and crafts, and I expected to practice them. Circumstances proved otherwise after my husband discovered the joys of knight errantry. He spent ever more time away from home, smiting the infidel in Spain or Germany or wherever the infidel might lurk at any given moment. I first learned to manage the estate so as to keep the wanderer in spare change. (Oh, those were harsh years. He'd return home and scold me violently for whatever I'd left undone.)

"Then I took up arms myself. This was almost four decades ago, and those were bad times in Provence. Bands of knights turned little better than bandits would surge up out of the hellhole of Italian wars in search of loot. My husband's retainers did their best, of course, but sometimes they were hard pressed enough that I had to join them. I discovered a certain aptitude for it. With practice, I became known as a warrior of some distinction. Troubadours added my stories to other accounts of women knights (and of course added praises of my somewhat exaggerated beauty in hope of grander largesse at my court). I gave instruction to the wives of knights gone crusading on how to protect their estates.

"It came to an end, and a new beginning, in 1179, the year King Louis called the estates to announce his intent to crown Philip his successor. My own lord was off warring (in Hungary, if I recall rightly), but even lords with more concern for their holdings answered the summons, leaving mostly we women to join with elders and the wounded to fend off those dreadful mercenary bands. I did too well for my own good, and my defense came to the attention of a wicked English mercenary, Sir Richard of Cheshire, who proved to be a Cainite. He forced himself upon me, hoping that my condition as freshly created vampire would distract me from my duties. It didn't, and in the end, he and his men fell back.

"I came to the attention of Count Olivere and have since placed myself under his tutelage. I explained to my husband that I've taken a vow to avoid the sun, and as long as the money keeps flowing his way, he cares very little. Some year soon, I'll have to build a new identity for myself, but in the present moment, I find that I'm able to perform the duties given to me better than ever before. The Curse of Caine is a terrible thing, truly, but it is also a blessing to be a woman of strength and ability. I believe that I honor God's words to us in performing as I do, and I accept the limitations of the Curse as a fair price to pay."

The Chivalrous Ancillae

Childer who took the Embrace more than a century or two ago remember when chivalry first appeared. Some preserve themselves in intellectual stasis, resolutely refusing to adapt, and for them, chivalry can never be anything but one more snare. More ancillae reject chivalry than either neonates or elders, I find. Neonates take it for granted as part of the world they grew up in, and elders are removed enough from intellectual fashion to regard it on its own merits. Ancillae remember the traditions of a few centuries ago, the ones chivalry is displacing, and see it as a threat to the world as they knew it.

Other ancillae don't automatically reject new ideas. Only vampires teetering on the brink of madness plunge into every intellectual fad, but there's room in most ancilla minds to consider the merits and drawbacks of changing their way of existence. They may compound their own personal doctrines out of many sources or commit themselves primarily to one view. Some ancillae find much of merit in chivalry. It offers a romantic view of a past they experienced directly, without sordid details they may wish to forget. It offers a continued purpose, since the world seems in no risk of running out of weak people who need protecting or enemies who need smiting. It encourages a balanced development martial prowess checked by courtly skills suitable for creatures that will be learning and growing for a very long time. It's also flexible enough in definition to provide some shelter

Chivalry's Enemies

A Cainite mind, like a mortal one, can only hold so many ideas. Over time, vampiric views of the world do change, but we retain some fondness for the ideas that moved us in life and fear or hate the ideas that drive them from the day's human society. Cainites accustomed to the profession of arms as simply a profession, and to the exercise of noble power untrammeled by notions of religious call, sometimes fight against chivalry as an idea and knights as individuals. A few such crusaders (if I may apply the term to them) spoke to me about their mission.

"God made us to rule, not to toady to priests and weaklings," was the common refrain. These rulers (and would-be rulers) of past centuries regard chivalry as undermining the true qualities of kingship and warrior prowess. Some of the anti-knights who spoke to me strike at chivalry in the realm of ideas. They act in various ways. Two displaced counts who spoke with me said that they simply seek out and destroy prominent knights or attempt to humiliate knights into breaking their vows. Others try to manipulate courts and clergy into repressing chivalry and its exponents.

I have not observed their efforts bearing much fruit yet. The mood of an era does not change simply because a handful of strong-willed individuals wish it to, but because the people at large respond to an inspiration. None of the would-be extinguishers of chivalry seemed to have any firm idea of what they might offer instead. Indeed, they are themselves testimony to why chivalry arose in the first place: It tempers power with responsibility and justice. Still, the strong have prevailed over the virtuous before and no doubt shall do so again.

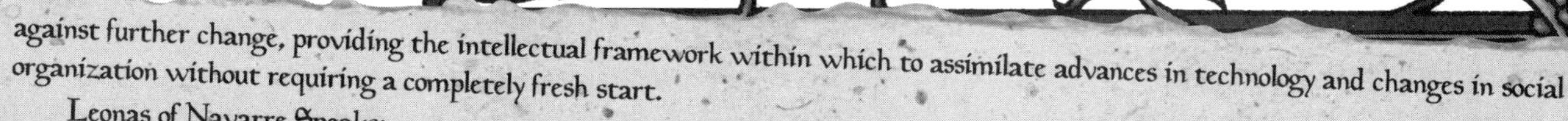

against further change, providing the intellectual framework within which to assimilate advances in technology and changes in social organization without requiring a completely fresh start.

Leonas of Navarre Speaks:

"I remember Roland and Charlemagne. They were nothing like the stories the youngsters tell each other now, of course: They were men of their time, who were more concerned with holding kingdoms together in the face of imminent destruction than in social nuances. I was a man of the time as well and did my turn fighting against the barbarians. Once that age ended, I found myself lacking a sense of purpose, nothing really seeming worth my while for the nights that would lie ahead.

"To put it simply, I went mad. I spent more than 100 years roaming the countryside as a near-mindless, ravening monster. The peasants in the Pyrenees no doubt still tell stories of the Beast of the Hills, which would bear down upon them at twilight. I existed that way for four of their generations. Then, one evening, I happened to hear a troubadour singing a song about Roland. He even mentioned me! That got my attention. I followed him for weeks, soaking in his accounts of a fantastical, pure, exalted version of the grim deeds I knew.

"I began to recover my sanity under his (unwitting) tutelage. I decided that a vision of the world that could redeem my experiences was worth following. God? Don't speak to me of God, I have no time for the spirit, if it exists at all. I care about the social ties among men and women and the notion of strength serving something other than itself. It's a peculiar, grand view of the world. I do not expect that it can prevail, but for now, it gives me cause, and perhaps, it will anchor my soul a bit during the next madness."

Roger of Amalfi Speaks:

"Meaning no disrespect to you, Master Simon, but for many of my generation, your peers in the blood seem to spend a great deal of time wallowing in the unrecoverable past. Unlike you, they do not seek to render their experience into instruction or guidance for those of us who came later, merely moon over what can no longer be. I spent my early centuries, as did many of my peers, frustrated by their self-indulgence and yearned for some goals to which I could attach myself and prove that there was yet room to build as well as to tear down in this world.

"I am, by nature, a warrior, so I turned my hand to war: against the Byzantines 600 years ago, against the Bulghars 500 years ago, against the Magyars and the Vikings 300 years ago. While all these wars gave scope for my might, none seemed likely to build anything of import. My sire continued to compare unfavorably the successor states to the wonders he remembered.

"The First Crusade changed that. For the first time, my sire was forced to admit that something at last might come of all my warmongering. He gloated some in the coming century, but I took that simply as that much more incentive to complete the task we began a century ago. In time, all the vestiges of his remembered empires will be swept away and a new, Christian empire will span the world from one end to the other. And it will exist because men of prowess, such as I was in life and am proud to be still, built it."

The Chivalrous Elders

Many vampires of my own generation, or an earlier one, remember the eras glorified in chivalric stories and songs. We know that Alexander the Great, Julius Caesar and Charlemagne were very different men than the troubadours portray; we know that King Arthur scarcely had a reality at all. Since we are no more united in our response to novelty than humanity is, we take up quite a variety of attitudes. Some of us feel amused by the legends constructed around complex and sometimes sordid realities. (I tend to favor this view myself, while respecting the impulse to good deeds that drives the storytelling.) Others of us are glad to see truths we'd rather forget glossed over in the songs. Still others take umbrage at what seems like a betrayal of important facts.

A handful of elders who have graced my halls with visits announce their intent to sweep away the notion of chivalry. These elders feel that chivalry rests on a dishonest foundation and desecrates what they regard as their accomplishments. So far, I see little sign of their efforts bearing fruit, but perhaps, in time, they may succeed in raising up alternative ideas and institutions. One particularly bitter Cappadocian who passed through Malta a decade ago actually claimed credit for introducing the idea of crusade, arranging to lure the most dedicated knights into doomed battle in the Holy Land. I am not moved to accept his claim at face value.

Most elders with whom I've spoken prefer simply to ignore chivalry or at least to make no particular fuss about it. Having seen other inspirations come and go, they observe knighthood, use it when it suits their purposes and watch for the next inspiration to emerge.

Elders change their minds about religion just as mortals do. Some elder knights adopt Christianity honestly, finding that it really does offer the explanations they need to understand their unlives. To some elders, Christianity's newness is itself an asset, suggesting a continuous unfolding of the truth. Other elders accept chivalry's notion of knights as chosen protectors while declining, in their hearts, to accept the Christian facets within chivalry. Sometimes, they even express their disbelief openly; history records some prominently skeptical lords. The moment such a critic of the Church falters, he is doomed, but success may justify a great deal of deviation for a long time.

Chivalry and Methuselahs

To most Methuselahs, chivalry seems like one more passing fad. On the scale of millennia, they may well be right. Whether it fascinates them, repels them or simply becomes one more tool with which to manipulate younger beings, their reactions need not make obvious sense to anyone else. They do not to me, at least not as far as I can tell.

Respectfully,

Simon ben-Yaakov

The Knight Who Forsook the Day

Knights lead. They lead charges in battle, they lead patrols and sorties during sieges, they lead their oath-sworn subjects in times of crisis. While sometimes they must delegate their authority to others, a knight who's absent too often from the public eye faces censure. The land and title given by a lord can be taken away; this doesn't happen often, but knights must show themselves worthy of the gifts they tend. First of all, then, a Cainite who masquerades as a mortal knight needs an explanation of why he's not seen during the daytime and must establish who acts on his behalf while he's hiding from the sun.

The Knightly Bearing

This chapter describes many problems that Cainite knights must confront. They do face all these challenges, and they generally prevail. Cainite knights have no time for whimpering or cowardice. Drawing on what they see as best in both Cainite and mortal society, they move through the world with confidence bred from demonstrated superiority. They carry the banner of social justice, leading in peace and in war. At least they hope to, and some actually manage it. If they succumb to doubt or despair, it's generally just a momentary lapse from which they rally in time to deal with the next challenge.

The Knight in the Shadows

Curses exist, and everyone knows it. Most people haven't seen many examples of really strong supernatural vengeance, but they know someone who has or a friend of a friend who has. It's no great surprise that a puissant warrior, razor-witted judge or righteous seeker of spiritual truth would run afoul of one of the many dark forces that taint the world. Holy men and women can lift many curses, but not all; God allows some to linger on for His own ineffable purposes. It's very sad when an otherwise worthy knight cannot face the sun because some monster or witch laid down a curse. A knight who demonstrates the desire to uphold his duties as best he can despite the burden may well earn the support and admiration of his subjects. Thus, a Cainite can turn the universal curse of his kind into what appears to be an individual one and make it work to his advantage.

As chivalry matures, knights take on increasingly extravagant oaths to distinguish themselves from rivals by superior dedication to the highest causes. Two hundred years ago, a simple oath to complete a pilgrimage to Jerusalem or Santiago de Compostela would show a knight's unusual holiness. After the Crusades, that's no longer so remarkable, and knights compete for greater honors: extended service in the Holy Lands or one of the knightly orders, the donation of important property and more eccentric displays. In the midst of knights swearing to pray at the door of every cathedral from Paris to Rome or to wipe clean the Holy Sepulcher with his tears, a Cainite can easily blend in. He simply declares that he's sworn not to face the sun, which is the light of the natural world, until all mankind turns to the Son, Who is the light of the mortal world. Or he might say that after a particularly humiliating defeat in a dawn raid, he's sworn never to see the sun again until he can prove himself a sufficiently brave warrior. Many excuses can cover the fact of never seeing the sun, and as long as the condition of fulfillment is sufficiently exotic, there's little difference between an oath good for the rest of a knight's life and one that might, in theory, end sooner.

A knight may avoid the sun for less cosmic reasons. Ladies who wish to test their suitors' commitments to courtly love can and do impose conditions. As this century draws to its close, it's not uncommon to see knights who wear only one color of clothing, venture forth only on certain days of the week or eat only certain foods, all for the love of their ladies. A knight who says that his lady commands him to avoid the sun for a period may encounter commiseration on her harshness, but is unlikely to face any more probing beyond that. An adventuring lady may likewise claim that she avoids the sun because of the command of her lord, a capricious man who tests her fidelity to his wishes. Such a story works best if the lord is far away or (better still) imaginary, of course. Actual lords and ladies can deliver the appropriate orders, however, particularly under the influence of Dominate.

Finally, a knight may spend time in the night and escape reproach because he's known to hunt monsters. Cainite knights may not care to share the kine with vampires outside the society of chivalry, and few things draw suspicion away from one vampire more than his triumphant destruction of another. A knight who takes up the mantle of monster-hunting gives up much of mundane life, sacrificing his own comfort and opportunity for the sake of others… as well, of course, as for the rewards and honors that

The Importance of the Story

The excuse a Cainite knight gives for avoiding the sun affects *every* aspect of his or her existence. Storyteller and player alike should spend time considering the ramifications of whatever excuse the knight chooses. If he's cursed, can the curse be lifted? Do priests and devout laymen urge him to pilgrimage and acts of piety to earn God's favor? If it's an oath taken to a loved one or someone else in the culture of chivalry, can he be released from it? What sort of self-obsessed person would bind a knight in ways that so thoroughly handicap his ability to perform his duties? If it's apparently born of religious devotion, what other signs of such zealous piety does he show?

A Storyteller bent on destroying Cainite knights could do it. All it takes is a few sufficiently nosy or narrow-minded mortal bystanders to shatter any cover story and bring the knight to Final Death. Doing so leaves little room for anything else to happen in a chronicle. Don't play this out with the player as the Storyteller's adversary. The Storyteller can and should require the player to make some effort at roleplaying the constant deception Cainite knights must maintain but then reward effort with reasonable success.

come from successful hunting. A Cainite can combine this explanation with any of the others: Perhaps a monster cursed him before its destruction, for instance, or perhaps he's taken an oath to avoid the sunlight so as to dedicate himself wholly to reclaiming the night (which God made along with the day) from evil.

Chivalry as Cover

Cainites of every age may use chivalry as a cover for their own activities without believing in it at all. The same factors that make vampires good rulers and commanders also make them good liars: When vampires practice to deceive, very few mortals can catch them at it except through sheer luck.

Once accepted as a knight, a power-mongering vampire has nearly unlimited license to pursue his personal ambitions. He must keep his mortal superiors satisfied and avoid triggering revolt among his vassals. Apart from that, he can get away with murder, literally.

Knights at the end of the 12th century still tell with shudders the story of Anheloch, a Bohemian count who made professions of chivalry and hosted knights come to fight against Teutonic pagans. He gradually grew jealous of the visitors' riches (he dwelled in a poor mountainous region) and, in the 1140s, took to killing some of them to steal their goods. Then, he blamed the deaths on pagan warriors and drew even more visitors bent on revenge, only to become more victims of his lust for gold. He sustained the deception for more than 30 years before slipping up in the presence of a young monk, who recognized a pectoral cross as belonging to the his deceased uncle. Anheloch confessed to the murders under torture and perished on the rack. Such abuses occur infrequently, but no land is altogether free of them.

To be an effective tyrannical knight, a Cainite either needs the protection of an acquiescent lord or needs to hold regional or national power on his own. Knights of lesser rank who abuse their power can only escape punishment by spending a lot of time away. It's certainly possible to play a character who "uses up" fiefs every few years and then moves on to adopt a new identity somewhere else, but the nomadic impulse runs contrary to most Cainites' desire for stability. Great abuses require great authority: The abuser must buy off or intimidate potential challengers. Cainites enjoy distinct advantages when it comes to simple power politics. As his regime endures, the tyrant becomes the butt of hostile stories, sermons and songs, but as long as resentment doesn't turn into active insubordination, subjects may rave as they see fit. Whining often defuses a rebellious spirit that could otherwise turn troublesome.

In time, an abusive lord must come into conflict with the Church. He may hope to find high officials willing to take bribes (in money, land, favors or some other suitable form) and seldom has to look very far. The upper reaches of the Church hierarchy are highly political, with few bishops achieving their office without a fine eye for useful alliances. Only the most genuinely devout bishop complains too loudly about other forms of unchivalrous behavior so long as the Church gets its cut of any ill-gotten gains. But then, true believers upset human plans as well as the schemes of Cainites.

But I Was Here First

A vampire who's held a domain for several centuries may find the world changing around him and providing opportunities for unchivalrous conduct. For instance, centuries after the end of the Roman Empire, northern Spain was a quiet place, and vampires there could rule almost as openly as the Tzimisce do in Eastern Europe. In the ninth century, peasants discovered the tomb of the apostle St. James in the extreme northwestern corner of Iberia. Within a century, pilgrims from all over Europe began flocking to Santiago de Compostela. All the lords of the roads to Santiago gained unexpected (and often unwanted) influence. A vampire inclined to rapine and plunder could conceal his crimes with very little effort. The medieval world is one where travel of some sort is far more common than the 20th century cliché would have it, and this provides excellent cover.

More Honor Than Riches

After a few generations of being divided among all heirs, even a large estate doesn't amount to much. Primogeniture, the inheritance of most or all of a legacy by the eldest male heir, is not yet universal in all areas. Population growth puts pressure on available resources (by the standards of the time, though all lands would seem thin and rarefied to later generations), and there's never enough to satisfy everyone's wants and needs. The typical knight oversees a fief barely capable of supporting his own household, his horse and military equipment and perhaps a few retainers. Supporting even a single squire often costs more than a poor knight can afford. Rather than towering over peasants from a sprawling castle far away, the poor knight often labors right beside them.

A vampire, of course, cannot tend crops or herds. (He can perform some of the work customarily done at night, like milking, if he can keep the animals calm.) If he doesn't inherit or win in fief enough to allow for hiring workers to fill in for him, he needs to acquire extra laborers quickly. Dissatisfied peasants go looking for grounds for complaint and can pierce many layers of deception when properly motivated. Fortunately, vampiric prowess makes it relatively easy to win ransoms and other trophies in sufficient quantity to pay for what the estate can't support on its own.

Even a knight who holds enough land and other resources to assign fiefs of his own likely doesn't have a great deal of luxury. Much of the revenue from his larger holding must go to maintaining a larger force of subordinate knights, squires and other retainers. He must keep reserves of money and supplies to deal with emergencies like famines and sieges. Any luxuries in his home or lifestyle come at the expense of something else — preachers who condemn indulgence as a dangerous sin actually have a point. A vampire who spends very much on vampiric shelter and the like without providing visible cover risks condemnation for greed, incompetence or both.

Not Only the Damned

Keep in mind that mortals may avoid the sun for all the reasons given here and more. Curses afflict fewer knights than vows and demands, of course. Cainites invent very few of the excuses pertaining to courtly love or sacred duty. Rather, they see mortals bearing those loads and appropriate the explanations. A mortal who hears a Cainite story involving any of these rationales won't think "How strange, I've never encountered that before," but something more like "Ah, another unfortunate (or extraordinarily devout) soul." Likely the Cainite is the first individual to use a particular rationale in the presence of a mortal observer, particularly one off major travel routes, but stories circulate far and wide of the lengths to which various passions drive knights. Cainites and their need for perpetual cover blend right in with the human landscape of inspiration and obsession.

Praying Without Ceasing

The increasing popularity of pilgrimage and crusade creates complications for Cainites. In the centuries between the fall of the western Roman Empire and the rise of successors to Charlemagne, religious relics and believers with True Faith tended to stay where they were. Vampires could learn which spots to avoid while maintaining the profession of religion, whether sincere or faked. As social networks reemerge and, in particular, as chivalry motivates knights to quest for tokens of holiness and bring them home, vampires must dodge through an ever more complicated maze of dangers.

The challenge of True Faith poses special complications for Cainite knights on crusade, discussed separately below. At home, vampiric lords must make sure that their resident priests and favored relics aren't too potent — vampiric needs can contribute to a substantial portion of the trade in fake relics, if the Storyteller wants to add a wrinkle to the trend. A knight who arranges to associate with overtly corrupt priests may expose himself to dangers he doesn't imagine: most vampires don't know much about the Cainite Heresy until its advocates come looking for them (see **Cainite Heresy** for the gory details). In addition to that vampiric menace, the lord's patronage of venal or otherwise sinful priests can attract hostile attention from reform-minded clergy, both superiors in the hierarchy looking to purge wickedness and outside reformers bent on shouting examples of the hierarchy's failings.

While the vast majority of knights do believe in Christianity, they don't all feel called to displays of fanatical zeal. For many knights, chivalry sets up knighthood as a pathway to God independent of the priests and their clerical hierarchy. Knowing that they act as God's emissaries in a wicked world, knights may or may not bother to pay a lot of attention to church attendance. A Cainite knight need merely say that he doesn't much care for the bleatings of un-martial cloistered men in robes or a Cainite lady allude to priests not always having been entirely gentlemanly in her presence, to avoid most questions about absence from church functions.

The Ladies of Shadow

The vast majority of knights are male, but women do sometimes run estates, patronize less wealthy knights and aspirants, travel as troubadours and even lead other knights into battle. Chivalry is a practical, as well as idealistic, view of the world. A woman who conducts herself according to chivalric code and succeeds in her endeavors presumably enjoys the same divine favor as a man doing the same things. Cainite women comprise a minority of women active in chivalry, but a larger fraction than their male counterparts. Cainite culture traditionally place less emphasis on single-sex roles, since gender matters less under the Curse. Chivalry allows Cainite women to exercise themselves in public in ways that few earlier cultures did — not just as healers and priestesses but as warriors and authorities.

A woman played a key part in the spread of troubadour poetry from its Muslim inspirations in Andalusia to the courts of Languedoc France. Wallada was born to Caliph al-Mustaki and a Christian slave; with her blue eyes and red hair, she was the subject of a fair number of songs by poets she sponsored. She also supported scholars of many kinds and appears in the dedications of books on philosophy and the sciences. Few Cainites could risk the visibility of someone like Wallada, but their influence can be substantial, even with the constraints of the Sixth Tradition.

A lady who simply discharges her expected social role need not have a dull existence. The lady holds real power in her lord's absence. Even while he's present, he generally leaves much of the routine oversight to her. She negotiates with buyers and sellers, deals with potential crimes that she'd rather not have come to the lord's attention and otherwise immerses herself in the affairs of the community. If her lord's fief includes significant resources, she (rather than he) most often arranges patronage of poets, artists and the like. In theory, her husband dedicates himself to the manly arts of war, which means that most or all of the rest of life lies within her sphere of influence.

The more prominent the lord's position, the more opportunities his lady has to engage in intrigue and adventure. The lady of a count, duke or king wields substantial influence. Her preferences shape artistic trends and even religious decisions, since flatterers and sincere imitators alike follow her lead. With a few well-placed commissions, she can elevate an obscure favorite or demote a popular client she dislikes. This isn't just a matter of fashion in clothes and art: It applies equally to construction and what later generations will call "infrastructure," the roads, canals, bridges and so on that tie together the pieces of a holding. When the lord's away, the lady also makes decisions on military matters; if enemies attack, she may even lead the troops into battle or supervise their campaign.

In the course of her routine, a well-placed vampiric lady interacts with every stratum of her society. She meets with priests at services and in personal visits, with artisans, with laborers and with the infirm or sick if she does any charitable service. In this steady social flow, she has ample opportunity to feed, to consider candidates for ghouls and even to recruit possible childer. The lady can be as aloof or as involved as she chooses with very little fear of suspicion, unless she's profoundly careless or unlucky in exercising her vampiric nature.

The ideal of the weak, helpless lady fit only for looking decorative actually comes from later centuries. The women of the Dark Medieval era don't have the luxury of being useless: There's always more work to be done than people to do it. When the men are away, the work doesn't suddenly stop. Women and men alike think of some jobs as more suitable or appropriate for women, but pressing need excuses deviations from expectations.

Chapter One provides additional details on the mortal woman's lot in the chivalric world. Chapter Five has extensive advice for creating credible and exciting female characters, both in spurs and as associates of knights.

The Knight at Home

Cainite knights of the Dark Medieval world share their living peers' concern with land. Like mortals, Cainites rely on

The Mechanics of the Estate

It takes one to five laborers to generate enough surplus to be worth a dot of Resources. The form of the surplus depends on the area: It can be tradable crops, wine, craftwork or anything else someone regards as valuable. It can also be labor itself, traded out wherever there's a need. That's the labor of one or two peasant families, supported by the rest. Women and children work, as well as men, in various roles, and their labor together adds up to Resources for their lord.

Ten laborers' surplus provides a second dot of Resources. It takes two to five families to support them (two if the families are unusually large and prosperous, three to five under more typical conditions). Fifty laborers' surplus provides the third dot of Resources. That's the working population of a typical village. A hundred laborers create the surplus necessary for the fourth dot of Resources, and 500 laborers' surplus provides the fifth dot. It takes several villages' populations to underwrite that much effort, and it's vulnerable to disruptions like war and plague. The Storyteller shouldn't arbitrarily abuse the privilege, but from time to time, it's appropriate to make the fifth dot of Resources unavailable until the calamity of the moment passes.

High-ranking nobles, in theory, have access to substantially more labor than five dots of Resources require. In practice, most of the extra isn't freely available. It's tied up in maintaining the land, buildings and other physical properties of the fief and in paying wages to staff, mercenaries and others who earn a living working for the noble. A lord can plan ahead: If he refrains from using the fourth or fifth dot of Resources for a month, the player can roll Wits + Seneschal, difficulty 10. If the roll succeeds, on the following month the lord has the equivalent of six dots in Resources. Each extra month of Resource conservation reduces the difficulty of the roll by one.

ASHEN KNIGHT

land to support them and their retinues. Cainites have even more reasons to worry about the complications of extended travel than mortals and, thus, join their fellow knights in making excuses to avoid most pilgrimages and crusades. A Cainite knight who stays near his holdings most of the time makes his existence simpler in some ways but at the cost of sustained scrutiny by his subjects and neighbors.

The Well-Tended Estate

No Cainite can ever go out to take part in planting or harvesting the crops. Many Cainites would feel acutely uncomfortable doing so even if they could, since agriculture hearkens back to Caine's own sin. A Cainite knight must tend his estate with the help of intermediaries. Labor doesn't just provide support for the community and the surplus that allows luxuries for the lord and his favored subjects. In the Dark Medieval world, work is a sacrament, as well as part of God's curse on Adam. Shared labor builds ties of fellowship among the laborers and can even inspire friendships across the gap between lord and commoner. Separation from shared labor means that Cainite lords must work to develop other opportunities for such ties or risk isolation and losing the support of their subjects.

A good wife — informed, capable of making decisions and with enough presence to win the obedience of servants — can be as important to a Cainite husband as to a mortal one. The knight must win her support, but it's not necessary that she actually believe the story he tells about why he avoids daylight. Instead, he can bring to bear the blood oath, as well as Disciplines like Dominate and Presence. As in past eras, wives of Dark Medieval lords cover for many failures, from mistresses to bastards a father chooses not to acknowledge, to personal obsessions and derangements. A supportive wife may even cover up cowardly avoidance of fundamental chivalric duties. She may be conditioned by Dominate or Presence, or she may simply do her duty to her lord for reasons of her own. The overly political nature of arranged marriages frees Cainites from some complications, since it's not expected that the wife must in every case overflow with love for, and devotion to, her husband.

An unmarried knight must find someone else to act as overseer of daytime affairs. If he can trust someone in his own family, that's a good choice. Almost every knight with an estate worth managing has needy relatives, one of whom might prove a good seneschal. If he's audacious, he might let his mistress oversee the estate routine like a wife would, but that inevitably attracts gossip and even clerical censure, unless the knight enjoys a great deal of prestige indeed. Most commonly, he turns to one of his retainers: an injured squire with a knack for management, an aged colleague too old for the rough-and-tumble of martial life or anyone in the knight's ranks who happens to catch his attention.

A Cainite woman in the noble and knightly ranks of society almost always needs to acquire a suitable husband. Social pressure frowns on women who refrain from both the bonds of matrimony and the call of the nun's habit. Once married, of course, the Cainite lady may use her husband as a convenient front, sending him away on long trips so that, in practice, she holds the power over "his" estate and affairs. For the full exercise of her power, she must either control his chosen overseer or arrange to be selected as the overseer herself. A docile husband attracts some jokes at his expense. If the wife does her duties well and gives him liberty to go errant, to war or on crusade, he may end up envied more than mocked by other knights, who'd also like to be free to neglect boring tasks.

Each Cainite lady must decide for herself how much control to exert. Simple force of will made manifest in Empathy or Intimidation often suffices — after all, mortal women in the same society manage to control their men without vampiric advantages, so clearly it's feasible. Making a husband into a ghoul works if the lady wishes to give him advantages for his knightly pursuits, though there's always some risk of attracting the wrong sort of attention. Furthermore, chivalric culture favors very elaborate displays of joy and sorrow, and a knight who's served as a ghoul for many years but somehow managed to break the blood oath might decide it's time to repent publicly and help exterminate the vampiric menace. Whatever means of influence the Cainite lady uses, she must take care to renew its application regularly.

Ghoul husbands offer one practical, if amoral, advantage. Should a serious threat from witch-hunters arise, the Cainite lady can sacrifice her husband, exposing his supernatural abilities after rendering him unable to implicate her through Disciplines like Dominate or Presence. The sacrifice may or may not appease the hunters, but it at least gives her some time to flee to safety.

The Fundamentals of Survival

Vampires must feed. Cainites who stand in the ranks of knights enjoy some distinctive opportunities to do so.

Mighty Servants

In the Dark Medieval present, a ghoul knight generally poses little risk to his vampiric master as long as the vitae keeps flowing. Treachery is possible but would expose the ghoul to all the complications of accelerated aging and loss of supernatural benefits. Any knight who stops to think for a moment — which admittedly excludes a fair number of them — refrains from betrayal at least until he's lined up a new sponsor. It is an age of heroic expectation. The tales of the time recount amazing feats, mingling historical fact with pious wish and sheer fantasy. Dark Medieval people expect more from the world than later, more secular views can allow.

Whoever the Cainite chooses to represent him in overseeing mundane duties must above all possess the Seneschal Knowledge. On most estates, Animal Ken is almost as necessary. By definition, the knight and his retinue have horses to tend, and livestock of all kinds provide trade goods as well as provisions and raw material for the people in the knight's charge. An overseer who lacks prowess in Crafts or Herbalism must maintain good relations with subordinates who know these skills. An overseer who doesn't start off knowing Law will acquire it over time, possibly along with Politics, depending on how important his master's estate is.

Knights habitually engage in violence. They get wounded. Every gathering of knights includes a fair number — sometimes an outright majority — with significant wounds. Few knights notice another bite or scratch, and wounded knights spend enough time having to lie down or otherwise be off their feet that their vampiric peers can feed with little risk of discovery. In a world where medicine is at best an inexact science, too, the symptoms of habitual feeding don't stand out against the background of poor hygiene and often-miserable diet. Note that non-chivalric vampires can and do exploit these same opportunities, and Cainite knights may even earn reputations as witch-hunters for destroying their rivals.

Cainites who hold fiefs can feed on their subjects, while Cainites errant can feed on the commoners of the areas through which they travel. In both cases, they must take some precautions. Death is common in the Dark Medieval world. Precisely because it comes so regularly, people know what it looks like. Commoners and nobles alike know the signs of famine, plague, common diseases, violence and so on. Death by exsanguination resembles nothing usual. Any vampire prone to losing control soon leaves a trail of corpses that rouse local interest in devils who need killing. Hiding all the bodies doesn't help much, as a pattern of mysterious disappearances also creates fear of supernatural predators.

If the Cainite knows for sure that other predators such as Lupines are in the area, he might try to make his victims look like those of another sort of attack. (Protean, for instance, provides a passable imitation of werewolf talons.) Then he can lead the hunt himself or put it under the leadership of a trusted subordinate. The problem with such hunts is that they're easier to start than to stop, and there'd better be something for the angry peasants to fall upon. If they feel that someone is hiding the truth from them, they may turn on any of the authorities in the area, including the Cainite.

The Knight in the World

Knights are men of action. Chivalry concerns itself with feats of arms, not with accounting or housework. Knights of every level of income like to spend time being active. Many of them become violent or abusive when confined to their estates; there's a limit to how far they can go in punishing peasants and bystanders before a higher-ranking knight calls them to account to their oaths of fealty. Fortunately for action-seeking knights, chivalry provides a variety of excuses to travel.

Richard the Lion-Hearted has spent only a fraction of his reign actually governing England from within English borders. Other kings also travel to take part in crusades, wars and tournaments, though most pay a bit more attention to their duties. At the bottom of the social pyramid, knights who can just barely afford to support themselves go wandering in search of paying work and the chance to earn ransoms. The duties of home and estate weigh most heavily on knights who aren't desperate (and therefore have little or nothing to lose) and who also aren't prosperous (and therefore enjoy enough sur-

Mechanics of the Hunt

The hunt itself consists in its most basic form of a series of resisted rolls, the hunting knight's Perception + Leadership against the target's Wits + Alertness, both difficulty 6. When the knight accumulates as many successes as the target has points of current Willpower, the knight's subjects succeed in finding the target, and combat ensues. Lupines are the most likely targets of such a hunt but not the only ones; consult **Vampire: The Dark Ages** and **The Bygone Bestiary** for other suitable creatures of the night.

If the knight directing the hunt botches a roll, he does something to give away his own supernatural condition. It could be as simple as a display of superhuman strength or as disastrous as frenzy in the midst of a crowd. Adjust the details depending on how severe the failure is, and emphasize roleplaying in the knight's quest for a solution.

Allow the knight to plan ahead. For each night before the hunt that the knight spends in preparation, let the player roll Wits + Acting (or Subterfuge, if it's higher). On a success, grant the player one extra die to use at some point during the hunt, either to boost a hunting roll or to help escape troubles (quick rhetoric, emergency use of a commanding Discipline and the like).

plus to feel at liberty to choose their own course of action). These mid-ranking knights form an important constituency in official excuses for action like crusades and wars.

A knight in search of a reason to travel can always find the infidel lurking somewhere that calls for an extended trip and war, from the Holy Land to Iberia. Closer to home, heretics may gather in sufficient numbers that loyal sons of the Church must gather to stamp them out. The Italian peninsula has at least one war raging at any given time and always requires mercenaries. No other major wars blot the landscape of Christian Western Europe in 1197, but minor struggles sometimes flare up brightly enough to warrant recruitment of outside help.

Before departing, a knight must make some arrangement to take care of his estate. If he's married, his wife may well assume the duty, or the knight may give it to a trusted seneschal or other assistant. If there's nobody on hand with prior experience in the position, he may have to trust to providence and pick whoever seems most suitable — a retired knight of the region, perhaps, or a priest or the head of a nearby Templar house. Knights who live close to successful monasteries sometimes give their estates into the safekeeping of the monks. (Sometimes a knight returns to find, to his embarrassment, that the brothers run his affairs much better than he can.)

The Ties That Bind

Storytellers and players alike need to keep in mind that oaths of fealty bind lords as well as subjects. The liege swears to protect his vassals, and the noble to protect his subjects. The knight enjoys substantial leeway in the details but does not have unlimited license to do as he pleases.

The knight must pay for services rendered, one way or another: If his foray abroad generates little profit, he can return to find himself in very tight financial circumstances. This simple reality accounts for a significant portion of the looting and pillage many knights do while away. It's the price they pay for the freedom to be excited for a while.

Whoever oversees the fief in the lord's absence must do everything the lord would: administer local justice, protect subjects, resolve disputes, see that the crops get in. Out of the surplus, if any, in all forms of revenue, the overseer pays his own expenses and then sets the remainder aside for the absent lord. The lord necessarily gambles on the overseer's trustworthiness. Will the overseer, in fact, pay what he should? Will he bungle things and reduce the value of the fief or provoke popular discontent? Will he sire bastards with the lord's wife? Will he, perhaps, arrange to discredit the lord and seize the fief for himself?

In addition to all these common concerns, a Cainite who turns his fief over to someone else's custody must make preparations to preserve his secrets. Stashed bodies and occult lore would be just the things to justify forfeiture of the fief and, perhaps, more dire penalties like being hunted for heresy and murder.

Cainites must arrange for their security as they travel. The fortunate few who know enough Protean to merge with the earth (whether by virtue of being Gangrel or through extraordinarily good ties with some Gangrel willing to teach the art) need not worry very much about it. Other vampires have to make sure they have reliable escorts and light-proof transportation. The proliferation of castles in contested areas of England, France, Spain and Germany in the 12th century makes vampiric travel easier by offering more havens, but the problem never goes away altogether. Vampires on the move inevitably spend days or even weeks at a time away from extensive human settlement. They learn to deal with its challenges, or they die. Storytellers who want to make the challenges really difficult should consult **Werewolf: The Dark Ages** for a full panoply of ready adversaries.

The Steed

By definition, knights ride. Chivalry evolves out of thought about the social meaning of the cavalryman's role. Become familiar with the **Vampire: The Dark Ages** rules on horses, and get ready to use them often in chivalric chronicles. Unfortunately, the Curse of Caine makes riding more difficult for vampires than for mortals: Animals' innate sense of Cainite wrongness reveals secrets vampires can hide from human senses. Cainite knights develop one or more of three approaches to the problem.

- **Animal Ken.** The more a Cainite learns about handling animals in general, the more effectively she can calm the fears of her steed.
- **Ghoul Steeds.** Once a steed's drunk the vitae of its master, the usual animal antipathy to vampires fades rapidly.

A ghoul steed offers several advantages, being faster, more enduring and stronger than any normal horse. Creating a ghoul may not be the right course of action, however, given that over time the steed develops a fondness for blood and flesh. The Cainite knight must plan ahead to account for his horse's unusual appetite. The more a Cainite knight travels in close company with mortal knights, the more likely it is that the ghoul horse attracts notice, leading, in turn, to suspicions directed at its rider. A vampire riding on crusade with such a horse can scarcely expect to escape detection, while a vampire traveling alone and with small, short-lived groups along the tournament circuit can avoid most problems easily.

- **Animalism.** This Discipline closes and eventually removes the gap between Cainite and steed. Even with the simplest power alone, a Cainite knight can soothe her horse directly. With the assistance of Ride the Wild Mind, the knight can merge her own soul with that of the horse and command it from within. Quickened Unity deepens the bond in some ways, though overuse of it jeopardizes the Cainite's sense of herself as distinct from the horse.

It's not necessary for Cainite knights to master Animalism, even though it's helpful in some ways. All vampires can make ghouls, and most vampires find it easier to arrange for lessons in Animal Ken than instruction in Animalism. Not all problems confronting vampires need to be solved through the use of Disciplines, and often, the Discipline may not be the best solution even when it's available. Animalism allows for some impressive feats, but human beings have throughout history shown themselves capable of amazing displays of horsemanship, too, without any access to vampiric powers. Vampires can excel in mortal fields of endeavor as easily (if not more so) as they can advance their unique abilities.

The Knight Among Peers

All knights spend some time at court, whether as invited guests (if they've performed noteworthy feats), summoned vassals (for rewards, punishments or just routine meeting) or as drop-in visitors whenever a lord cares to receive company. Cainite knights almost all settle into their cover stories about absence during the day by the time they first visit court, but they must prepare to go over the ground again as they meet knights who haven't yet heard the story. Knights with records of valor and heroism get support from their peers — "Ah, yes, it's a tragic affair, but look how well he bears up under it" — while knights known for cowardice and ignoble behavior find rumor running against them.

Few courts of the 12th century resemble the opulent splendor portrayed in later tales. The constraints described above in "More Honor Than Riches" apply to lords as well as vassals. A county-wide meeting likely happens in a bare castle room with rough furniture, not a splendid chamber dedicated to the task. Knights in the field economize even more, using temporary chambers or borrowed rooms wherever they can

Storytelling the Court

The more exalted the roles characters fill, the more formal and "courtly" the court itself becomes. Characters who struggle for survival as knights errant and minor fief holders seldom, if ever, experience the great pageantry of which troubadours sing. Characters who hold major duchies and counties mingle regularly with kings and potentates and move in the midst of events that become the seeds of later epic poems and stories. The more powerful the characters, the more likely they are to change the course of history. Players and Storyteller should work out in advance how they feel about the prospect of diverging from history: It's great when everyone agrees on what they want and terrible when they don't.

Whatever the social strata of the characters, court may be very important or fairly unimportant in a particular chronicle. If players love political intrigue, then pull out all the stops. Troubadours gather material for their songs and satires and love to learn secrets. Cainites' rivals use the minstrels, and so should the characters. The servants of whichever lord hosts the gathering seek to learn what's going on, so as to offer good advice, and engage vassals in exchanges that include mutual deception, careful negotiation and, sometimes, even honest cooperation. The lord's rivals attend or send representatives to official functions and make bids for the loyalty of others. Travelers bring news, good and bad, from afar, while visionaries try to rouse support for crusades, pilgrimages and other pious undertakings. When a knight falls in battle or to disgrace, all the others who might inherit part of his fief maneuver for the chance to claim their share.

If players would rather emphasize other matters, keep court simple. Do play out characters' interactions with their lords, but feel free to handle the rest through a few die rolls, just to check for unusually good or bad results. Some knights play the game of politics very intensively, and others don't, so there's precedent for the characters being involved as much as suits them but no more.

A malicious Storyteller can use the challenges of court life to destroy a Cainite knight character. Don't do so unless the players are ready to make new characters. Court pressures can force a Cainite knight to flee to preserve his secrets, on the assumption that being thought a criminal or heretic is better than being thought a vampire. Again, make sure that players understand what's at stake, just as before any radical change in the characters' place in the world. Players ready for some fresh challenges and interested in roleplaying the conflict of human ideals and vampiric needs may find flight from court just the hook they want.

If the Storyteller wants to bring game mechanics to bear, require players to make Willpower or Self-Control rolls when their characters face provocation to use their vampiric abilities. In most cases, the standard difficulty of 6 is sufficient; don't raise the difficulty very often. Cainite knights have experience dealing with these things, after all, and if the difficulty is too high, then no Cainite can ever sustain the illusion of mortality.

find the space. Knights from Western Europe write with envy and amazement of the ancient wonders of Byzantium and the East, making it clear how different those halls are from the knights' own simple places. The most impressive edifices of the chivalric world are cathedrals, and they're not where knights generally gather to do business.

Though the practice doesn't become common until later centuries, some monarchs of the Dark Medieval world do engage in "royal processions." A king on procession pays a visit to selected nobles, generally ones he wants to distract and bankrupt, and makes an extended stay with each of them. They're required to pay the expenses of hosting the king and all his courtiers for as long as the king deems appropriate, and complaints make the host look petty or as if he has something to hide. Cainite knights face even more challenges, as it's harder to escape a royal summons to join the king on a hunt or at a fair or for a meeting than to evade lesser knights.

Cainite knights must police themselves (and their fellow vampires) against exercising more authority than their mortal positions warrant. It's so easy to draw upon Cainite powers and make everyone in sight yield to vampiric commands. When a knight does that to his lord, however, it's insubordination, if not outright rebellion; the lord is justified in responding with punishments from humiliating drudge work to the removal of knightly status altogether. When humans lead, vampires who wish to take part in the society must submit.

Cainites hostile to chivalry cite this as one of the major problems with the whole idea. It inverts the proper flow of authority. Cainites may be cursed by God, but they're fit, so pre-chivalric vampires say, to rule the kine. Advocates of chivalry respond that the ideal of making strength serve justice suits Cainite as well as kine and offer the hope that virtuous service may lead to redemption. In the meantime, chivalry provides scope for heroic action without all the complicated exercises vampires must normally perform to avoid attracting attention. The combination of ideal and entertainment makes submission a reasonable price to pay, at least for some vampires.

Every knight has a lord. Lords give orders and expect their vassals to obey as long as the orders fall within the scope of oaths of fealty and the general morality of chivalry. Even if some Cainites see the feudal order as a complex game, the mortals who participate take it seriously. The ties of fealty are, as most knights see it, the only bulwark against the twin evils of tyranny and chaos. The feudal order rose in response to the real need for social organization after the fall of the Roman Empire and its successor states and provides the framework within which whatever peace may be found can flourish. Chivalry sets boundaries on the sorts of conflicts knights can indulge in and their scope for independent action.

Knights who refuse to accept orders from their sworn superiors threaten the cornerstone of the whole system. Their superiors, their fellow vassals and most other knights in the area join forces to stamp out the threat. The feudal system provides room for a certain measure of independence and certainly doesn't require perfect morality — great monsters can flourish within the system. Like all social systems, however, it does require public acceptance from its participants. Insubordination that stays discreet and quiet draws little condemnation, except from the sort of zealot that temperate adherents to chivalry generally ignore anyway. Public refusal strikes at the fundamental principle of loyalty and must be addressed at once. Friends of the rebel gather to remonstrate with him, to plead for a show of repentance and submission. Rivals challenge the rebel to duels and trials by combat. Enemies may even mount a war in hopes of claiming land and resources to incorporate into their own holdings. The more serious or prolonged the rebellion, the more severe the response: A single act of disobedience seldom triggers a war, while years of sustained resistance almost always do.

In this situation, Cainites enjoy a distinct advantage. Their superior and supernatural abilities make it possible for them to manipulate lords into not giving awkward orders. The tricky part is in making the manipulation focused enough that the lord's lack of independent will doesn't attract attention itself, perhaps leading to calls for doctors and priests to investigate the malaise. Weak-willed lords lose respect, and without respect, no system of personal authority lasts very long. Intervention behind the scenes leaves the public chain of command intact, and therefore, makes it easier for insubordinate Cainite vassals to go about their way.

Tournaments

Cainites can take part in tournaments only in limited ways. Most of the battles take place during the day, when only vampires with amazing (Methuselah-like) levels of Stamina and Fortitude can be active in any meaningful sense (and they have other priorities).

Cainite neonates and ancillae with a fondness for tournaments introduced the custom of the "midnight tournament." These foreshadow later developments in reenactment and formalized presentation in tournaments. The battle area is necessarily smaller than in regular tournaments and marked off by torches (concealed and decorated so as to reduce the risk of frenzy). The combatants wear bright garb and decorations intended to catch the light, so as to make them stand out in dark surroundings. Most battles take place on foot rather than horseback, since the risks of injury to horses are too great.

The early midnight tournaments, starting around 1150, brought together only Cainite knights. As word spread of the opportunity for fresh challenges, mortals began taking part as well. While midnight tournaments pose no threat to the popularity of regular full-scale tournament brawling, they offer an interesting alternative and plenty of chances for knights to show their prowess in unusual ways. In addition, the generally confused environment of midnight tournaments reduces the risk of exposure for Cainite knights a little too careless about use of their powers.

All tournaments include a halo of non-combat social activities. Knights gather to visit, trade stories, socialize, pursue romantic liaisons and simply spend time together.

Daytime tournaments create substantial complications for Cainites and test cover stories as thoroughly as summons to courts do. Midnight tournaments allow some nocturnal activity, but most mortals don't stop all daytime affairs simply because it would be convenient for the vampires among them to do so. Cainite knights who wish to take part in tournament social life must bring to bear all the cleverness they can muster.

Cainite ladies face almost as many obstacles. They're not expected to fight among the ranks, of course, but they are expected to watch, to bestow favors on the knights they choose to sponsor and to help award prizes to the victors. A lady who somehow never manages to attend these gatherings undercuts her social standing and needs a good cover story; even chronic illness won't serve all the time. On the other hand, a Cainite lady can do as well as any other at exhibiting her crafts and providing hospitality for evening and night events. She can even make substantial show of piety by attending all the late-night and predawn church services that local priests conduct in hopes of bringing some religious conviction to the brawling knights.

Male and female Cainites alike can exploit tournaments for their own ends. In the press of the crowd, it's relatively easy to cultivate potential feeding stock, ghouls or even childer. Knights and bystanders do die at tournaments, whether in battle or due to food poisoning, bungled robbery and other complications. One more death doesn't stand out nearly as much as it would in less crowded circumstances.

The Knight's Duty: War

In the Dark Medieval world, people in all social strata sometimes go to battle. Peasants band together to defend their lands against bandits and also provide the bulk of military levies in times of actual war. Shopkeepers have to defend their goods, while merchants routinely travel armed to deal with challenges on the roads. Nobles' claims to exclusive right to the use of weapons (some specific weapons or any deadly force at all) still attract debate. The first such claims circulated in the last few decades, and it will take more than a century for them to become widely accepted. For now, in an environment where civil authority can't be relied on in most locales, individuals and impromptu groups of all kinds defend themselves and their interests.

Knights enjoy popular respect when they actually do what they profess as their calling, using their strength to protect the weak. Insofar as claims of noble monopoly on weaponry prevail, they do so because knights show themselves worthy. Conversely, bad knights breed popular suspicion and efforts to secure peace and safety some other way.

Wars Near and Far

Many knights have few obligations at home. Their fiefs are small, their retainers few in number (if any exist at all), and they almost always have someone capable of managing the

Me and Mine

When Cainites ride to war, they seldom do so with clan concerns foremost. Vampires may fight to defend their sires, protect their childer and cooperate with like-minded Cainites, but "clan" as an abstract concept means little to most vampires. Religion, ethnicity, point of origin and common interests all matter more — in the vast majority of cases — when vampires consider how they'll respond to challenges. The generalizations about clan in this section shouldn't dominate characters' thinking, and for every trend, there are exceptions and counter-trends.

The great movements of the era, particularly the *Reconquista* and the Crusades, do bring some vampires together along clan lines. Nevertheless, Storytellers don't have to worry about precise conformity with generalizations about the clans unless it suits their particular chronicles.

estate in their absence. Most knights constantly need more wealth than they have. So they go wherever there's a chance to make money and have adventures. Wars rage on the frontiers of Christendom, each with special significance to Cainites in addition to its human dimensions.

• **Iberia.** The most tangled knots of Kindred politics occur in and around the *Reconquista.*

The Assamites pursue their own agenda, which has less do with backing the Islamic powers because they are Muslim than with some complex scheme outsiders do not see. All other clans use the Assamites as bogeymen, mysterious figures who might be tools of any enemy, from a hostile Antediluvian to Satan.

The Lasombra and Toreador fight on both sides of the line between Christian and Muslim, attacking their own kin with as much (if not more) ferocity than they muster against outsiders. The eldest in each clan generally prefer to sit out the war, but neonates and ancillae feel compelled to take action. Generational tensions rise along with religious ones. Vampires of southern and western Iberia tend to regard Islam as the heir to thoughts the vampires wish to preserve, while vampires of northern and eastern Iberia see in Christianity a promise of world order and redemption. No single vampire's attitudes have to conform to the map, however, and dissent flourishes on all sides.

The *Reconquista* doesn't move in a simple, straight line. Cities in the center of the peninsula, like Toledo, change hands repeatedly as the front between Islam and Christendom slides north or south and as factions within each side compete for control. Thus a Lasombra or Toreador scholar who remembers when neither Islam nor Christianity ruled the land may have to consider his profession of allegiance anew every few years or decades. Do he and his childer identify with the current victors and hope that the tides do not turn? Do the vampires try to steer a middle ground of independence and hope that no fanatics on either side take enough umbrage to stamp them out? Every choice comes with risks.

The Brujah also take part on both sides of the *Reconquista*, but then, fractiousness is nothing new to their clan. Nor are their numbers so large — as the *Reconquista* became ever bloodier, many Brujah schemers turned to less turbulent areas where they could work on smaller-scale plans in peace. They pursue their old vendetta against the Ventrue through a variety of mortal agencies — Brujah can be found among both the most fanatical advocates of chivalry and its staunchest enemies, aiming at whatever they see as weak points in their enemies' social structures.

• **The Baltics.** Where the Iberian enemy seems to roll in riches, the targets of knights warring in the lands around the Baltic Sea seem scarcely human at all. The tribes east of Germany resist Christianity and Frankish-inspired culture with passionate loathing. Their long-term prospects offer no hope: Trapped between eastward-expanding Germany and westward-expanding Russia, the space open to pagan, only partially settled existence shrinks. The battle rages on throughout the Dark Medieval era, for centuries after **Vampire: The Dark Ages**' time period. Observers on the spot seldom see the Christian victory as preordained, and as the battle continues, the defenders don't always lose.

The first northern crusade begins in 1147, with muddled origins. The decree — instigated in large measure through the efforts of Bernard of Clairvaux — is in part a response to lackluster results in efforts to recruit northeastern knights for a new crusade in the Holy Land. The Danes, Saxons and Poles are all relatively new to Christianity, which is still spreading and has been established less than a century in most Baltic lands. The call for crusade gives knights in the region an opportunity to prove their zeal without the need to go all the way to the Holy Land and authorization to make war on their eastern neighbors until the Wends and Western Slavs either convert or perish to the last man. For the next half century, conflict rages across northern Germany and Poland, the Christian frontier moving east in fits and starts.

The Telyavelic Tremere play a small but significant part in pagan resistance to the crusaders. They most often concentrate on their fellow vampires, using blood magic to identify Cainite intruders and remove the invaders. Sometimes they also contribute to weather manipulation and other grand magical efforts at defense, but as often as not, find their efforts of this sort stymied by rival magic (and True Faith).

The wars in northeastern Europe provide little glamour. Instead of sunny shores, knights ride through dark forests in often-wet weather, blazing trails and trying to deal with enemies who know the land vastly better than the intruders do. Vampiric factions take part in the struggle, seeking sometimes to use human forces as their tools, sometimes participating in human-led movements. Vampires have cultures as well as clans, and many do not forget their origins. Gangrel and Tzimisce dominate the resistance to Teutonic expansion, while Ventrue lead the push out of Germany into Prussia, Poland and Lithuania.

The Teutonic Knights

The northern crusades include no great orders to rival the Templars or Hospitalers, but that changes in coming decades. The knights of the Hospital of St. Mary of Jerusalem, founded at the start of the 12th century, petition the Pope and the kings of northeastern Europe for the right to become a new military order. Even as negotiations proceed, they demonstrate their worthiness through leadership in battle and recruitment. The knights get their wish in 1198, when they formally become the Teutonic Order. While the Baltics never rouse quite the fervor of the Holy Land, kings and lords from across Europe put in some time fighting in the Teutonic Knights' campaigns. Prescient vampires who make places for themselves in the order early on can spend the ensuing decades building influence among most of the major courts of Europe.

A given chronicle can diverge from history. It seems a certainty that some group will earn papal authority to lead the Teutonic crusades, but it doesn't have to be that particular group. A chronicle focusing on characters strongly committed to crusading could include the emergence of a new order founded by the characters, instead of or in addition to the Teutonic Knights. Perhaps a rivalry to match that of the Templars and Hospitalers could spring up.

• **The Byzantine Frontier.** North of the Holy Land, the Byzantine Empire faces ongoing hostilities with the expanding Seljuk Turks. Byzantium is losing, though few of its leaders and even fewer observers from Western Europe realize it. The Seljuks advance across Asia Minor, absorbing the Byzantine Empire province by province and preparing for the day when they'll sweep through Constantine's city and put an end to the empire. In the meantime, individual knights and whole companies find ready employment with the Byzantine army, which relies heavily on mercenaries.

Much of the conflict for the Byzantine Empire involves no more chivalric issues for Cainites than for mortals. The Tzimisce contribute more vampires to the Byzantine effort and have no use at all for chivalry. They do not drive out chivalrous vampires who wish to assist in the war against the Turks, they simply make their contempt for chivalry clear. Western European vampires who persist in arguing the merits of chivalry find themselves forcibly ejected from Tzimisce-organized forces; the ejected knights may then leave or fight independently, as they choose. On the Muslim side, Assamites and others offer advice to the Turks on dealing with European vampires and otherwise remain aloof from the fray. Assamite elders care more about the conflict for the Holy Land, where European vampires congregate in much greater numbers.

• **The Holy Land.** Three separate crusades and centuries of pilgrimage have brought many European Cainites to the Holy Land. Muslim and Jewish Cainites are even more numerous, leading to conflicts that often bypass matters of clan and chivalry altogether. See **Jerusalem By Night** for an extended discussion of Cainite involvement in the Holy Land.

The War Against Evil: Crusades

To most knights (as to most Christians) the papal summons to crusade *feels* different than the usual rallying for battle. The Pope isn't considered infallible as later theologians will proclaim him, but he's still the first-ranked individual in Christendom, heir to the throne of St. Peter, God's vicar on Earth. When he names an enemy as the enemy of all the faithful, that moves the conflict to a higher plane than a mere tussle over resources or personal honor. Christians in the Eastern communion regard the Pope as merely an archbishop with delusions of grandeur, but the call to crusade finds some willing listeners even where the patriarchs' version of the faith holds sway. Most Christians, when they stop to think about it all, long to see Christendom united, and in theory, crusading does that. Sometimes, it even does so in practice, to varying degrees.

People seldom act for just one reason. Knights sincerely believe that they do God's will and simultaneously look forward to the loot they'll earn sacking heathen cities. Both motives are true, despite being contradictory; it's part of the human condition. The same sorts of contradictions appear in vampiric thought. Vampires go on crusade to earn God's forgiveness and do His will and also to strike at old personal foes, seize valuable new havens and gain influence over the kine for their upcoming moves in the War of Ages. Cainite knights join crusading armies to exploit the rich concentration of blood, to scout out fresh opportunities and to monitor the behavior of human allies, underlings and puppets. All of these agendas rest side-by-side in vampiric minds with the pursuit of holiness.

Likewise, Cainite knights may decline to go on crusade for multiple reasons. Not absolutely every single available knight can go on a given crusade: Someone needs to stay behind to administer justice and keep the peace. A Cainite who doesn't wish to deal with the complications discussed below may present himself as making the heroic sacrifice ("I must let others fight for God, while I secure our homes") and parlay the respect earned into later diplomatic advantage. If he appears too eager to avoid the crusade, he risks being accused of cowardice — his sacrifice must seem genuine, made reluctantly.

See **Jerusalem by Night**, Chapter Two, for a history of the Crusades in the Holy Lands, and page 48 for an overview of the crusades in northeastern Europe.

The Beginning: Mustering

Crusade begins with the Pope's bull identifying the part of the world needing Christian liberation and summoning the faithful to their task. News spreads rapidly, but not instantly. Rumors generally circulate before the Pope makes his decree; often the bull follows on the heels of months or years of public debate as to whether a particular crisis warrants a crusade. As the call goes out, kings and high-ranking nobles assemble their

forces. The whole machinery of the feudal hierarchy creaks into motion: Each superior in turn commands the service due from his vassals, who call on their own vassals and so on down to the individual knights with nobody to serve them.

It takes time for armies to gather. A minimum of weeks passes, more often months. Knights must all arrange for others to care for estates. New equipment of all kinds becomes more expensive, and anyone willing to make loans or "gifts" rakes in the profits. (The most greedy find themselves marked for later revenge as wicked profiteers upon the cause of righteous justice.) In some crusades, a full year elapses between widespread distribution of the bull and the final gathering of troops for departure.

In the interval, ambitious individuals and groups maneuver for advantage. A lord whose forces muster quickly shows himself worthy of the trust given to him by his own superior — and his troops may end up making local war on less worthy lords while they wait for the crusading army to depart. On the other hand, a lord whose vassals gather the crops and make good plans for the well-being of their fiefs, even at the cost of some delay in mustering, shows merits of other kinds and may well end up awarded management (temporarily or permanently) of assets previously assigned to his rivals.

The chaos of muster provides excellent opportunities for vampires. Prey gathers thickly. Hygiene suffers even in the best-prepared temporary encampments, so few observers notice or worry about temporary weakness and other symptoms of feeding. A typical army ranges from hundreds to a few thousand soldiers, plus several times their number in squires, cooks, baggage handlers and other servants and support staff. They sleep in tents, under whatever cover they can scrounge, or in homes whose owners they evict, temporarily or permanently. On the road, they spread out across the countryside, the forward units of the army hours or even days ahead of the rear. The army moves as a dirty, dusty mob (unless it's raining, in which case it's a dirty, muddy mob), with little coordination or discipline except on special show occasions.

Vampires who work together enjoy unprecedented opportunities to plot and manipulate human targets in coordinated fashion. They can also work together to foil, confuse or outright destroy human hunters getting too close to the vampires' own secrets. Vampires who use their powers more or less openly may demonstrate greater-than-human prowess in impromptu tournaments, diplomatic gatherings and the like. Vampiric ladies mingle with their mortal counterparts as well and may build their own networks of influence, which they have time to strengthen once the armies depart.

The Road to the Enemy

Crusades almost always happen at the borders of Christendom (apart from crusades against internal heresies, and those don't become common until after the era of **Vampire: The Dark Ages**). Just as it takes time to assemble armies, so it takes more time to move them. An army travels at the speed of its slowest members or develops stragglers. A large

group of mounted knights and foot soldiers with their accompanying provisions and supporting laborers moves at half the speed of a small group of mounted men or even less than that. Detachments ride ahead to scout terrain and deal with small-scale obstacles, both physical (unbridged rivers) and social (recalcitrant lords). The army may fragment along the march, but it cannot risk arriving piecemeal anywhere near serious adversaries, or it will face almost certain defeat as each piece succumbs to resistance and counterattacks.

Vampires who enjoyed an easy, rewarding existence during muster now face many more challenges. They move with large groups of violence-loving, edgy men bent on finding excuses to attack possible enemies. The armies seek to do God's will but also to enrich themselves in the process. Discovering a monster in the ranks would provide a fine opportunity to seize all the creature's resources and transfer them to the brave souls who found the thing. Vampires therefore need to exert extra caution; everything they know about social finesse may be required to compensate for a bit of bad luck or an especially nosy fellow crusader.

In the Dark Medieval world, lighting at night is scarce. Crusading armies move en masse, with many tents of similar design — while there's little mass production, there's common wisdom about what works and what can be made quickly. A tired and possibly drunk knight can all too easily stumble into the wrong tent. Troubadours tell funny stories about the mishaps resulting from such errors. For a Cainite, finding a mortal stumbling in while he feeds on a chosen victim might not be funny at all. Knights (and squires and servants and others in an army on the move) conceal stolen loot in the tents of others, then frame them for the theft. A Cainite who's been quite careful about his vampiric practices could nonetheless end up facing hostile questioning about offenses he didn't actually commit at all and risk exposure of his true secrets. A knight looking for a place for a quick twist with his chosen lover might well think that the quiet tent of that cursed or oath-bound knight who's out and around after dark is just the place and find more than he bargained for. The whole panoply of human foibles manifests itself during army travels, and others' vices can expose vampiric secrets just as easily as the vampire's own carelessness.

In addition, crusaders travel with every holy relic (real or fake) whose owner can be persuaded to let it go. A strong crusader force positively reeks of holiness, and even though only a small fraction of the artifacts or their guardians radiate True Faith, every little bit makes it worse for vampires. Many vampires seek excuses to travel as members of outlying forces: scouting ahead, making side missions, bringing up the rear, anything to get away from the core of the army.

Traveling vampires can feed on the natives of the areas their armies march through. In one sense, this is an easy, nearly risk-free undertaking. The vampire won't be back until the crusade is over and may well not return the same way even then. Among so large a gathering, any revengeful hunter is unlikely to find the right target. On the other hand, it takes just one obviously vampire-drained body to turn the whole army into volunteer witch-hunters. It's widely known, or at least believed, that Satan sends extra minions of all sorts to attempt to ruin a crusade. Even lukewarm believers can rouse to fervor when confronted with a supernatural threat to the righteous cause.

Fraud, Pious and Otherwise

Vampires worried about the dangers of real relics can substitute their own. Vampiric craftsmanship reaches heights most humans never attain, through superior dexterity and skill. In addition, vampires can apply their distinctive Disciplines. Most useful of all, but not readily available to most knights, is Chimerstry. A Cainite knight with a Ravnos prisoner might extract lessons upon pain of Final Death or with the aid of mind-controlling Disciplines; no Ravnos is likely to want much to do with knights voluntarily.

The War

Many aspects of crusading differ little, if at all, from their counterparts in any other war. Strategy and tactics do not go on holiday simply because the Pope blesses the undertaking. Generals have to put forth extra effort to keep zealous troops in line, but there are few fundamentally new challenges involved. Vampires among crusaders face the challenge of accounting for daytime absences — with Christendom at stake, many crusaders pressure their comrades to forsake lesser, personal commitments. Cainite Knights find plenty of opportunity to call upon both their mundane abilities and their Disciplines. In some cases they must risk outright mind control to create the illusion of obedience or wipe out any inclination to question… and then watch in hopes that no uncontrolled outsider comes by at the wrong time.

Some vampires arrange to serve as messengers, scouts and spies, all assignments that don't require rushing into battle with the main mob. A knight who develops a reputation for keen insight can enjoy a certain amount of personal privacy as long as good information keeps coming. Likewise, a knight who shows he can carry important information to distant recipients quickly and reliably usually enjoys freedom from too many inquiries. Kings and commanders have too many other things to worry about to spend much time asking why something actually works as well as they'd hope.

The longer the crusade drags on, the more urgently vampires seek secure havens. Vampires with any notable skill in estate management help themselves by volunteering to run strongholds and captured territories; others fend for themselves however they can. The homes of enemy leaders taken prisoners, randomly dominated peasants forced to provide a hovel and command centers of the crusade may all shelter vampires from daylight, but all carry some measure of risk. Nor can vampires afford to forget that Christians do not have a monopoly on True Faith.

Dark Medieval battles happen during daylight hours. No vampire, even the most Fortitude-equipped, can spend any meaningful time in the midst of a daytime struggle.

Returning

Few crusades end in glorious triumph. Under the best of circumstances, the crusaders return home more or less as they went, but tired, carrying whatever loot they obtained and burdened by injuries, from minor to catastrophic. Exhaustion wipes out most religious fervor while simultaneously sharpening what remains: The mass of the army poses less monster-hunting threats, but the dedicated few may more than make up for the laziness of the rest. No matter how thoroughly the crusaders vanquished their rivals, war takes its toll.

If the crusade ended in something less splendid than victory, passions run high as everyone, at all ranks, searches for scapegoats. The righteous cause must have been betrayed, and great reward might come to the observant soul who can identify and reveal the traitors. Even a hint of supernatural prowess other than saintly aura provides an excuse, and careless vampires must flee to escape destruction. Careful vampires can feed freely, and forward-thinking Cainites establish far-flung networks of influence and dependence when resolve runs low among the kine.

Most crusaders lack the energy for the sorts of random activity that can expose a temporary haven. The major risk now comes from angry locals on watch for weaknesses in the crusading army, so as to win back some of the stolen loot and perhaps injure or kill an oppressor along the way. A vampire with linguistic and diplomatic talent might even covertly aid this sort of quest for revenge, depending on how devoutly he takes the cause. Sufficiently flexible consciences can reconcile assisting un-Christian attacks on fellow Christians if the targets have some wickedness in need of punishment.

Once home, vampire and mortal crusader alike must reenter society. The return to (relatively) peaceful life seldom goes smoothly. Accustomed to danger and reward alike in greater measure, the crusader finds his domestic situation small, dull and cramped. On the other hand, he generally needs extended rest and recuperation. His recovery depends, in most cases, on his old assistants, his wife if he's married and the retainers he arranged for when departing. His well-being now requires him to accept greater than usual support from precisely the people he usually orders around. Tempers fly, and petty acts of violence mar many knightly households for years after a crusade. The details of accounting and estate management often seem less than enthralling, and the fortunes of many fiefs depend on how well the knight's underlings can manage despite his bored intervention.

Once settled, crusaders reflect on their experiences. Success breeds confidence. So, perhaps paradoxically, can failure, if a bold enterprise failed because of superior opposition. The opposition confirms the seriousness of the challenge and provides room to hope that perhaps a future battle, better prepared, could yet carry the day. Failure can also suggest that the fault lay in sinfulness on the part of the crusaders rather than in the rightness or lack thereof of their cause. Vampires deal with their personal stories much as mortals do: In this matter, at least, the gulf between Cainite and kine is small.

Blood and Fealty

As much as neonates rile against the traditions of their elders, the teachings flowing from sire to childe ensure a certain amount of clan unity. While there are many variations and exceptions, stereotypical views on human affairs do hold a certain kernel of truth in them. Even if chivalry does not actually fascinate every Ventrue in Europe, most have heard of it and know that their fellows have taken an interest. The following clan perspectives, then, should serve as a default attitude, although one subject to change due to other influences.

The Clans Without Chivalry

• **Assamites:** Knights are enemies, pure and simple. In Spain and the Holy Land, knights lead the attack on everything the Assamites value. Chivalric ideals find no welcome in Assamite minds. (Many Cainites from other clans who share an affinity for Islam also take this attitude.)

• **Followers of Set:** Sutekh's childer don't really understand chivalry very well. It's new and strange. They study it diligently, looking for weaknesses they can exploit, but that's all part of their calling.

• **Ravnos:** The Ravnos hate knights as much as Assamites. Mounted warriors slaughter all the peoples Ravnos move among and justify it as God's will. The Ravnos plot their revenge, bringing to bear all their arts of deception to discredit, then destroy, the predators.

• **Tremere:** What use do magicians have for the trappings of knighthood? Tremere can and do advise the courts of the mighty, but they have no interest in venturing into battle as part of the thick-witted mob, however finely dressed.

• **Tzimisce:** The Fiends are warlords, not prancing idealistic fools. They approve of chivalry insofar as it hobbles their enemies in self-imposed mental shackles. Beyond that, they care only that it not infect their own ranks. A few Tzimisce lords provide assistance to the Byzantine army (which often battles crusader armies who regard anyone not under their own banners as "the enemy") and to Muslim and pagan armies fighting on the edges of Christendom.

An individual Cainite from any of these clans might decide that chivalry calls to him. If he answers and becomes a knight, he can expect little sympathy from most of his lineage. They regard his decision as folly at best, wickedness at worst. Some try to persuade him to give it up, others may even try to attack him as a threat to their own concerns. Some members of his clan may offer him acceptance, whether genuine or as part of a scheme against rivals within the clan. (The War of Ages seldom takes a holiday, and any unusual behavior might offer a competitive advantage.)

Alert Cainite knights from other clans offer outcast knights shelter, sometimes for altruistic reasons, sometimes simply to acquire another grateful pawn. An outcast knight might end up actually gaining significant power, if he attends to his own self-interest while intrigue swirls around him. He might just as easily decide to flee the whole mess and hide himself among mortal knights, trying very hard to keep all Cainites at bay.

The Clans With Some Knights

• **Cappadocians:** While most of Cappadocius' childer pursue scholarly paths, not all shun physical exertion. The clan's hereditary pallor requires explanation, and any Cappadocian who takes up a knight's duties had better be very good at it, so as to defuse suspicions of secret sins. Some Cappadocians rise to the challenge in part as a snub at their clan's recent necromantic allies, demonstrating that the real heirs to the blood have better purposes than skulking around trying to command the dead.

• **Gangrel:** Chivalry implies a social order most Gangrel would rather avoid or destroy. Some of the Animals find it interesting and join the ranks of knights for various reasons. It's a good way to go adventuring and mete out a fair amount of destruction, and it's appealing to some of the *einherjar* who've lacked any regular opportunity for looting since the end of the Viking era. Other Gangrel find chivalric notions of honor appealing; some hope to use their status as social leaders to nudge mortals away from the worst failings of Christendom. Devoutly Christian Gangrel are few and far between, and most Gangrel who practice chivalry emphasize its secular aspects.

• **Malkavians:** The Madmen don't do anything as a group. Various Malkavians react to chivalry with everything from fanatical devotion to passionate detestation. Malkavians who do become knights often win mention in stories and songs as recipients of special divine touches — or, sometimes, infernal blandishments in the form of deranged visions. The one certainty is that Malkavian knights won't blend in anonymously. Whether as strategic or tactical innovators, oracles, poets, sages or ungovernable hotheads, Malkavians attract notice. They tend to be either very good or very bad knights.

• **Nosferatu:** Most Lepers preserve themselves by operating in secret. A few step forward to hide themselves in plain sight through simple expedients. Knights who go constantly masked or visored show up in many stories: It's an unusual commitment but by no means unheard of. In a world still full of hideous diseases, some Nosferatu can even travel unmasked, attributing their defects of appearance to a near-fatal encounter with pestilence. In addition, Obfuscate allows a Nosferatu to present any desired face to the world. Nosferatu often have a love/hate relationship with chivalry, since it simultaneously encourages pride in mere violence and stimulates the desire for purity and noble achievement. A knight who competes in tournaments and wars with full command of Potence can humble a great many arrogant peers, as well as protecting many innocents from tyrants' wrath.

The Chivalric Clans

• **Brujah:** The Brujah miss very few interesting new ideas; chivalry's held the clan's attention right from the emergence of various strands of pre-chivalric thought. By no means do all Brujah accept chivalric ideas, but many Zealots find within chivalry aspects that suit their various agendas. Great Brujah lords strive for perfection of prowess and virtue, while land-starved neonates with poor prospects seek to prove the superiority they're sure lies within. Some Brujah emphasize the aspiration to holiness; others simply like having lots of opportunities to hit people without witch-hunters rushing to respond.

• **Lasombra:** Muslim Lasombra loathe chivalry as much as Assamites. Christian Lasombra, on the other hand, delight in it, and it is ubiquitous throughout Christian Lasombra domains. The Lasombra seek to use chivalry to tame barbarous impulses among nobles, strongly backing efforts to play up the sacred role of chivalry and clerical involvement in chivalric ritual. Lasombra sponsor some of the Iberian and Languedoc troubadours who spread early Grail romances; the handful of Lasombra in Germany likewise back minnesingers developing sacred themes.

• **Toreador:** The development of purely Cainite knightly orders is almost entirely the product of the Toreador fascination with chivalry and chivalric romance. Many Artisans also become (or sponsor) troubadours, deepening their association with the ideals of the romantic knight. There are, of course, Artisans of a more martial ilk, who find beauty in the purity of combat and not the lilt of song. These Toreador often leave the gentile courts of their princes for the darker pleasures of crusade. Muslim Toreador have nothing to do with chivalry; it's a perennial source of debate when the clan gathers in meetings that cross religious lines.

• **Ventrue:** Chivalry marks the last glorious era of Patrician interest in power and leadership rather than commerce. When knighthood withers, the old dreams of clan kingship wither with it, replaced by dreams of authority through finance and other channels. That's the future, however; in the Dark Medieval world, no clan provides so many knights at all levels as the Ventrue. For motives ranging from the basest power lust to the most sophisticated yearning to unite and order troubled kingdoms, Ventrue take up arms and ride across Western Europe and beyond. Wherever knights gather in significant number, Ventrue move among them. Fewer Ventrue take up solitary questing, leaving that to Nosferatu and other clans. The Patricians prefer to show their authority over others, in addition to their own individual excellence.

• **Caitiff:** A Cainite who commits himself to chivalry may go years on end without knowingly encountering another vampire. Lineage doesn't matter in these circumstances. For a vampire who's been rejected by the community of his own, finding a place in human society often looks very appealing. Freed of any particularly close association to Cainite history, Caitiff often experiment with new ideas. Chivalry suits many innovators very well.

Clan Versus Liege

Chivalry begins with the exchange of responsibilities. The liege grants land, title and power to his vassal in exchange for promises of service of various kinds. The vassal receives status, income and the lord's promise of protection and support so long as the vassal discharges his duties. A knight who takes oaths of fealty and then breaks them faces punishments beginning with widespread distrust, passing through loss of the liege's gifts and ending in imprisonment and even death for treason. While most knights enjoy a great deal of freedom in discharging their duties, the duties are very real.

Of course, some vampires serve other vampires. A forward-thinking sire can Embrace his chosen childer and then arrange for them to publicly become his vassals. If the sire and childer get along, a fief ruled over by a united lineage can be immensely strong, holding a whole county in its sway for generations. If, on the other hand, sire and childer quarrel, then the lineage fief can be even weaker and more chaotic than the feudal norm.

Serving the Past

Vampires often move to the centers of power in the age they inhabit. Nearly every visible throne of king, Pope or other human authority figure casts a shadow within which Cainite manipulators lurk. Often the manipulators overestimate their own influence: Society moves for reasons besides the whim of individual rulers, and there are limits to what decrees can accomplish. Nonetheless, even an ineffectually manipulative Cainite learns a great deal about how courts work after a few centuries. A vampire who once participated in the affairs of Imperial Rome, Athens, Carthage or Babylon knows tricks that occur to precious few mortals of the Dark Medieval age.

A politically experienced elder or Methuselah brings to bear all the advantages of her wisdom but also all the pitfalls of long-made assumptions that no longer apply. If she can keep aware of how the world changes, however, she can carve out a niche for herself on almost any scale. It takes only a fraction of her accumulated knowledge to fend off mortal rivals, crippled by a mere lifetime of experience, leaving her free to pursue her own interests. If she persists in trying to rule in pre-chivalric fashion in a land where chivalry holds sway, she may become the villain of a story about how virtuous knights slew a tyrant or witch and freed her subjects to better rule. No single vampire can fend off challenges forever — every reign ends. Her childer and vampiric vassals face difficult decisions, as the chivalric code doesn't draw a firm line as to how far vassals should go in serving a doomed lord, particularly one who does not herself honor chivalry.

Some elder Cainites had nothing to do with earlier eras of government but like to claim they did, out of nostalgia or pride. Some formerly apolitical elders patronize the troubadours who tell historical tales, offering suggestions on "what it was really like" suitable for Dark Medieval myth-making. Others simply set out to recreate kingdoms they think they

remember, with results ranging from the eccentric (dress codes that mandate togas) to the disastrous ("republics" whose senates are composed of illiterate and confused knights). Many elders who wish now to step into politics after centuries of withdrawal attempt to lead directly, only to attract the attention of witch-hunters. Somewhat more clever fledgling rulers work through intermediaries — including younger vampires raised up to act as secret regents on behalf of undeclared kings, as well as mortal tools. Younger Cainites and mortals alike don't always make complacent pawns, however, and nostalgic kingdom-building seldom lasts for many years, let alone decades or generations.

Cainite knights who serve elder vampire lords do not have *boring* lots. Good or bad, their time as vassals to their own kind likely stand out in the annals of chivalry.

Ghoul Knights

Mortal servants blessed with the gift of vitae share many of their masters' concerns, but not all. Most obviously, the ghoul need not fear the day, but must fear the loss of vitae.

Ghouls make wonderful knights. The default Discipline of Potence is just what a chivalrous warrior wants, and there are no useless advantages when it comes to acting as a leader of men and protector of the innocent. Over time, the ghoul can rise to superhuman levels of skill, supplementing the gifts that come through the blood. As long as he's discreet in his receipt of vitae, he can escape nearly all the monster-hunting dangers that threaten his master.

A ghoul lady likewise enjoys many opportunities. If she wishes to fight, she can do so remarkably well, whether in her own persona or in disguise as a man. If she chooses to retain the lady's role, she can be a formidable guardian of the people and lands of her lord while he's away. A ghoul with social Disciplines as well as Potence makes an extremely competent overseer and can readily maneuver herself into positions of influence in the estates around her by dint of advice and command.

Ghouls seldom retain devout faith. The act of drinking the regnant's vitae raises too many religious issues. It's easier for the regnant to rationalize the process as a gift; the regnant isn't submitting his own soul on a regular basis, as opposed to dealing with the once-for-all-time curse of the Embrace. The ghoul owes his power to a very blasphemous-seeming process that leaves little room to escape the reality of dependence on a damned creature for personal advantage. Whether ghouls start as believers or not, it's hard to maintain conviction in those circumstances. Any ghoul who can hang on to the hope of salvation may well turn into a raving fanatic, covering uncertainty beneath a rigid shell that leaves no room for negotiation.

A ghoul knight, therefore, fits many of the criteria for fame as a wicked knight: strong, intelligent, courageous but devoid of Christian charity. It's so easy to cow others, so hard to remember the long-term benefits of cooperation and submission when the chance for power lies close at hand. Troubadours sing the downfall of wicked knights — in the end, there always seems to be some righteous champion available to overthrow the wicked and restore the blessings of proper authority to oppressed souls. A long-lived ghoul may have the experience of building and losing one sanctuary after another, until he learns discretion or meets destruction.

Storytelling the Ghoul Knight

A ghoul knight needs to find a vampiric master to serve. The ghoul can help maintain his master's cover, at home and abroad, and in return, can accompany his lord on all sorts of adventures not otherwise open to knights low on the social scale. A good troupe concept is one or more vampiric lords surrounded by ghoul knights; together the troupe can solve the challenges that ghouls or vampires alone would have more trouble overcoming.

Give thought to the motives of a knight who accepts the offer of service in a vampire's retinue. **Liege, Lord and Lackey** provides many possible answers to the fundamental question of what makes serving a vampire worthwhile. The circumstances of chivalry offer several more possibilities:

- **The Challenge.** A clever vampire lord offers the knight a true test of worthiness: Can the knight retain his commitment to chivalry while working in the shadows? Can he, perhaps, show the lord through example the superiority of the new way?
- **The Trap.** The knight accepts his new lord's offer so as to study the lord's assets and knowledge from close proximity. In due time, the knight thinks, he can smite the creature and claim all those belongings as his own. In the meantime, he serves well because he must earn the lord's trust. Whether masquerade becomes reality depends on how strongly the knight finds himself wishing to retain his original purpose after a few years (decades, centuries…) of enjoying the rewards his lord can offer.
- **The Opportunity.** An able but unimposing knight may have great difficulty rising through the ranks, given the occasional bit of bad luck when the lords who'd promote him happen to watch. A careful vampiric observer can spot neglected talent and offer the knight fresh scope for the exercise of his abilities. The lord may recruit the knight for a period of service with the promise of help in promotion thereafter. If the knight finds the rewards of his vampiric lord sufficient, the term may extend indefinitely.
- **The Sanctuary.** Whether through his own fault or the malice of others, the knight now faces censure and probable punishment for some offense. He could simply do as other knights do in such circumstances and flee to some remote land under a new name. The vampiric lord offers the knight another opportunity: more protection and distinct, fresh opportunities.

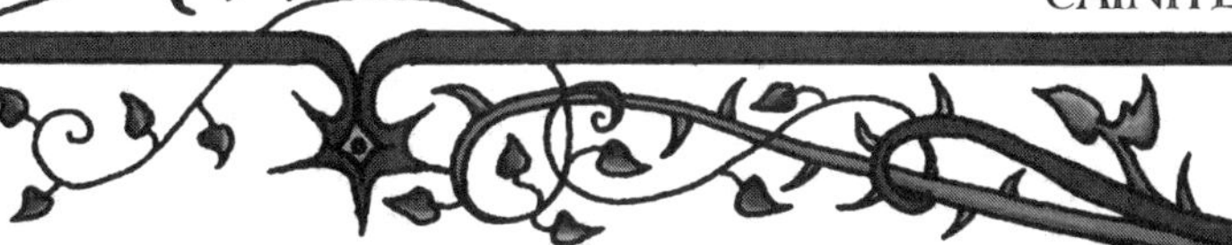

Chapter Three: Knightly Orders

Spiritual things are in place, not like bodies by the contact of dimensive quantity, but by the contact of power.
–St. Thomas Aquinas

Membership in a knightly order is, to many, the epitome of true chivalry. Owing fealty to Pope and king, the great orders form a nexus between Church and state like no other occupation. Because of this, they are almost all occupied with those areas where temporal and religious powers agree: the fight against infidels. Indeed, the greatest of these orders, the Templars and the Hospitalers, form in the Holy Land and others arise out of the Spanish *Reconquista* and the battles in Eastern Europe against local pagans. Some Cainites come to these orders to pursue their own chivalrous ways, but more seek to use them as power bases against their rivals. Some dedicated followers of chivalry have even founded orders of their own.

The Militant and Hospitaler Orders

The Crusades and their intermingling of war and religion inspire the fledgling orders of knighthood. From the combined need to take Jerusalem by force and to maintain Christian faith and sanctity arise trained bands of warriors, dedicated both to their king and their God.

Such divided purposes do not always sit together easily, especially now, when clergy and courtiers scheme and plot to gain the upper hand. In order to wear the sword of knighthood, candidates must be dubbed by a monarch, while to belong to the clergy, they must be confirmed by the Pope. Therefore, to rise above the status of upstart pretenders, an order of would-be chivalric heroes need the approval of both Church and state — and, even then, survival is not guaranteed. Any number of knightly orders have been sponsored by various monarchs or by the Church, only to fade away almost immediately. Orders that flourish despite the odds gain both military and economic power throughout Europe and the Holy Land.

Generally, most prestigious knightly orders of the day fall into two classes: militant and hospitaler. The former exist for warlike purposes, while the latter supposedly serve the sick and weak. Some orders combine the two aspects from inception, while others take on other roles over time. Many orders begun on the highest of principles degenerate into bands of mercenary profiteers or worse, becoming little more than well-equipped hordes of killers.

The Knights Templar

No single group attracts more attention and controversy in the 12th century than the Poor Knights of the Temple of Solomon, or Knights Templar. To its supporters, the order embodies the fullest vision of chivalry: knights as warriors of the Lord, an independent estate bound to the service of God. To clerical critics, the order (like its rivals) encourages insubordination and courts infidelity, while secular nobles fear the order's independence from their control. The Templars wear a distinctive white mantle emblazoned with a red crusader's cross.

The order begins in obscurity. In fact, the order's own records don't state for sure just when it was established. In about 1118 (give or take a few years), the French knights Hugues de Payens and Geoffrey de St. Omer and several others took an oath of poverty, chastity and obedience before the Patriarch of Jerusalem and committed themselves to protecting pilgrims on the roads through the Holy Land. Almost immediately, the Templars attracted support from struggling esquires and powerful nobles alike. Hugues was Count of Champagne and bore many of the order's early expenses; Fulk, Count of Anjou, soon joined him. In 1128, the Council of Troyes commissioned Bernard of Clairvaux to draw up a rule for the order.

Bernard immersed himself in the task. He was already famous throughout Christendom as an influential member of the Cistercian Order, a monastic group at the forefront of efforts to reform the Church within the framework of radical orthodoxy. The rule he produced for the Templars embodied every idea then circulating about knighthood as a holy calling. He backed up the rule with extensive propaganda; *In Praise of the New Chivalry*, which he wrote in the 1130s, became the manifesto for the religious side of chivalry. He contrasted the sinful indulgence of secular knights with the manly, devout purity of the Templars. His rule remains in effect in 1197.

The Templar Rule

Templars give up private property. All their goods belong to the order, and the order's superiors can reassign all material belongings as seems appropriate. Templars observe a rigid dress code, banning all luxury and finery in favor of garments entirely in white, black or brown and made of simple fabrics. Each knight gets one mattress, one bedroll and one blanket, which should suffice. (The rule does make provisions for extremes of heat and cold, but only through the temporary loan of extra material.) All Templars in one of the order's strongholds take their meals together, observing monastic silence and decorum. Their meals include meat no more than two or three times a week (and on Christmas, All Saints Day, the Feast of the Assumption and the Feast of the Twelve Apostles), and they eat in pairs to make sure no member eats too much or too little.

The master of each house wields almost complete authority over the brothers there. He can assign them specific duties, issue or take from them everything from clothes to weapons and allow or forbid them from offering counsel to others. Brothers who resist face the repeated warning that anger against a superior goes against God. No brother can have a locked or sealed container, and any letters he receives are read to him, if the master approves of the message. All gifts given to brothers become the property of the house, under the master's control.

The ban on personal property does not keep Templars from holding fiefs, however. Most notably, Templars can own and administer estates and retainers if won in battle against the heathens or if the estates make it possible for Templars to fight heathens more effectively.

The rule aims to produce knights who feel no fear of death in a righteous cause because they know with confidence the state of their own souls and lack any of the worldly entanglements that would restrain them from boldness. It generally works, too. The Holy Land holds less than 2000 Templars, and about the same number or fewer work in Europe. They achieve victories out of all proportion to their numbers, dwarfing the accomplishments of large armies.

Individual knights can take the oath of membership for a fixed term of years or for life. Many join the Templars for a few years and take what they've learned to pursue more secular careers later.

The Classes of Templar

A master oversees each house. Knights compose most of the membership, supported by light cavalry known as *sergeants*. Farmers and non-combat chaplains support the warriors.

The Grand Master of the Knights Templar, currently Gilbert Erail, gives direction to all other Templars. The Seneschal and Marshal assist him. Traditionally, they operate out of Jerusalem, but now use other holdings in the reduced Outremer. Immediately below them are the conventual officers. The Commander of the Land of Jerusalem maintains the order's treasury. The Commander of the City of Jerusalem operates the master chapter house (or, at least, did until Saladin's conquest), and the Commander of Acre does the same for the order's second largest house. The Draper sets standards in wardrobe and furnishing and coordinates supplies for the order. The Templars divide the rest of their operations into provinces, each with a master and a commander: Tripoli, Antioch, Poitiers, France, Hungary, England, Aragon, Apulia and Portugal.

The Growth of the Order

In short order, impressed lords, kings and priests grant the order a growing variety of exemptions from normal rules. By the middle of the 12th century, the order pays no taxes and enjoys immunity from *all* authority except direct papal command. No prince of the world or of the Church can command Templars do anything: The rest of the world *asks* the Templars, who accept or not as seems wise to them.

The order's members build and maintain castles throughout the portions of the Holy Land that remain under Christian control, from Château Pélérin, south of Acre, to Baghras, north of Antioch. In addition, smaller bands of Templars operate out of all the crusader-controlled cities, escorting travelers on the roads and patrolling borders in search of opportunities to beat back encroaching Saracens. Templar doctrine encourages its members to be the first to advance and the last to retreat, which means that many Templars die in battles from which others would have fled or avoided in the first place. Such heroic deaths only inspire more support and admiration, since chivalry places little emphasis on carefully calculated self-interest: Templars do what most knights only wish they felt brave enough to do.

Lords who feel that their lives may have been less than holy donate land and goods to the order by way of atonement. Merchants who wish to prove the extent of their success give valuable gifts. Peasants wishing to offer thanks and support a

The Battle of Hattin, 1187

In the 1180s, Reynald de Châtillon, the Prince of Antioch, was known and feared throughout the Holy Land for his caravan attacks and pirate raids. Meant to terrorize Muslim merchants and townspeople, his assaults were notoriously brutal and threatened to destabilize the cautious peace established in Palestine following the Second Crusade. The Count of Tripoli, one Raymond, was an astute observer of the situation and urged Guy of Lusignan, King of Jerusalem and nominal lord over all the Christian princes of Outremer, to practice diplomacy and stop Reynald from provoking the Saracens. His counsel was ignored, with predictably disastrous results. As Reynald's raids continued, an angry Saladin eventually dispatched armies into Outremer, and before long, he had besieged the unfortunate Raymond's wife at Tripoli. Even at this critical juncture, Raymond advised caution, declaring that he would rather lose his wife than the entire Kingdom of Jerusalem.

Alas, his offer of sacrifice was also ignored. Instead, Guy chose to engage Saladin in battle on the impetuous advice of Reynald and Gerard de Ridefort, the Grand Master of the Knights Templar (whose charges later suffered the brunt of Saladin's fury). Moving toward Tripoli, the Christian armies of Outremer camped by a dry well between two hills known as the Horns of Hattin. Raymond noted their dubious tactical position and declared the end of the kingdom.

In this assessment, Raymond was correct. On July 4, 1187, Saladin's forces had the Christians completely surrounded and cut off from any source of water. When Raymond led a charge of his household knights, the Muslims let him through and then closed the circle once again. Raymond wisely returned to his wife at Tripoli and lived to fight another day. The rest of the Christians weren't so lucky: Dying of thirst and battered by wave upon wave of Saladin's cavalry, they were finally overrun. Saladin spared Guy and many knights, holding them in Damascus for extremely lucrative ransoms. However, he also made sure to personally decapitate Reynald and ordered his pacifist Sufi holy men to execute the surviving Templars and Hospitalers. Worst of all, Saladin even captured the True Cross, one of Christendom's holiest relics. Jerusalem fell shortly thereafter.

Hattin was perhaps the worst military disaster of the Crusades, and it cost Christians the vast majority of the cities and lands they had won during their first two ventures to the Holy Land. It led to the Third Crusade and exposed the tactical and strategic flaws in chivalry's military ethos. Bravery, nobility and devout faith simply cannot overcome a weak position, poor intelligence and an addiction to an outmoded offensive mindset. Raymond of Tripoli understood this, but men of his sort are a rarity. Far more common are the Reynalds of the world, men who go on to repeat Hattin's mistakes again and again.

(For more on Hattin and its effects on the Cainites of the Holy Land, see **Jerusalem by Night**.)

worthy cause make their small donations. Every class in Europe contributes to the Templar coffers, and it all underwrites building one of the most effective fighting forces in Christendom. While individual Templars continue to abide by standards of poverty, masters and commanders cut dashing, fashionable figures at courts across the continent.

During full-blown crusades, the Templars often clash with the leaders of crusading armies. By papal order, the Templars submit to crusader leadership, but antipathy runs strong in both directions. The Templars resent the extent to which their intimate familiarity with the land and enemy goes unappreciated, while the crusaders find the Templars fanatical and lacking in strategic sensibility. Both claims have much truth in them, which only makes the matter worse. Templars tend to shine brightest in between crusades, when they can operate on their own or in collaboration with select small forces.

Current Conditions

While the Templars maintain extensive holdings and support in Europe, the heart of the order — the Holy Land — is in disarray. Saladin's conquest of Jerusalem and virtually every other inch of Outremer in the 1170s and 1180s stripped the order of its most important holdings, including the Temple of Solomon itself. The actual fall of Jerusalem came after the catastrophic defeat at the Horns of Hattin, when Templar and Hospitaler tactical advice led the Christians into an untenable position. Both orders paid a heavy price as Saladin executed 200 of their number. As the Saracen leader put it, "these more than all the other Franks destroy the Arab religion and slaughter us." (For more information, see the sidebar, below.)

The Third Crusade brought some prosperity back with the recapture of Acre and other areas and the rise of more reasoned Templar leadership. In 1197, much of the order's prestige is restored, but it remains alienated from its true purpose — Jerusalem. As the drive to recapture the Holy City is slipping more and more into politics and inter-Christian conflicts, the order's attentions fall more and more toward Europe and matters of finance.

Templars and Mammon

The order becomes involved in money lending not long after its founding, starting with an 1135 loan to a would-be pilgrim to the Holy Land in exchange for the right to run his estate while he's away. Throughout the 12th century, the order's assets grow, and various masters and commanders take the initiative in putting some of that wealth to use. They underwrite travel expenses, help out allies in various sorts of need and offer their services as arbiters and representatives. Inevitably, they become entangled in secular affairs, often to the detriment of the order's local reputation. The order's greatest asset is its reputation for purity and devotion; loansharking schemes undermine that image.

In the Dark Medieval world, the order's commitment to financial involvement remains hotly debated. Some of the order's leaders feel sure they can work with secular affairs

without losing track of the order's mission, while others feel just as strongly that masters enjoy no more freedom from corruption than the rank-and-file brothers do. Money makes so many desirable goals more obtainable: better equipment, extra reserves of supplies for Holy Land fortresses in case of siege, more reliable transportation and so on. Money also draws the attention of those who work with it. While gifts do not stop pouring in, surely some concern for the future is in order, they argue. Step by step, the order's financial managers find themselves focusing on what would be good for the order's investments rather than what serves the order's purpose.

Characters who belong to the order can (and should) take part in this debate. It's by no means too late for the order's members to decide to restrict their involvement in worldly affairs, assigning a few brothers to handle necessary funds and passing the rest on to non-Templar beneficiaries. Voices call for reform throughout the life of the order, and though in history they go unanswered, don't deny characters the chance to help make a difference.

Cainite Templars

No Cainite can discharge the Templar obligations of knighthood. It's simply not possible for any vampire to attend all the daytime church services or function as a member of a military unit that fights almost all its battles during the day. Further, the Templars include many more believers with True Faith than a comparably sized sampling of dedicated crusaders at large, let alone a wider range of the population.

Dealing with True Faith poses the greatest problems. Many Cainites do sincerely wish to adopt the order's goals and win for themselves perhaps some spark of divine favor. Vampires can wish to protect pilgrims and repulse the forces of Islam as sincerely as any mortal. It's just that some of their fellow knights and many Templar buildings repel even the most earnestly crusading vampire. A few Cainite would-be Templars become cynical and seek to corrupt the brothers of a particular house so as to remove the aura of faith. More Cainites seek (consciously or otherwise) for houses where faith runs strong but not too much so, trying to find the middle ground between faith that actually transforms the world and opportunistic unbelief. That ground is narrower in the Templar movement than elsewhere but not impossible to find.

The Templar Rule does make provision for injured and sick knights to serve in whatever capacity their disability allows. Templars have some experience with curses (see below) and do not reject knights who are otherwise useful members of the order. So, while a Cainite cannot act as a regular member of the order, he can do something in a support role. He might act as a quartermaster, a physician, a guard during the night hours, a scout, a messenger or any other function that doesn't require riding into battle during the day. He will always be second-best in the eyes of other Templars but may still seem useful.

Templars and the Secret Powers

Templars encounter more supernatural beings than most mortals of the Dark Medieval world. The orders' prominent role in crusading makes it a target of all those who wish to foil the Crusades, including vampires, werewolves and magicians. Templars tend not to distinguish or classify the monsters they encounter, summing all such beings up as "Devil's spawn." A few Templars specialize in detecting and destroying the creatures that haunt the night (and day) as a secret part of the order's mission. Templar devil-hunters usually operate in small groups of their own under cover stories authorized at the order's highest levels.

Devout Cainites can and do sometimes join in the hunts. The right story of an evil curse or other misfortune — if necessary, coupled with Dominate — allows a Cainite to apply his own familiarity with vampiric existence to track down vampires hostile to the order. The vampire may or may not have any special insight into the circumstances of other monsters, but preternatural speed, strength and other powers often come in handy when the monster-hunters close with their prey. With the right Disciplines, Cainite Templars can go places and deal with opposition that no mortal could hope to win against. The order looks with favor on these secret warriors and rewards them generously for work well done.

Among the order's supernatural foes, Muslim magicians create the most harm. The mainstream of Muslim society rejects magic just as thoroughly as Christendom, but on both sides of the wall of belief, practitioners of various forms of arcana flourish in the shadows. The sort of curse a Cainite Templar might claim to be under really can strike his mortal brothers; the magicians who dedicate themselves to fighting the order have mastered spells that command health, luck and even time itself. Some of the Templar bloodshed in mass executions goes to power dark rituals, just as some necromancers in Christendom use the blood of unbelievers for their own ends. Cainites who learn the still-developing Discipline of Thaumaturgy may become formidable assets to the Templars (even though the practice of magic becomes a point of accusation later).

Clans and the Order

• **Assamites.** A handful of Assamites have operated under deep cover within the order at various times, and at least one does so still. In general, they serve as loyal and effective brothers, while waiting for the moment strike. They also contribute to the push to confine and remove True Faith from the order, though they hope to avoid the notice of other vampires while doing so.

• **Brujah.** Many Brujah find the order unsettling. Part of this is a strong dislike for the petty fact that the Brujah didn't invent the order. The more removed a Brujah knight is from his clan's obsessive philosophizing and utopia-building, the more likely he is as an individual to find the order appealing. Thus, Brujah Templars tend to appear where the Brujah clan is relatively weak, particularly in Italy.

• **Cappadocians.** Few Cappadocians join the order directly, but throughout the Holy Land, some members of the clan provide services as doctors. In the Holy Land, the Cappadocian appearance actually provides a bit of an advantage because however unnatural it may seem, it's very clearly *not* Saracen. In Europe, where the enemy lies far away, Cappadocians find less acceptance from Templars.

• **Lasombra.** Many Lasombra priests attack the order's independence, fearing the consequences of a powerful force so far removed from normal accountability. Lasombra knights usually prefer to serve in existing armies and, during crusades, clash unpleasantly with the order. Lasombra intervention contributes to the order's slow growth in Spain and Portugal.

• **Malkavians.** Malkavian visionaries flock to the order, serving it however they can. Bernard's vision resonates powerfully in the minds of vampires seeking a fresh approach to the problem of moral conduct in an immoral world. In addition, the sheer fervor many Templars bring to their work inspires vampires looking for an object of fixation — for these deranged souls, any such zealotry will do.

• **Ventrue.** No clan provides more Templars than the Ventrue, and no clan takes a more active part in the debate over money lending, with Ventrue partisans of both extremes. Some Ventrue see the order's greatest strength as its purity of focus, free of the corruption regular institutional life creates, and want to take whatever measures prove necessary to keep the order from becoming just another bunch of worldly knights. Other Ventrue see commerce as a tool with which to undercut traditional institutions mired in sin and decadence, and regard financial involvement as an entirely appropriate extension of the order's mission. The participants in the ongoing debate include individuals who will become prominent both in the main clan and the *antitribu* in future centuries, and both sides will evoke the memory of the Templars as an experiment gone wrong.

The Ventrue directly contribute little to the innovations Templars make in accounting and management. What the clan's members usually provide are negative examples and teachings, born of experience of the many things that *don't* work when trying to manage widely spread estates.

The Knights Hospitaler

The Order of the Hospital of St. John of Jerusalem is the most famous and enduring of the hospitaler orders. Despite the distress it causes religious authorities in Europe because of its lack of accountability to them, the order remains instrumental in establishing the legend of the crusader as a holy soldier of Christ and in building the ideal of a spiritualized warrior. Indeed, a number of its members will eventually be canonized or sanctified, including Peter of Imola and Saint Gerland.

The members are predominantly French and Italian but do include a few Spanish knights as well. Their sign is a white Maltese cross against a black field in times of peace and against a red field in times of war. One of their chief strongholds, the Crac des Chevaliers, is among the largest and best-defended of crusader castles and hosts, at some point, almost all those who travel through Outremer.

Guillaume du Crac donated this imposing castle perched on a volcanic hill in Kerak, southeast of the Dead Sea, in 1142. In 1193, the order had the keep enlarged and fortified and has successfully defended it despite the waning Latin fates in the Holy Land. In its expanded state, the fortress is so large that it contains an entire town enclosed within its walls, with a church and chapel, aqueducts, cisterns, courtyards, stables, living quarters and large halls.

Birth of the Order

The Hospital of St. John has existed since the time of Christ, but served at that time only as a place of healing for pilgrims. In 1099, Gerard (known as the Blessed and who ran the hospice) made it possible for the order's subsequent development by assisting the crusaders in their siege of the Holy City.

Hospitalers and other faithful tell a near-miraculous story of Gerard's endeavors during the siege of 1099. Hearing that the city was under attack by Christians, he rushed to the walls and joined the city's defenders — only instead of throwing stones, he tossed out loaves of bread to replenish the crusaders' supplies. The Muslim authorities promptly arrested him and dragged into court in chains, but the witnesses to his crime were left dumbfounded when the loaves they'd kept as evidence turned into stones as they were held before the governor. Cainites in the Holy City speak of Malkavian or Ravnos involvement in this transformation, but both faith and simple lies run strong enough in Jerusalem to account for the tale without the blood of Caine.

Gerard's efforts earned the crusaders' gratitude as well as their hefty financial contributions. Whether due to his personal influence or to general European enthusiasm for the Crusades, the newborn order gained an astonishing array of holdings within the span of a very few short years. In 1114, Gerard received an entire province in Portugal and territories in numerous Western European countries followed soon thereafter. In addition, throughout the early part of the 12th century, the religious power of the order increased thanks to a series of papal bulls and privileges permitting such extensive authority that bishops could no longer interdict Hospitaler churches.

By 1130, the hospice-infirmary in Jerusalem was large enough and prosperous enough that it had to hire mercenaries to protect its patients from bandits. Within a few years, Gerard's successor Raymond du Puy militarized the hospital to the point that it took part in both the dismally unsuccessful attack on Damascus in 1148 and the subsequent triumphant capture of Ascalon in 1153. Knights Hospitaler were prominent in the fighting at both battles. Soon enough, these knights became as militant and famous as the Templars.

The Hospitaler Rule

The Knights Hospitaler, many of whom fall into the loose category of "holy laymen," at first followed a variant of the Rule of St. Augustine, but have come to observe their own rule. Raymond du Puy and Roger des Moulins, among the earliest Grand Masters of the order, drew up that unique rule and, eventually, it becomes influential enough to be adopted by a number of the religious hospitals. A slightly later adapta-

Richard the Lion-Hearted and the Hospitalers

Richard I of England became a hero after the campaigns following the siege of Acre during the Third Crusade. Steadfastly by his side was Garnier de Naplouse, Grand Master of the Hospitalers, as well as a large contingent of de Naplouse's fighters. The Christians' shared success did not seem to gain Richard's favor for the order, however. The king refuses to arbitrate in the increasingly rancorous disagreements between Hospitalers and Templars. He supports the splitting away of the fledgling Teutonic Order out from under Hospitaler control — infuriating de Naplouse's successor, Geoffroy de Donjon, who blames Templar influence for the Hospitalers' loss of the subordinate order.

tion of the original rule divides members into three classes: knights (*fratres milites*), chaplains (*fratres capellani*) and sergeants (*fratres servientes armigeri*). Others associated with the order function as servants in the houses owned by the order or work on the order's farms.

In its final form, the Hospitaler Rule winds up similar to that of the Templars, although not quite as extreme. Knights and other members of the order swear the threefold vow of chastity, poverty and obedience and can own no personal belongings beyond bread, water and clothing — the last of which must be of poor quality. Unlike the Templars, though, the Knights of St. John choose to affiliate with orders of hospitaler sisters, many of whom work directly with patients. Occasionally, claims surface of these associations sponsoring women fighters, only to be vigorously denied by abbesses and sisters of the orders involved.

Cainite Involvement

The order has close ties with certain Toreadors. Unbeknownst to all but a select few mortals, the powerful Toreador Alphonse des Rosiers sponsors a secret sub-order within the Hospitalers, the Knights of the Sable Rose. A group of highly accomplished ghouls make up this inner clique, and they are loosely tied to a wholly vampiric Brotherhood of the Sable Rose based in Flanders. Carel vanden Driessche, current Master of the Brotherhood, is patiently and quietly campaigning to bring the two forces into even closer alignment — thus far with little effect.

What the Roses have accomplished is to quietly protect the order as a whole from the sort of supernatural persecution endured by the Templars. Vanden Driessche, a skilled politician and warrior, has forged careful alliances with some Toreadors of Islamic stock and, through them, with members of the vizier caste of Assamites. This has hardly made for peace between Muslim and Hospitaler, but it has helped keep the most militant Assamites from focusing their attention on the Brotherhood or the order as a whole. If the Hospitalers ever realize the extent to which the secret knights in their midst have altered the course of their battles, it is difficult to predict whether they will be pleased or infuriated.

The Order of St. John's Toreador patrons fear that other Cainites have taken an interest in the Hospitalers. Indeed, in 1158, the talented de Puy vanished mysteriously from Verona, during a tour of Europe on which he was warmly received by numerous heads of state and lavished with gifts. Des Rosiers used all his resources to find the vanished Grand Master, convinced the Lasombra-backed Cainite Heresy had "recruited" him, but never did. Two years later, the humans of the order finally gave up hope and named Auger de Balben as their new grand master.

In addition, of late, numerous Christians living near the Crac des Chevaliers have claimed to see a misshapen gray figure haunting the rocks around the keep late at night. Far more people spreading this rumor are implying that the monster is somehow under the Hospitalers' control than that it is attacking the order's defenses.

Other Militant Orders

The Templars and Hospitalers, as the most prominent warriors to hold and retake Jerusalem, cast the longest shadow of the various militant orders. However, Outremer is far from being the only place where knights take up the cause of Christendom, either out of purity of spirit, desire for glory and bounty or both. Indeed, the Teutonic Knights, whom history will remember as the third great order, are on the verge of forming and leading a "holy" battle against the pagans of Northern Europe. Following are some of the other important and noteworthy militant and hospitaler orders across Europe.

The Order of Calatrava

King Sancho III of Castile founded this militant order in 1158. The king had searched in vain for someone to hold the fortress of Calatrava; the stronghold had been won back from the Muslims but subsequently abandoned by the Templars, who

Hospitalers and Templars

Opposing human motivations and hidden Cainite rivalries have conspired to make the Order of St. John clash on a regular basis with the other major order of the region, the Templars. This rivalry greatly weakened the defense of Jerusalem before its fall in 1187 and continues to cause difficulties for various political entities attempting to work with both orders. Little love has been lost between the two orders since their inceptions, and no reconciliation seems possible.

For the time being, however, the rivalry continues. In the wake of the terrible defeat at Hattin, both orders are all the more anxious to reestablish their power and reputation. In the shadows, Cainites and ghouls tied to each group are waging a silent battle, trying to either eliminate or displace their opponents.

found it too difficult to keep. Raymond, abbot of the Cistercian monastery of Fitero, volunteered his services. The lay brothers of his abbey became soldiers of the Cross, while many of the warriors who came to their assistance adopted monastic habit. Their mark is the distinctive cross fleury, in red.

Persistent rumors hold that a parallel Calatravan order has been founded for women too wayward or too difficult to be dealt with, but most scoff at the very idea for now. In 1219, however, a formal Ladies' Order of Calatrava will indisputably be founded — to supersede any trace of the earlier, unofficial order, many claim — although its ranks fill mainly with wealthy patronesses rather than fighters.

The Order of Christ

Also known as the *Schwertzbrüder*, *Ensiferi* or Swordbearers, this Livonian order is not to be confused with the later Portuguese Order of Christ. Albert, first Bishop of Riga, has just created the Knights of Christ this very year of 1197, intending them to spread the faith throughout the Baltic Provinces, as well as to protect new converts from pagans. The white mantle and red cross distinguishing this order resemble the garb of the Templars, with the notable addition of a red sword — hence the name *Ensiferi*.

This order bears the dubious distinction of being open to people of any rank. Its numbers are already swelling with aimless adventurers who indulge themselves in pillage and carnage even more excessive than that committed by other crusaders. Despite its name, this order provides excellent cover for Cainites who enjoy the ironic pleasures of Church-sanctioned bloodshed.

Cainites and the Spanish Orders

The Lasombra position in regard to the Spanish orders is very much up for debate. The Magisters have yet to formally commit themselves to either supporting or opposing any of the Spanish orders. Many of them are passionately interested in the *Reconquista*, but the Moors and Christians among them cannot agree on the expulsion of the Saracens from Europe. However, the clan's attachment to El Cid and his ideals is quite deep (see **Libellus Sanguinis I: Masters of the State**, p. 17). While only a few individual Lasombra are officially on crusade themselves, many are pulling strings in the abbeys and monasteries elsewhere.

The Brujah of Spain are certain, one way or another, to oppose whatever position the Lasombra take. Some have indeed surreptitiously joined the Order of Calatrava, while others seek to utilize another prominent Spanish order, the Order of Alcantra. This knightly order was founded sometime after 1156 by the brothers Suero and Gomez Fernández. The Alcantran Knights enjoy some military success before unfortunately and apparently inexplicably becoming embroiled in the civil wars among the kings of Aragón, Castile, León and Navarre — thus violating their oath to take up arms only against the infidel. Many claim this conduct concealed Brujah rage against the Lasombra.

Destiny

The *Ensiferi* are not a long-lasting order. Of their two grand masters, the first, Vinnon, will be murdered by an unidentified assailant in 1209; the second, Volquin, will fall on the field of battle in 1236 along with 480 knights of the order. Whether this degradation and eventual massacre comes at Tzimisce hands or results from simple internal strife and human resistance to the order, the results are equally dismal for the *Ensiferi*. Some of the surviving brethren petition to be allowed to enter the Teutonic Order and linger in a shadow existence as a provincial branch entitled the Knights of Livonia.

The *Ensiferi* are already encountering dark enemies for which they are ill-prepared. Their desire to conquer and slaughter in pagan lands brings them into the fringes of traditional Tzimisce territory, and some of the Fiends don't hesitated to strike back. Adventurous Cainites riding the wave of holy slaughter face "demonic hordes" of hellhounds and *vozhd* war-ghouls. The open nature of the order has diluted what little protection faith might have granted them, and the battles are hard indeed. The mortal heads of the order are clueless as to the true nature of the "pagan degenerates" they are fighting. Even without Tzimisce interference, the order is doing far more to enrage the pagans than to either convert or suppress them. Fear and madness are slowly creeping up the ranks, and the Swordbearers have a hard battle ahead.

The Order of the Hatchet

The *Orden de la Hacha* is very nearly the only official order of the time open exclusively to women. Raymond Berenger, Count of Barcelona, founded the Catalonian order in 1149 to honor a band of brave women who, armed only with axes, defended the town of Tortosa from a Moorish attack. Those admitted to the order and made dames are exempt from all taxes and take precedence over men in public assemblies. Their device is, of course, a battle ax.

Most of the Dames of the Hatchet have, predictably, stayed in the homes they fought so valiantly to defend; women fighters in the Holy Land, or even other areas of Europe, who pronounce themselves members of the order face some degree of skepticism and scrutiny. The court of Barcelona is disinclined to elevate any new women into the order, so it seems meant to die out with its original members. The Dames of the Hatchet, however, provide one of the painfully few opportunities for women to fight openly and be praised rather than condemned. It is entirely possible for other nobles to follow Raymond's example and elevate exceptional women in exceptional circumstances.

The order was at first entirely mortal — the original group was made up of women ready to defend their homes, not manipulative Cainites seeking mortal recognition. Without much chance of new membership, vampires have not directly

infiltrated the Dames, but certain enterprising Cainites have expressed more than passing interest in some of the ladies. Mencá de Planes and Agueda Gitarda are considered to have been the organizers of the hastily assembled crew and must indeed be both charismatic leaders and clever tacticians to have scored their dramatic victory. Several prominent women among the Spanish Lasombra have let it be known that the order is under their protection, and most expect several neonates or ghouls to come from their ranks.

The Order of Cyprus

Also known as *l'Ordre du Silence et de l'Épée* (the Order of Silence and the Sword), this order got its charter sometime before 1195 from the titular King of Jerusalem, Guy de Lusignan. Based on the island whose name they bear, the Cypriot Knights are bound to provide a stronghold and refuge for those times when Christians do not fare well in their battles in the Holy Land.

This order has proven a boon for a small cabal of Tremere attempting to investigate the mystery of Acre. Cainites far and wide fear that city, supposed to contain some power inimical to the unliving. Perhaps because, as it is said, Acre contains fragments of the True Cross, vampires attempting to enter the city reportedly burst into flame. The Order of Cyprus, with its relative isolation and lack of exposure to any heated combat, serves as an excellent shelter for these Usurpers. They masquerade as scholars (and even one "cursed" knight) associated with the order. They glean information from knights traveling from Acre and send others to pursue leads within the city. They must use extreme subtly when doing so, as even ghouls seem to fall ill when entering Acre. Their tentative exploration has, of yet, produced no solid results.

The Tremere in Cyprus are very much aware of the potential consequences of their presence. If they succeed in discovering a mystical power in Acre or even in analyzing what is potentially an aspect of True Faith, they will have gained powerful leverage in dealing with other clans and greatly advanced their own magical studies. The Tremere know they are not the only Cainites interested in Acre. Rumor holds that several Cappadocians are pursuing their own form of study in the area, and at least one mortal envoy fell victim to an Assamite attack.

The Order of St. Thomas of Acre

Sometimes called the Order of St. Thomas of Canterbury, the date of this order's creation and indeed even the true identity of its founder, remain mysterious. It undeniably came into existence in the Holy Land around the time of the Third Crusade, and members argue that it was Richard the Lion-Hearted himself who granted the order his authority. At first the knights of this order confined themselves to caring for the poor, burying the dead and ransoming captives, but they soon turned to more military endeavors.

This is a predominantly English order but located in Acre itself. The Order of St. Thomas finds itself perpetually lacking for funds — unlike the Hospitalers, who receive large donations from grateful beneficiaries. For other orders, obtaining and selling always-scarce food supplies serves as a reliable source of income, but the Knights of St. Thomas have little luck in establishing such an arrangement. Enduring a great deal of pressure both from members of the Church and from within its own ranks to either shut down or merge with the Templars, high-ranking knights of the order are determined to resist such a move by any means possible.

Because Acre is anathema to the childer of Caine, the order is largely immune to their influences and intrigues. Some Ventrue have tried exerting influence from England without great success, and their ire may well explain the knights' lack of backing. The order's presence in Acre seems also to have given its knights some glimpse of the secrets within the Templars and Hospitalers. The Order of St. Thomas has begun to suspect that evil has taken root among the knights surrounding it. The rank and file of this order is growing increasingly paranoid about their relations with the other militant and hospitaler orders, and the grand master has been training small groups of men he trusts. Soon, he thinks, they will be ready to seek out and destroy the monsters concealing themselves throughout the Holy Land.

The Order of St. Lazarus

As a measure of their reckless disregard for personal well-being, these knights proudly wear the symbol of a squared-off cross in green, the color identified with the prophet Mohammed. After all, they have nothing left to lose; they bear the dread disease of leprosy.

At first, the peaceful Order of St. Lazarus — sometimes called the Order of St. Ladre — ran a hospital and leper house (a *ladre*) just outside the walls of Jerusalem. Eventually, other militant orders began to place their leprous knights under the hospitalers' care. Since the disease often progressed slowly, leaving men able-bodied for quite some time, it was natural for sufferers to begin to protect their fellow patients from infidels, brigands and marauders. The order quickly became a militant one, with its most notable patron no less a figure than Baldwin IV, the leper King of Jerusalem.

Even after the fall of Jerusalem to Saladin in 1187, the order has persevered. It now has several leper houses in the remaining Christian lands of Outremer and continues to care for the sick and fight for the Christian cause.

The Lazarene Nosferatu

The Nosferatu — often accused of originating the plague of leprosy — have a natural enough association with the Order of St. Lazarus. The Lazarene Order provides an ideal cover for Nosferatu activities — these knights proudly proclaim themselves "the living dead" and "the men who walk alone." Zealous Nosferatu have thus been presented with an opportunity to leave their shadowy ruins and catacombs and openly involve themselves in the affairs of the Holy Land. Many welcome the chance to do penance in the service of God.

The Nosferatu involvement goes deeper than using the order as cover, however. The Hospital of St. Lazarus has been in existence for centuries, and one Nosferatu, most recently going by the Frankish name of Guillaume, has called it his own for much of that time. When the militant order grew up around the hospice, Guillaume made its leadership his own project. He purposefully revealed his vampiric condition to Gerard, the order's dying grand master. Gerard expressed sympathy instead of revulsion, and Guillaume rewarded him with the Embrace. Guillaume would subsequently Embrace Raymond, Gerard's successor, under the same conditions. In the aberration that was the Christian Kingdom of Jerusalem, these Lepers found purpose in their own form of chivalry.

With the return of the city to Muslim hands, the Nosferatu and the Lazarene Knights had to flee. Raymond brought several childer and leprous ghouls to Constantinople under the shelter of the Nosferatu there. Gerard and Guillaume seem to have simply vanished, but Raymond fears they fell to Kothar, the Leper elder of the city, who had his own grudges against his Christian clanmates. They may have found shelter in the other leper houses of the order, however.

Secular and Minor Orders

The great age of secular knightly orders is not yet come. The Knights of the Garter and of the Golden Fleece are yet to be imagined, but the legend of the Knights of the Round Table is available for those who wish to draw on it as a source. Generally, the *fons honorum*, the origin of true knighthood, is considered to require both papal and temporal authorization; hence the religious bent of the crusading orders.

Orders founded without either secular or religious approval tend to fade away rapidly. Because many orders exist for only a few years, bear confusing and conflicting names or are "invented" by scoundrels for various reasons, it is difficult for many to conclude with finality which of the minor orders are imaginary or apocryphal and which are merely obscure. These minor orders include:

The Order of St. Catherine of Sinai

This much-persecuted band came together near the end of the 11th century to provide escorts to pilgrims visiting the tomb of St. Catherine in the monastery by the same name, on one of the summits of Mount Sinai. It remains unclear whether its member knights consider themselves to have either secular or religious authority, since the careers of various patrons wax and wane. Rumors in Cainite courts hold that the order is the fabrication of a single vampire, although this benefactor's identity shifts from story to story. Although unreliable, these

stories may explain why the Assamites seem to have taken a particular interest in this group — and not a beneficial one. The order's numbers are dwindling as knights fall victims to attacks that (to Cainite eyes) bear the silent signature of Haqim's childer. The slaughter of both knights and pilgrims has enraged some young Christian neonates, further exacerbating Cainite tensions in the Holy Land.

The Order of St. Michael's Wing

Alfonso Henriques, the first King of Portugal, founded this order in 1147 in commemoration of his victory over the Moors. Popular wisdom holds that St. Michael himself appeared on the battlefield to aid the soldiers of the Lord in battle. Cainites who listen to certain other sources believe that the avenging figure was no angel, but rather a Brujah warrior known as Nuno da Silva. The Zealots have a vested interest in protecting the fledgling kingdom; whatever his personal motivations, da Silva — if that is indeed the true identity of the seemingly divine figure — certainly fought like one imbued with heavenly fervor.

The order's stated mission is to fight infidels and to defend widows and orphans, but its single purple-embroidered feather is not often seen outside of Portugal. Lack of papal confirmation seems to be condemning this order to obscurity, which may be a sign of the Lasombra putting a stop to undue Brujah influence.

The Order of St. Helena

This self-proclaimed order is composed of lady fighters who have chosen to model themselves after Helena, mother of Constantine. St. Helena is venerated by the Church for having uncovered the lost cross on which Jesus was crucified. She distinguished the True Cross from the crosses on which the thieves were hung by taking the advice of Jewish sages who counseled that each of the three crosses should be touched to dead bodies; the holy cross would thus be identified by its ability to restore life to the dead.

The three women who founded the Order of St. Helena wish to emulate the order's namesake in striving to identify and pursue truth and holiness. Hedewigis, Ermengarde and Sancha all chose to abandon their families and titles in favor of a new family of independent women. They have adapted and simplified the arms bestowed upon Helena in the early Middle Ages to serve as the order's device: a black double-headed eagle, bearing on its breast a red shield marked by a gold cross.

Former camp followers who grew frustrated with the corruption and hypocrisy staining the shining ideals of the Crusades rub shoulders in the Helenite ranks with noblewomen disgusted and disappointed by the failures of their so-called holy warriors. The test for these dedicated women is to somehow manage to armor and equip themselves, which requires more money than many people of either sex are easily able to amass; most do so through persistent scavenging and clever bartering. Having thus amply demonstrated their resourcefulness even before their arrival at the order's keep outside of Tyre, they then receive training both in the art of combat and in a monastic discipline which exceeds in its strictness that of many other militant orders.

Although scorned and mocked by the established orders, the Order of St. Helena has so far escaped organized resistance, primarily because of its accumulated resources and virtuous reputation. The sheer defiant eccentricity of the order, as well as its very existence, flouts all the rules of both Eastern and Western society. In addition, the Lady Knights of St. Helena have embarrassed the Church several times by thwarting schemes they considered unworthy of Christians. Already, several zealous knights have earned abundant rewards for removing, sometimes forcibly, some of these headstrong women to convents, where they can be kept under a close eye and taught to do more useful things than take up men's weapons.

Fortunately for the order, the Patriarch of Antioch and the Patriarch of Jerusalem are currently far too busy arguing over whose jurisdiction includes various portions of Tyre province to make any formal plans regarding what to do with the women making their home in the disputed territory. This situation is only temporary, but in the meantime, the order persists and attracts women who wish to partake of the knightly lifestyle; more than one of these also suffers from a strange curse and is unable to venture out during the day....

The Crafty Maid's Policy

Some women choose rather flamboyant means of acquiring the items they need. For example, a popular song (familiarized in numerous variants), tells the story of how one attractive young woman tricks a gentleman into giving her a prized possession by saying she craves what lies between his legs. He eagerly promises to give her what she wants, with his two friends to serve as witnesses — only to regret his folly when she goes galloping off on his undoubtedly well-bred and well-trained horse.

As always, such roguery is safer for characters in songs than those out of them. Highborn women have an advantage in that their status shelters them from some repercussions of independent behavior, such as being unceremoniously tossed into dungeons; lowborn women, especially those without fathers or husbands, have no such protection.

Spurious Orders

Stories of knightly orders circulate like wildfire among the songs of the troubadours and the whispers of the courts. Many of these are fanciful creations, intended to provide examples to young knights or add legitimacy to an established power structure. Storytellers, however, can make use of such orders, by deciding either that they are in fact real or that some enterprising knights have decided to make fiction into fact. They may also simply use them as background material, the subject of stories overhead by the characters. Such apocryphal orders include:

• **The Order of the Dog and Cock:** Legend has it that Clovis I adopted Christianity in 496 CE and that the first of his barons to follow suit founded *l'Ordre du Chien et du Coq*, an order noted for its profound and unquestioning loyalty to the king.

- **The Order of the Royal Crown:** Charlemagne is supposed to have founded this order sometime before his death in 814 CE. The Knights of the Royal Crown are completely undocumented but, actually, somewhat historically plausible given the Frankish monarch's lifelong devotion to the Church, and certainly, the great king's strife against heathens and pagans might well inspire other Dark Medieval zealots.
- **The Order of the Civet:** *L'Ordre de la Genette* supposedly took its name from a great victory over the Saracens, after which the conquering knights discovered a trove of civet furs in the enemy camp. The Civet Knights, as unlikely as their story sounds, are generally accepted as conquering heroes. Stories vary widely as to exactly what they use for a coat of arms.

Fraudulent Knights

A Cainite could do rather well by claiming to be a member of an invented order or of an order no longer in existence. Such self-named "knights" are free from duties, responsibilities and inconvenient bonds to monarchs, yet may enjoy — however fraudulently — the status and privileges due to a crusader. In addition, they have no more need to invent excuses for failing to attend Mass or avoiding a battle commencing in the middle of the day, since they no longer have compatriots to check up on their actions.

Such deceptions are practiced both in the Holy Land and in Europe. Discovery poses the risk of complete social disgrace among mortals, as well as the disdain — or worse — of those vampires who actually respect the goals of chivalry. One clever yet foolish Ravnos, posing as a battle-scarred crusader, skillfully talked his way into a grand feast at Rome only to have the misfortune to discover entirely too late that the dark, taciturn gentleman seated across from him was none other than Fabrizio Ulfila. That most potent Ventrue manipulator spent nearly all of the evening listening quietly to the Charlatan's wild tales of daring exploits. The next night, the Ravnos was found wandering the worst part of the city, all but witless and incoherent save for his blind insistence that he was, in fact, a two-headed donkey.

On the other hand, Sir Emelrich von Hildesheim returned from his travels to his native Saxony with enough newfound wealth to establish himself as a landed baron, and none are willing to question openly either the startlingly short duration of his trip or the decidedly small number of stories he has to tell. Whatever voyages von Hildesheim made have decidedly not improved his temper, and former crusaders passing through his demesne do well either to confirm loudly their acquaintance with him and his noble deeds or else to travel particularly quickly.

The Order of the Swan, A Cautionary Tale

The Order of the Swan (*l'Ordre du Cygne*), a French order, is said to have been founded around 711 CE by a chevalier called Elie or Eslie to mark the occasion of his marriage to Béatrix, daughter of Thierry, Duke of Cléves — a marriage which took place solely because the chevalier had been instrumental in liberating the duke from enemies surrounding his castle. The order was secular from its very inception and never managed to rise very high above those roots. In fact, it quickly fell from what little grace it ever had.

Within a few years, the order suffered under successive reigns by vicious and depraved grand masters. Truly faithful members fled, while those seeking personal gain thronged to the sign of the Swan. Eventually the order's machinations became so blatant and so distasteful — at one point members were actually caught in the act of attempting to kidnap the young daughter of a wealthy merchant — that local lords imprisoned most of its knights and burned its keep to the ground. Some genuinely chivalrous souls, no matter how short a time they had been members of the order, were irremediably tarred by the brush of its evil reputation.

The Order of the Swan would be held up to this day as a warning example for would-be knights, save that outside of one or two obviously exaggerated horror stories, few traces remain of the defunct order.

The Cainites of France remember it, however, and know the lesson it teaches. Indeed, they say the duke had run afoul of the Lasombra Marianne Deseaux, and it was she who engineered the siege of Cléves. When her plan failed, she tuned her ire to the order and created its corruption through subtle interventions over the years (an undesirable candidate here and there achieving entrance over objections, missives from potential allies somehow going astray). She even Embraced a few select knights and then cast them out — to wander the world remembering their failure.

Cainite Orders

Bertin strove vainly to soothe the horses. No matter how he whispered in their ears or gently stroked their coats, something about the unfamiliar scene drove them half-mad. Had he been less busy or perhaps less sensible, the young squire himself might well have faltered: The familiar clearing had somehow shifted into an utterly unrecognizable landscape, possessed of sounds and smells alien to daylight.

At last the horses stood more or less still, trembling and snorting. Bertin turned his eyes to the circle. With a small shock, he realized that it was the foreign knight newly come from Salvatierra, fighting on foot with Sir Maugier, in such a bout as Bertin had never seen. The combatants blurred against the motionless stands swiftly enough to make the flickering torchlight look torpid. Like thunder from lightning, the clamor of blade against blade or shield was oddly detached from the spectacle.

The noble spectators in the stands were transfixed. Bertin could not hold back the remembrance of a cathedral choir he'd seen

once, blank-eyed, uncannily still and breathing in unison just so, preparing to sing an unearthly hymn.

There are a handful of exclusively Cainite orders acting in Europe and the Holy Land, paralleling the mortal knightly companies. These exist in addition to the Brotherhood of the Sable Rose, the Cainite order-within-an-order operating within the Hospitalers (see p. 63). In these orders, vampires may continue their dedication to chivalry while having the freedom to acknowledge their natures and abilities. These groups are under Toreador control; other Cainites are, as of yet, generally unconvinced of the wisdom of founding vampiric chivalric orders, although they may apply to join if they so desire. These orders are the philosophical heart of the still-developing Via Equitum — the Road of Chivalry.

The White Company

A fraternity of supposedly spotless integrity, these knights strive to uphold the ideals of honor, obedience to God and celibacy — the latter being practiced in their case both by abstinence from sexual and romantic love and by physical self-control in terms of feeding. They wear pure white, unmarked sashes or tabards.

Doña Lupa Manrique, once the cherished daughter of an ancient and noble Castilian family and now a Toreador of consummate gentility, leads the chivalrous band. Manrique has steered the Company in one particular direction: Rather than chase Saracens aimlessly about the desert sands, these noble knights stay closer to home in order to avenge crimes against truth and honor. They especially abhor oath-breaking of any sort and have been known to go to extreme lengths to track down and destroy both mortals and Cainites who have failed to keep faith with serious vows.

The troubadours of the Toreador clan endlessly sing of the Company's exploits under Manrique's command, and most Cainites susceptible to tales of romance and heroism are happy to listen. Manrique's deadly skill at tourney is no less highly praised than her grace and austere elegance. Yet some question Manrique's untiring dedication and speculate as to some personal tragedy in her past that might be more responsible for her brilliant career than pure idealism.

The Fellowship of Our Lady

William Grey, an English Toreador who followed the First Crusade, claims he received a vision of the Virgin Mary, Queen of Heaven, while traveling through Syria. Taking the apparition to heart, he founded this tiny band of Cainite knights dedicated to the Virgin and gave it the mission to protect and assist women. He and his fellows believe their holy task will eventually free them from vampiric taint. The Fellows wear the mark of the white lily but are seldom met with — their numbers never rise above nine.

Grey not only carefully scrutinizes the character of those who seek to join the Fellowship, he refuses even to consider any who were not knighted as mortals. He has even gone so far as to reject those he thought were elevated for unworthy reasons. Grey places humans above Cainites in almost all

things, and this policy has stirred up no small amount of rancor among more traditional vampires.

Grey and Ogier Fouinon, the Ventrue prince of Avignon, have recently had a bitter falling-out. Some suspect that the dispute arose over the ramifications of Countess Saviarre's potential patronage of or affiliation with the order. Others claim that Grey, in his blithe disregard for politics and diplomacy, declined to admit to the order a knight favored by Fouinon. As a result of the feud, the Fellowship's name has been besmirched by accusations of heresy, which conveniently tie in to the decline of Marianism in the mortal world.

The Order of Chanticleer

This order is comprised of zealous demon-hunters and slayers of Baali. Many vampires of different clans have set aside their differences and joined this order in their passion to rid the earth of demonic taint. These knights, who often alienate other Cainites with their aggressively violent piety, pride themselves on testing the limits of their endurance by exposing themselves to the rising sun — the stylized rendition of which serves as their blazon. Some members of the order also identify themselves by wearing a rooster's feather for a helmet plume.

In Europe, the Order of Chanticleer is trapped in limbo, torn between their goal and the desires of a few Toreador elders not happy to see their accomplices in hedonism persecuted. Infernal occultists have managed to identify and destroy knights while they were helplessly enmeshed in the snares of clan politics.

In contrast, the Chanticleerans are free to devote themselves to the hunt in Outremer. They proclaim their great successes in driving the Baali outside of Damascus even further underground and pride themselves on having given the Final Death to a powerful Cappadocian who had bartered with the forces of the Devil. One notable setback, however, occurred when an entire company was lost during a rather foolhardy expedition to uncover the Baali stronghold of Chorazin. Aerial and terrestrial demons actually tempted several knights into evil; those who resisted seduction simply met Final Death.

One of the members of the Order of Chanticleer, Edythe Swift, has so angered elders throughout England with her outspoken criticism of what they consider wise restraint that they have declared a blood hunt against her.

Edythe truly has been a thorn in the side of many Cainites, and it seems likely that at least some will respond to the call. It remains to be seen whether the order will close ranks around her or even if other vampiric orders will come to her aid. This blood hunt has the potential to become a political disaster entangling knights of many different clans, especially if Edythe refuses to disappear quietly.

Controlling the Cause

The orders of knighthood are generally each under the rule of their own grand master. Though he is, in theory, the humble

The Dispossessed, A Ghoul Order of Sorts

Marian often wakes to the sound of her own voice repeating her name slowly and distinctly, over and over. She wishes she could stop. The ones she finds herself speaking to are long since gone.

She was nothing then, and she is nothing now, she knows. The handsome lord, his bright lady, they would not have recognized her name had they heard it. But their trusted reeve had been kind to her. She claimed to be willing to serve as the lady's maid and so earned passage along with the three of them to Jerusalem.

Of the first two weeks of their stay, she has little more than a blurred memory of heat, dust and incomprehensible babbling. Flashes of recalled pleasure with the unlovely but gentle reeve sometimes return to her. But the night the lord and lady were turned away from the party they'd counted on attending, their joyance took priority over that of their lowly servants.

She hadn't known she was with child until she saw the blood seeping from between her legs as well as from her other wounds. Even with that sudden hurt penetrating her mind, the twisted ecstasy flowing through her kept her prone and unresisting. When she woke the next day, weak but alive, it was the memory of her lord and lady calling her by the wrong name that returned again and again, to wipe out the images of her lover's death.

As the crusading tide ebbs and flows against the shores of the Muslim lands, Cainite influence has also risen and fallen. Some vampires who travel to the Holy Land are unwary and find their existences ended through carelessness. Some lose interest in whatever caprice involved them in the seemingly endless struggle. Some suffer defeat in the interminable politicking within clans. For whatever reasons, left behind are their attendant ghouls and retainers. Many cannot survive on their own, but some of those who can have now banded together in Jerusalem. They pay the fee of pilgrimage to the Muslim authorities and gather in the Holy City.

The members of this ragtag assemblage will never disclose too much or too incriminating information about their former masters, for to do so would be to damn themselves as well in the eyes of the Church. But they sometimes seek out and comfort those whose lives have been damaged by Cainite intervention, and on a very few occasions, they have dared to resist machinations they considered intolerable.

The ghouls and lost souls in their huts on the edge of town would have a hard time escaping persecution if not for two factors: the first being that most mortals sense something disturbing about them and tend to leave them alone and the second being the protection they receive from certain Malkavians and Nosferatu. The latter have on occasion found them useful — voluntarily so, of course. The former seem simply to find them amusing.

servant of both the monarch and the Pope who sponsor his order, it is the grand master who is responsible for supervising the religious observances and practices of those knights beneath him, leading the order's military activities and furthering the often-conflicting goals of Church and state.

These grand masters exert tremendous power and influence. On occasion, they arise as natural commanders, but as one might expect, the positions are far more often hotly contested. Wealth, status and political pull are certainly factors. Depending on what temporal or religious interests are involved in the knighthood in question, martial skill or economic savvy might also be deciding factors.

Following the grand master in most orders is a hierarchical structure consisting of chaplains, knights and sergeants, mirroring the triple nature of medieval society. In addition, administrators have to be appointed to supervise donations, many of which come in the form of estates throughout Europe.

All these positions can facilitate the acquisition of power and wealth for Cainites to an even greater extent than they can for mortals. The drawback is that such situations expose vampires to numerous risks. It does an ambitious vampire little good to have carefully plotted over the course of years to take control of a minor order if, shortly after he does so, several mortal knights possessed of blindingly powerful True Faith take up residence in the order's keep. Of course, there are always means by which such a situation may be dealt with, but a master who loses the support of his knights or his religious may find himself deposed or worse.

For those who genuinely believe in the causes they serve, ascending to the rank of a grand master is a glorious apotheosis, a goal to be achieved by painfully few. As noted above, two of the masters of the Order of St. Lazarus, Fra Gerard and Fra Raymond, received the Embrace as reward for their exceptional piety and for services rendered to the Nosferatu; neither one was able to continue in his former role, and both assisted the order secretly after their "deaths."

Considerably easier for vampires to maintain are roles as advisors or assistants to the heads of various orders. Many Cainites have become invaluable figures in the running of strongholds both at home and in the Holy Land, effecting great changes even though they are almost never acknowledged as the authors of such.

Neither Liege Nor Order: Rogue Knights

Sir Robert de Lindesey surveyed his small but noisy band of warriors with a pleasure surpassing even their own current drunken exuberance. He thought they'd fought well that evening, remembering to keep their shield wall together and almost always following his bellowed instructions with suitable speed. The information he'd gotten from that bloody little snake of a Setite was dead on — the caravan had been no match for his vicious crew.

He examined the looted jewels with a practiced eye, having already divvied up the coins. The only thing nagging at him now was the skinny fop who'd escaped. To de Lindesey's way of thinking, that one had the bearing of a courier and was presumably still carrying whatever papers he'd been holding. Annoyingly enough, the Serpent hadn't mentioned any such person. Wasn't worth chasing some lackey halfway to Calais, though, not when he'd gotten all the valuables and a good night's fighting besides.

Not all the knights who went on crusade stayed gone. Yet, not all of them have returned quietly to their homes, either. Some decided they liked the unfettered lives they'd led far from the direct control of law or family and the looks of lands they were passing through on the way home. They settled down to careers of pillage and robbery.

Local governments find it extremely difficult to deal with these traveling marauders, not least because the knights are usually far more experienced and better equipped than the representatives of law and order. The Church decries their activities but often finds her most extreme measure — excommunication — scorned by now-hardened mercenaries.

Although they make the lives of peasants and merchants miserable, renegade knights are often quite useful for nobles who have dirty work they need done, are engaged in squabbles with other nobles or wish to avoid their own requirements of knightly service to the king. Would-be conquerors with deep enough pockets have been known to employ them, in defiance of their notorious untrustworthiness. In addition, they are often caught up either deliberately or inadvertently in Cainite politicking.

Rogue knights have offered many rationales for their self-serving activities. Some perceive themselves as prototypical Robin Hood figures (though that name, as such, will not gain its cachet for many years yet to come). Others, disillusioned after years spent to little purpose in the Holy Land, note that their worst excesses pale in comparison to the rampages taking place there. Many younger sons who were sent to gain glory on crusade are too ashamed to return home without having made either a name or a fortune. Some have abandoned their mortal lives entirely after being Embraced in foreign lands, and now struggle to create new existences.

In a way, it seems fitting that these disreputable knights exist. The medieval love of symmetry demands balance and knighthood as it is practiced in the Dark Medieval embodies both the brightest and darkest aspects of human and inhuman beings.

Chapter Four: The Order of the Bitter Ashes

He asked nothing but justice of Heaven, and of man he asked only a fair field.

–from the Chronicle of the Cid
(trans. by Southey)

On the fourth day of creation, the Bible says, God created the greater light of the Sun to rule the day and the lesser light of the Moon to rule the night. Both lights serve as reminders of the divine Light from which all other created things spring. The Curse of Caine cuts vampires off from the Sun but not, some vampires hope, from the divine Light itself. While most Cainites reject any thought of submission to the Light, a few Cainites turn individually or as a group to serving the Light as best they can in a night that can never end in anything but fiery Final Death.

The Order of the Bitter Ashes gathers together Cainite knights who take up the burden of guarding relics that are tangible evidence of God's presence in the world. They lead a difficult existence, their unique opportunities balanced against equally unique challenges.

History

A few vampires have sought the Light almost since the very first nights of Caine's curse. Understanding comes slowly, progress toward holiness even slower: For every three steps forward, there are at least two steps back, and often four or more.

A few key people and eras mark the road toward what might (in the end) prove salvation for Cainites. Members of the order, and the Cainites they hope to recruit, argue about just which markers count the most and why.

Akhenaton and Moses

Two great leaders rose in Egypt within a generation of each other.

The Pharaoh Akhenaton preached a single god over all other gods and spirits, and identified him with the Sun. Akhenaton's reforms did not outlast him — the old priesthood reasserted its prerogatives before the pharaoh's corpse had finished cooling. In the meantime, Akhenaton's ideas found favor with Cainites who remembered that their own condition stemmed from the curse inflicted upon Caine by a powerful spirit or god. Some vampires decided that, in fact, their curse came from the single true god, and that, in service to him, they could win the redemption Caine himself rejected. Others felt that the god who levied the curse was nothing more than a petty local force, who could be overcome by service to the god who is the Sun.

The prophet Moses gave new identity to the nation of Israel and (unwittingly) sparked fresh argument among spiritually-minded Cainites. Many vampires refused to have anything do with Moses' god and pursued their own paths. (See **Dark Ages Companion** and **Book of Storyteller Secrets** for some examples of vampiric mysticism more removed from Jewish and Christian thought.) The Cainites who accepted the truth of Moses' teachings responded with mixtures of fear and hope: hope that the newly named God might explain what they must do to redeem themselves, fear that he would never accept them. The vampires most inclined to fear God and least hopeful of his good intentions withdrew from the Middle East, seeking sanctuary that might endure some future day of judgment.

Vampires who found hope, or the possibility of hope, in the Jewish message continued to follow the evolution of the Jewish nation. A few particularly brave (or desperate) vampires settled in Jerusalem itself. Others watched from a distance, making a trip into the Holy Land every few generations or sending emissaries on their behalf. They continued to argue among themselves about which elements of the Jewish faith were true and which were false (or incompletely true), never reaching agreement and all passionately sure of their own correctness.

The *Grails Covenant* Trilogy

Vampires seldom act for just one reason, and over time, their plans acquire many convolutions. Observers must decipher the machinations as best they can. When vampiric plans cross, so that observers see different facets of an extended undertaking across the centuries, stories emerge as the observers attempt to account for what they've seen.

The Order of the Bitter Ashes here differs from the version presented in the *Grails Covenant* trilogy of novels by David Niall Wilson. One way to use the novels is as inspiration for the accounts provided by vampires the characters encounter in the course of a chronicle. The novels offer the sorts of twists and changes that many vampires expect of each other and sound plausible enough in the midst of an environment where spiritual power manifests regularly.

Storytellers can also, of course, decide to make some or all of the novels' setting true wherever it disagrees with the version presented here.

Vampires Fleeing God

A determined vampire willing to endure hardship can travel very far indeed. Single vampires, and a few small communities, can be found anywhere they think God won't see them. They do their best to avoid all other Cainites and often seek to avoid humanity as well. Some hoard vast lore, while others are simply deranged. Many of the God-fleeing vampires are very old and very powerful; encounters with them far more often end in the quick death of potential rivals than in anything productive.

The Gatherers

A coterie of vampires formed in the century after the Exodus to study more closely the new religious movement. Some of the coterie's founders believed strongly in the Jewish faith, others shared Akhenaton's solar monotheism, and still others held different ideas. What held them together was the mutual conviction that the one god spoke at least some of the time through the new teachers and prophets and that some artifacts associated with these divine messengers carried power which vampires could use. It didn't take long to discover, for instance, that a stream where one of Israel's judges regularly washed might sometimes soothe a vampire's frenzy or restore lost blood or otherwise mitigate the Curse of Caine.

The coterie's founders called themselves the Gatherers, since their primary undertaking was the gathering and protecting of holy relics. (A few individuals held out for "the Arguers," claiming that argument was the coterie's real primary mission, but they eventually yielded.) The coterie did not then and never has achieved a real consensus about god's identity or concerns. Their discussions always veered from theological argument to the only realm where they could reach agreement, the care of relics.

Captivity and Return

The fall of Jerusalem to Babylon in 597 BCE galvanized the Gatherers to systematic action. Until then, they'd proceeded on a case-by-case basis, with no real long-term plan. Now, the Gatherers realized, they needed to coordinate their efforts. Many relics passed beyond their grasp, but by intercepting and infiltrating some of the caravans of loot headed for Babylon, the Gatherers recovered hundreds of holy treasures. For centuries, the Gatherers had found shelter in the caves on the east side of the Jordan; now, they undertook systematic construction of safe havens.

The Gatherers waited out the era of Jewish exile, filling the time with theological debate and travel. They circulated throughout the Middle East, studying alleged prophetic lore and revelations. A handful went even further: into the wilds of barbaric Europe, across the African desert and over the mountains of central Asia. More than half of the far travelers never returned. Those who did make it back to the Jordanian caves brought fascinating tales but few signs of the divine wisdom the Gatherers sought. Whatever the exotic insights of the mortal and supernatural denizens of these other lands might be, the rest of the world offered little that demanded the Gatherers' attention.

It was during this era that the Gatherers reached general agreement that the truths they sought must lie somewhere in or near the Western monotheistic tradition. They agreed that god was unitary (or perhaps dual), not plural, and that he seemed to pay particular attention to the peoples of the Fertile Crescent. Debate continued about all the particulars.

Fresh controversy erupted when Jews returned to Israel. Should the Gatherers return the artifacts they'd harvested? In the end, after almost a century of intense argument sometimes punctuated by direct violence, the Gatherers decided not to. As vampires, the Gatherers could ensure continuity of protection in ways that no mortal community could, nor would they be so likely (they thought) to succumb to passing fads and fervor. The Gatherers' Disciplines offered modes of protection unparalleled in mortal capacity. A minority of the Gatherers argued then, and continues to do so now, that this all merely rationalizes the selfish desire to hoard relics. The minority believes the true mission of the Gatherers should be to restore relics to worthy mortal keepers.

The Turning Era

The centuries before and after Jesus were filled with prophets and messengers, offering up many prescriptions for the world's ills. A significant number of the Gatherers found Jesus' teachings convincing in some sense, though they continued to argue (as they still do now) about whether he was the Messiah and, if so, what that meant. Others favored Simon bar Kochba or the Essenes or any of the countless other claimants of new truths.

The order made several disastrous attempts to openly influence humanity in the declining centuries of the Roman Empire. The Gatherers seldom speak of such things in the 12th century. On at least three occasions between about 200 and 500 CE, the order attempted to create a network of mortal believers dedicated to the task of systematically harvesting holy objects. In every case, the network turned into a cult of its own. On at least two of these occasions, the mortal believers ended up slaughtering the Gatherers involved, believing that vampires must have come to exploit the harvested objects.

Around 250 CE, the order came into possession of one of its greatest treasures, an oracular head. This is the actual severed head of a Middle Eastern man. When supplied with blood (it's placed in a shallow pan, so that it can absorb blood through the neck) and supplicated with the proper rituals, the head regains a semblance of life and utters prophecies. Sometimes it speaks of what's happening in the present moment, sometimes of the future; it has never been heard to speak of any past event. Particularly when it foretells the future, it does so with a complex symbolism that combines Jewish imagery with an apparently personal collection of allusions and metaphors.

Since the head cannot or will not speak of the past and since it had passed through many owners before the Gatherers acquired it, the order doesn't know whose head it is. The most popular theory attributes it to John the Baptist, whose beheading is a matter of common knowledge and who was in life a well-known prophet. Other Gatherers speculate that it is the head of one of Jesus' disciples or even of Jesus himself — the Jordanian cave archives include several paintings of Jesus' soul ascending to Heaven out of his decapitated body. A persistent though never popular interpretation says that the head belonged to Pontius Pilate; the objection that he was probably not Middle Eastern in origin goes unaddressed. A few stalwart Gatherers who reject the Jewish tradition altogether believe the head to be Akhenaton's.

With the fall of Rome and the rise of Byzantium, the order entered a period of quiescence. Individual Gatherers continued to travel the world, but the order collectively abandoned efforts to interfere with human affairs. Century by century, their stores grew, and that seemed sufficient.

The Rise of Chivalry

The 12th century opened with the worst shock the order ever received. Gatherers of the 11th century didn't realize that they'd been discovered by necromancers loosely allied with the Seljuk Turks. The magicians spent 20 years studying the Gatherers. In 1101, the magicians hired the services of several extremely powerful Assamites (trading them favors for use in disputes within the clan) and assaulted the order's stronghold in Jordan.

The defenses held for a while, long enough to enable a third of the Gatherers to escape with the most valuable artifacts (or at least the most portable). The other two-thirds perished along with their holdings when the magicians simultaneously collapsed the caves from above and released corrupted ghosts from below. In a single night, the work of more than 1,000 years disappeared.

The survivors scattered for years before converging on the Castle in the Lake (see p. 83). They decided that while their past efforts to work with humanity had gone badly, perhaps it was time to try again. The Gatherers needed allies if they were to have any hope of surviving future attacks like the one in Jordan. Another great debate ensued. It ended in 1123 with the decision to create the Order of the Bitter Ashes.

The Knights Templar provided the primary inspiration for the new order. Various Gatherers had crossed paths with the Templars and been impressed by their dedication. Since Templar goals overlap with the order's in some ways — particularly in the thwarting of evil forces — the first thought to emerge from Gatherer debate was to model a new organization on the Poor Knights. Then Gatherers suggested recruiting the actual Templars they'd worked well with in the past. Both suggestions found favor. The name for the order came from *The Book of Nod*, a work devoutly studied by Gatherers. The order's profession to abide by God's decree (or that of His angel Uriel) that Caine and his childer "eat only ashes," the Gatherers hoped, would suggest the human desire for abasement and repentance, as well as the specific condition of Caine's curse.

The next question, and the one over which the Gatherers argued the longest, was about power. Should the Gatherers simply Embrace their chosen agents? Or should they do something special? The Gatherers finally settled on the use of an artifact they believed to be the Holy Grail. As with the oracular head, the Grail's true origin is a mystery. It came into their custody only in the eighth century, and by then, it was impossible to trace back a valid history. The Grail has strong power and radiates an aura of holiness, and it might be just what its defenders say it is. Even if it isn't, it's a cup blessed in some other remarkable way, so the fact of its holiness wouldn't disappear even if it could be established that the cup had never been near the Last Supper. Many Gatherers feared to let the Grail out of the strongest seals within the Castle in the Lake, but others pointed out that isolation had already proven fatal.

Having decided to act, the Gatherers did so quickly. It took only a few months to identify 23 candidates for the Grail Embrace. All accepted. The order knew what it was looking for: a particular combination of piety and ruthless ambition, so that a knight would be willing to risk his soul for the holy work.

The initial Grail Embraces all took place in the Middle East, since the order exploited its Templar contacts there to gain information, but the order's focus of activity quickly shifted to Europe. Across the continent, important relics lay in abandoned or concealed strongholds at least as often as in well-attended churches and the citadels of the powerful. While the order has not turned its back on the Middle East, its primary focus is now Europe.

The Current Order

The order's own leaders sometimes represent the order's organization with the help of an orrery, a model of orbiting spheres like those that chart the movements of the planets. At the center, like the fixed Earth, stand the Gatherers. They watch but seldom move, even to reach out to their servants within the order. The Grail Knights orbit like planets sharing the same celestial sphere. The founding knights swing a little closer to the Gatherers, more recent recruits further away; all share in the same responsibilities and honors. Mortal servants surround the Grail Knights: Mortal knights, informed servants and ignorant tools stand at successive removes from the heart of the order.

Bitter Destiny

The Order of the Bitter Ashes, for all its high ideals and accomplishments, does not survive into the modern nights. As the age of chivalry comes and goes, so too does the order it spawned. Yet, the order's demise is not just a matter of changing times, but instead, of crusade and inquisition. The faith the order so valiantly tries to protect will eventually eat it alive.

Early blows come as the ravages of medieval politics and loyalties swallow up the order's holdings. The Albigensian Crusade is but a few decades away from tearing down the order's Pronvençal holdings. As the Iberian frontier pushes further and further south, the order will also be less able to mask its activities amidst the chaos of the *Reconquista.* When the Inquisition rises in the coming centuries, the order's few remaining strongholds will also fall.

The fate of the Gatherers is less bleak, and they do survive into the Final Nights. They keep their own counsel, however, and few know of their existence. Some claim they have sponsored other experiments like the order throughout the last few centuries. There may also be a few stray Grail Knights who escaped the Inquisition. Most survivors did so by compromising their ethics and so lost the gifts of the Grail, but some Noddist scholars maintain that at least one Grail Knight kept the faith and is still out there.

The Mission of the Order

The Gatherers charge the order with three positive duties and one negative one:

• The order protects holy relics, rescuing them from wicked custodians and preserving them for sacred use.

• The order provides guidance to vampires seeking redemption. This guidance most often comes indirectly or cloaked in mystery, as the order fears imposing its will on troubled souls in moments of crisis.

• The order assists vampires who seek release from the world, through inspiring courage to greet the Sun, allowing contact with relics that destroy vampiric flesh and vitae or granting access to other means of leaving the world and entering the realm of the divine.

• The order fights monsters of all sorts, all beings who consciously serve evil powers.

To Protect the Relics

The Gatherers do not feel at liberty to spend much time in the presence of the mortal men and woman who might (or might not) be god's messengers. These ancient Cainites know that the Beast lurks under their veneer of reverence, waiting for the time to strike. To expose holy men to the risk of becoming the Gatherers' own prey is simply unacceptable to them. So the Gatherers settle for rounding up the physical traces left behind by self-identified prophets and teachers. Whatever the truth of the messengers' contact with god, their lives sometimes do leave discernible power imbued into places and things. Unfortunately for vampires bent on seeking the divine, the remaining power can be used for evil and selfish purposes just as easily as for good or constructive ones.

Practitioners of magic put relics to all sorts of uses, extracting raw power to support other rituals, as well as making use of distinct abilities that the relic item or place possesses. Particularly powerful relics change hands often, both as gifts and through theft or fraud. The Gatherers find it ironic that the most tangible traces of god's passage become so surrounded by death, corruption and vice of every sort.

To remedy this situation, the order acts to remove relics from guardians the Gatherers deem unfit. The methods of the order begin with straightforward asking. In some cases, lords who find themselves the custodians of artifacts of great power and mysterious provenance may become tired of constant efforts to snatch the artifacts away and quite voluntarily turn them over to knights with an aura of holiness. Sometimes the order works in conjunction with its few friends in the clerical hierarchy, arranging for relics to come into possession of an allied bishop or priest who then turns the relics over to the order. While the order frowns on deception for selfish ends, its members do sometimes simply lie, claiming clerical authority they do not have.

On occasion the order's emissaries decide that a relic's current owner can, in fact, take proper care of it. The decision not to take ownership usually entails an offer of instruction in the defense and worshipful use of the relic, so that the owner can make the best use of her fragment of the divine. These lessons, which may take months or even years, can be quite tricky because the knights will do their utmost to hide their Cainite nature from mortals.

More commonly, the order decides that a relic's current owner abuses it or simply can't guard it properly. With all due regret for the sins they may commit along the way, order knights scheme to remove the relics from unworthy guardians. Wherever they can, they spirit the objects away thanks to the gifts of Caine. The order can and sometimes does mount full-blown assaults on the strongholds of the wicked, but only as a last resort.

The standard procedure calls for two knights and their retinues to call on the owner of a relic the order seeks. If overt requests fail, then the knights attempt subterfuge. Only if that fails are the knights permitted to summon the assistance of their fellows.

To Guide the Searchers

Members of the order with talents in disguise (whether purely natural, based on Disciplines or drawing on some other source) spend one year in every 12 traveling incognito among other Cainites. The order's other members help prepare cover stories, working with allies when possible and through direct deceptions of their own when necessary, to provide the order's guides with a plausible background: a sire, connections to clan and other communities of interest and a story explaining where the knight has been recently.

This sort of deception is not, on one level, very difficult. Even Cainites cannot, in most cases, readily get detailed information from foreign lands. A few good points that people on the scene can verify make it easy to make claims about remote situations. On the other hand, knights don't just live in holes. They travel on crusade, errantry and personal tasks of many kinds. Furthermore, they tell each other stories about notable deeds. And some Cainites have impressive networks of informants indeed. A good order background may take years or even decades to arrange, with stories of the knight's early deeds set loose to make their way around the chivalric world. When the knight himself appears, he doesn't come as a surprise.

Darker Reflections

The Order of the Bitter Ashes and the Gatherers who sponsor it are rare examples of Cainites with pure intentions. Although they are not entirely free of intrigues and personal machinations, for the most part, they truly believe they are doing a service to humanity and to god (however they choose to see god). Unfortunately, good intentions have never been a guarantee of pure results.

In a chronicle about redemption and self-sacrifice, the order is a useful example, a guidepost to help vampires find a way to reconcile their curse and their faith. In chronicles dealing with moral ambiguity and the reality of evil, however, a pure-as-driven-snow order is less useful. Simply turning it into another cynical vehicle for Cainite power-mongering, however, is no better. Following are some ways to add some ambiguity and moral shadow to the order, while still preserving its central good intentions.

• **Bad Seeds:** The Gatherers are as cautious as they can be in recruiting members for the order, but they are not infallible. Cainites are masters of deception, and a less-than-moral candidate might well insinuate himself into the order's ranks. Surviving the Grail Embrace (see p. 87) requires a certain purity of spirit, but the vampiric squires, aids and archivists of the order have no such ritual to go through. A cabal of such aids more interested in acquiring information and influence than in purity of spirit could be quite damaging. If the bad seed is one of the Gatherers, then the damage is all the worse.

• **Rival Views:** The Gatherers and Grail Knights are not homogeneous. Most of the Gatherers have witnessed the growth of Christianity and know full well that it is but one of many faiths. The knights are more tied to Christian dogma but still hail from a variety of backgrounds. Because of this, they can and do disagree on courses of action. Conflicts in which one knight wishes to sack a Jewish (or Christian or Muslim) house of worship that holds relics and another wishes to protect it can escalate into divisions throughout the order. Gatherers can and do have bitter disputes about what qualifies as a true holy object and who is worthy to protect it. Conceivably, rivals could send the knights they sponsor into the field against one another.

• **Shades of Evil:** Just as there are different views as to what is holy, there are different views as to what is evil. Few Cainites have any moral trouble dispatching Baali invoking Satan, but "pagan sorcerers" and "depraved spirits" can be another matter altogether. If a Grail Knight finds his vile enemy was protecting holy relics of her own faith, his victory may seem hollow indeed.

• **Touch of Corruption:** A longer term problem lies in the very nature of the order. The Grail Knights and the Gatherers hoard holy items on the assumption that they are best suited to protect and keep them. This assumption may well be totally flawed. Indeed, mortal bishops and prelates would surely argue that accursed creatures like the childer of Caine would corrupt whatever holy items they possessed. It is altogether possible that the chests of sacred relics kept in the Castle in the Lake are slowly turning dark under Cainite influence. The more ancient pieces in the Gatherer's care may even be irredeemably corrupted — almost an invitation to subtle infernal influence.

Not all order members travel as knights, though the vast majority do. Some present themselves as clergy — and, in fact, some actually are or were at one time. Less frequently, an order member travels as a merchant, scholar or other member of the lower classes. This sort of disguise occurs most frequently when the order needs information about a specific situation or individual that may not be well covered by the chivalric grapevine.

The major purpose for extended travel under false identity has nothing to do with relic harvesting. The order looks for vampires who show signs of seeking Golconda or whatever they may understand as redemption. (The term "Golconda" is widely known among vampires, but it's not universal, and many vampires prefer to think of redemption in terms of mortal religions.) Vampires fail to find redemption far more often than they succeed, and any seeker on the road to God's grace generally treads it alone. Vampires may or may not believe in a god capable of both curse and forgiveness, and most prefer not to think about it much. Every redemption-seeking vampire must reinvent most of the work of her predecessors, whom she's unlikely to find until after achieving holiness herself. The order seeks to bridge the gap between intention and consummation.

Identifying a vampire deserving of the order's help takes time. The signs of an open heart don't always light up the night in obvious fashion. The seeker might be well known for religious devotion but equally likely might seem simply rebellious or confused to other vampires. The order's emissaries spend time observing Cainite coteries and communities from afar, focusing in on the individuals who seem least inclined to accept their condition as an unchanging given. Then comes the delicate work of establishing just why these vampires are dissatisfied. Mere lust to regain mortality doesn't interest the order, nor does the hunger to become a new Caine. Only the desire to regain God's favor concerns the order. In most cases the order simply ignores other vampires, though, on occasion, an emissary may arrange the destruction of a vampire who seems particularly likely to succumb to infernalism.

The order believes that each vampire must earn her salvation. So simply appearing in full splendor with a full set of instructions wouldn't do; it undercuts the effort necessary to make redemption meaningful. Instead, the order confines itself to hints and suggestions. Some clues deal with immediate issues. The order's emissaries offer advice on how a vampire on a Via the order favors — principally the Roads of Chivalry, Heaven and Humanity — can improve his standing. An emissary may offer not just advice but weeks or months of companionship as a vampire weathers the trauma of abandoning a Via the order thinks dangerous, such as the Road of the Beast. On other missions, the emissary offers clues dealing with matters much further away: how to survive the ravages of a Beast that senses itself near extinction or a prophecy of some future crisis that the vampire might remember and draw on in a moment of need.

At no point does the order provide direct instructions. Its members offer hints, suggestions and allusions. At most, as in the case of Road change, the order supports a vampire in the completion of a specific task, and then the order's emissary removes himself from the scene so that the vampire may continue on his own spiritual journey. Once the emissary identifies a suitable target for inspiration, a direct meeting may well never happen at all. The emissary may speak in dreams and telepathic messages or instruct witting and unwitting mortal agents or even arrange signs in the landscape. The order favors indirect communication in every case except when a direct word seems truly necessary.

Judge Not, Lest Ye Be Judged

The Gatherers teach their disciples two paired truths: The order's members have the moral right to arrange the destruction of vampires communing with dark forces, and the order's members bear moral responsibility for the outcome. A questing knight who mistakenly accuses another Cainite of infernalism and arranges Final Death for his target must pay the same penalty himself when his error comes to light. The order assigns knights abroad in the world to investigate occasions of arranged destruction independently, so as to establish the validity of claimed evil. Order members favor less drastic measures in part because no action short of Final Death brings such after-the-fact scrutiny. No order member long survives once he embarks on a deliberate crusade of abuse, and every order member strives for humility — but pride does not die altogether. Few vampires like having their judgment questioned; in this the order still belongs to the larger society of Cainites.

To Free the Purified

The strongest-willed of Caine's heirs need no help escaping the world. When they're ready, they face the Sun or confront some other challenge capable of overwhelming them. However, very few Cainites have that much willpower.

Vampires seldom decide to commit suicide on a whim. The decision to abandon the material world comes only after decades or (more commonly) centuries of trying to find some way of resolving a vampire's moral qualms about the Cainite condition. Many vampires who feel this moral struggle find their answers in their Roads, turning to external standards as some sort of consolation that, in the end, virtue will be rewarded. The Gatherers themselves disagree on the moral responsibility of virtuous Cainites.

The order's policy is simple: Help vampires seeking God to determine their own sense of what must be done to obey universal moral law. If the answer proves to be service as a Cainite, then the order provides opportunities. If the answer proves to be self-extinction to escape the Curse, then the

order helps with that. Order members apply abilities and Disciplines to stimulate the escaping vampire's courage and determination. Cainites who wish to make recompense for the harm they've done can call on the order for help in providing specific services as long as the order's identity remains secret. Finally, vampires who cannot muster the courage to destroy themselves may call upon the order to arrange a quick end to their curse. A swift conflagration usually does the job.

To Vanquish the Wicked

Three of the order's charges concern helping the righteous, whether worthy individuals or blameless inanimate objects. In theory, none of them require conflict, though relic protection all too often involves combat and stealth. The fourth charge, however, is all about conflict. Order members must fight supernatural evil wherever they find it.

The order focuses on very specific sorts of evil. It does not intervene in any misery, however monstrous, created by mortal men and women. The Gatherers agree that if god wishes to punish humanity, he can do so, and he does not need the order to act as his instrument. Above all, the order focuses on evil vampires and the harm they do, most especially through the practice of blood magic in its various forms. The order also pursues monsters of every sort who originate outside the material world, from the distant past or somewhere else outside the scope of human society.

A few knights dedicate themselves entirely to this quest. Sometimes the order assigns them to monster-hunting, particularly if they suffer from some condition that makes social interaction difficult (Nosferatu, most commonly). Some knights voluntarily take up the vocation. Of the order members who've met Final Death, more than three-quarters died on monster hunts. The Gatherers impress upon knights the seriousness of the enterprise and the very real risks of failure. Since the Gatherers begin by selecting for strong will as well as virtue, the challenges do not dissuade many would-be monster-hunters from their calling.

The nature of the monsters the order confronts varies as widely as the seasons, the climates of different parts of the world and the phases of the moon. Vampires gone amok, vampires transformed by blood magic, demons and other vile spirits, creatures out of the lands of the dead or the realms of disembodied souls; the order confronts them all. The order searches for the lairs of infernalists, invades the dens of ogres and chimera and pushes into every unexamined corner of the world. Wherever possible, the order prefers not to let others know the monster was ever there, but this can't always happen. Inevitably, tales circulate of great heroes fighting strange creatures not only in distant wilderness but in the heart of Europe's palaces and churches. Wherever monsters go, the order follows. To protect its secrets, the order spreads deliberately false stories and attributes its victories to plausible substitutes.

The Composition of the Order

The ranks of the Gatherers are closed: They do not recruit and do not accept volunteers. Once every few centuries, one perishes, and the survivors take the passing as one more sign that the world's history is indeed finite. The Gatherers believe that they embody a unique moment in history and that to include vampires who weren't part of it would be to betray their hope of redemption.

The Grail Knight

The Gatherers choose knights who prove themselves worthy and offer them a drink from the Holy Grail. The Gatherers believe that, over time, they will give the Grail Embrace to 144 knights, 12 childer for each of the signs of the zodiac (or each of the tribes of Israel, depending on which Gatherer explains the theory). Upon imparting the Grail Embrace to the last of these, the Grail will, the Gatherers' prophets say, shatter or simply transform itself into indiscernible empyrean substance. The order began with 23 knights and has now grown to include 42. Another 17 were Grail-born but have since fallen in battle or otherwise met Final Death, so the Gatherers have granted a total of 59 Grail Embraces thus far.

The Gatherers perform the ritual of the Grail Embrace only once a year, beginning on the night of September 28th, the eve of the Christian feast day of Michaelmas. The ritual begins when they mix their own blood with holy water in the Grail and pray over it for a full night. They then let the Grail sit unattended during the full day of Michaelmas. The chosen recruit drinks from it at the start of the next evening. The single sip the Gatherers offer from the Holy Grail works a miraculous, if traumatic, transformation on the Cainite knight. The blood-water mixture burns through the vampire's veins, calling up the Beast in a final challenge. The pain and internal struggle ends only when the vampire feels the burning kiss of the next dawn's light (and then seeks shelter).

The Grail Knight remains a Cainite but one unlike any other. He does not feel the craving for blood because his own body replenishes its stores of vitae. His skin becomes a very soft, pure white — even if he wasn't Caucasian before the Grail Embrace and even overriding the Assamite darkening and other supernatural features. This skin tone isn't quite like albino pigmentation (or lack thereof); it resembles fresh snow lit indirectly. The Grail Knight's skin glows as if reflecting moonlight, but it cycles opposite the Moon. That is, his skin shines brightest in the new moon and holds almost no luster at all when the Moon is full. (The Grail Knight can suppress this glow through force of will, but it takes sustained effort.) He becomes partially immune to vampire anathemas, so that while sunlight, fire and the like do hurt him seriously, he's not so completely at their mercy.

The blood of the Grail Knight is fundamentally different from traditional Cainite blood. The blood of a Cainite burns in the veins of the Grail Knight and vice-versa. Mutual feeding and blood oaths become completely impossible. The Grail Knight cannot create childer either.

See "Playing Among Bitter Ashes," on page 86, for the mechanics of the Grail Embrace.

The Entourage

The Gatherers assign 10 assistants to each Grail Knight. The entourage provides the knight with aids, companions and advisors but also serves as the training ground of future candidates for the chalice. Indeed, all the Grail Knights served at least several months as squires or in other positions in an entourage. The current composition of the entourage reflects centuries of experience and experiments in fulfilling the order's mission. The combination of Cainite and mortal members (and warriors and scholars) gives the entourage the flexibility of action so important to its diverse missions. Note that titles in the entourage denote rank within the order and may be separate from rank in the mortal world — a vampire who was a knight and lord in his breathing days may still serve as a squire, loremaster or man-at-arms in the order.

Knights and squires rarely discuss such things, but the mortals in the entourage also serve as emergency provisions. While the Grail Knight need not feed from others, the various Cainite squires and men-at-arms are not so lucky. Lost in the deserts of Syria, they may have no choice but to feed on their living fellows.

• **The first squire** is always a Cainite whom the Gatherers consider a serious candidate for the Grail Embrace. He's generally assigned so as to complement the strengths and weakness of the Grail Knight he serves. Thus Grail Knight scholars and courtiers have first squires skilled in matters more martial. The first squire has the authority to act on the Grail Knight's behalf in emergencies, and the rest of the entourage follows his orders unless the knight specifically countermands them.

• **The second squire** is also a Cainite and most likely a neonate from chivalric culture. The Gatherers see him as a potential candidate for the Grail Embrace but one who needs more experience and testing. If both the first squire and the knight are disabled, the second squire gives instructions but usually leads the entourage to an order sanctuary at the first opportunity. In the normal course of events, the second squire studies the strategy and tactics of his superiors and oversees the routine chores of provisioning and the like.

• **The third squire** is almost always mortal. The Gatherers agree on the importance of humility in their undertakings and on the need to remind Grail Knights that they don't possess all knowledge. The third squire's primary responsibility is to study holy teachings and offer moral commentary on the events unfolding around him. He is, in some ways, the order's equivalent of a court jester, speaking the truths that would otherwise go unsaid. He also tends to the knight's equipment and studies the specialties of the first and second squires, so as to become better rounded.

• **The three men-at-arms** are just what they sound like: commoners trained and experienced in combat who assist the knight and squires. The leader is often a Cainite who accepts the order's beliefs but does not himself wish to become Grail Knight, for whatever reason. The others can be Cainite or mortal. Occasionally a knight decides to accept a man-at-arms position to teach himself humility; more commonly, the men-at-arms aren't eligible for chivalric standing or don't care to seek it. Many are good at tasks besides combat, from medicine to scholarly studies — the order prefers not to recruit anyone who can do just one thing well.

• **The loremaster** is generally the least physically fit member of the entourage and specializes in the life of the mind, studying widely in human affairs, the nature of the physical world and everything else that comes to hand. Experience shows that almost any datum might prove an important clue at some point, so the order instructs loremasters to examine the world without a great deal of emphasis on what seems practical. This command doesn't always apply, of course; in the midst of a specific mission, the loremaster concentrates on the immediate task, like everyone else in the entourage. Between moments of single purpose, the loremaster ranges widely — often separating from the entourage for a few days at

Mortals and the Grail

Only Cainites may drink from the Grail in the Gatherers' ritual. They once believed that mortals might benefit from the transformation as well but were proven sadly wrong. The last mortal candidate for the Grail Embrace burst into crimson flames and (in a last act of defiance) leapt upon one of the Gatherers, destroying him.

Mortals can, however, drink the blood of a Grail Knight. In such a circumstance, the blood has the same effect as that of a regular Cainite of four generations lower than the knight's actual generation. If the mortal becomes a ghoul, her available Disciplines are hence more potent (see **Book of Storyteller Secrets**, p. 75, for more details). The blood is also highly addictive, causing the mortal to crave it above all else. Soon enough, a blood oath will be in place.

The Gatherers strictly forbid their knights from feeding mortals in this manner. It causes slavery and degradation contrary to the order's holy mission. Some knights, however, find it all too useful a tool.

The Gatherers are also concerned about the implications of mortals not being able to drink from the Grail. They have yet to decide whether this troublesome fact is an indication of the corruption of the Grail (by the Embrace ritual perhaps), of the relic having a non-Christian and purely Cainite origin or whether it is an omen of ill times ahead.

a time — in pursuit of knowledge about everything. The loremaster is usually a Cainite

• **The steward** takes responsibility for the physical operations of the entourage. He secures shelter and food, keeps supplies in order and so on. It may not be glorious work, but it is necessary so that the other members of the entourage can go about their business without unnecessary hindrance. The steward is always a mortal — his responsibilities simply require activity during the day.

• **The scout** often travels separately from the rest of the entourage. The scout investigates unfamiliar situations, whether it's the concealed tensions in a town where a monster might be hiding, the weaknesses of an evil magician hoarding relics or the best of several paths through a stormy mountainous region. The order looks for individuals who combine speed with stealth. Many scouts are vampires Embraced as children or young adults — the Gatherers find that such premature vampires are the most likely to turn to self-destructive evil if not reined in and seek to make an asset of their fragile condition. The scout may be a mortal or a Cainite.

• **The anchor** is a position left deliberately open. The Gatherers consult with the Grail Knight and the permanent members of his entourage to see what talents they need to insure greater chances of success for a particular mission. Thus relic-seekers may add a priest or magician, while monster-hunters likely add another man-at-arms or martial squire.

The Commoners

Every one of the order's chapter houses requires several dozen mortal servants to attend to its needs, just like every castle or inn does. The only distinguishing feature of the order's properties is that the people who work there share a dedication to the order's ideals. Many of these attendants do not know any details about the order. They serve a fraternity of "holy knights" who protect relics and suffer dark curses. Only the most senior seneschals know the full truth.

The Havens

The order maintains a network of strongholds, so that its members can spend time in safety without overly long treks. Through networks of intermediaries, the order bought a total of 10 castles from either the Knights Templar, at times the Templars needed money more than they needed more holdings, or lords equally in need of money. These all

The Women of the Order

The Gatherers are almost all male, and so are most of their recruits. The order does include some women, just as chivalry at large does. Women stand out in the order, whether in all-female entourages or primarily male ones. The order's meritocratic approach makes it no harder for them to prove their worth, as long as they earn a bit of respect from the men around them.

Scotland, the Order and Prophecy

The order's most potent seers say that the Knights Templar will fall and that Scotland will become a haven for them. Many of the order's members retain a filial fondness for the Templars and look forward to the day of reunion.

serve as satellites of the order's true home, the Castle in the Lake (see p. 83).

• **Provence** holds three order castles, the greatest concentration of the order's strength in the 12th century. From the outside, they blend in with the general culture of Languedoc, apart from a somewhat stricter attention than usual to the forms of Christian orthodoxy. They host tournaments, receive minstrels and troubadours and participate in the affairs of the communities around them. The high traffic in independent and questing knights makes it easy for order knights and their entourages to blend in without notice.

• **Scotland** holds two order castles, in addition to the Castle in the Lake. Both are modest, simple structures, originally built for defense in the constant wars between Scottish and English factions. Before the dedication of the Castle in the Lake, they were major repositories of relics. Now they act primarily as meeting places for when order members speak with their former Templar brethren and other participants in chivalric life.

• **Germany** holds a single order castle. It stands in wild lands, near the sites of repeated clashes with heathen warriors. The German members of the order concentrate on repelling pagan incursions in search of Christian artifacts, on which (they believe) pagan magicians work corrupting transformations. They are not affiliated with the emerging Teutonic fighting orders, though they sometimes cooperate on matters of mutual interest like devil-hunting.

• **The Holy Land** holds two order castles. Both are former crusader castles damaged by Saracen attacks and renovated surreptitiously. They appear ruined from the outside, with all their usable rooms and chambers concealed carefully.

• **Iberia** holds two order castles, both in the northeast. They sit several days' ride from the major pilgrimage routes. One or more entourages are always based at each of the three, and they keep an eye on pilgrims carrying relics. They do stop greedy bandits who prey on such pilgrims, but the order is far more concerned with supernatural manipulators seeking the treasures for their own.

For several decades in the mid-12th century, the order held a third Spanish castle on the Bay of Biscay. It fell in the course of an epic battle. The order had uncovered a large enclave of Baali in caves overlooking the bay, not very far from small towns with docks the order used to load relics and other treasures for shipment to their Scottish holdings. The knights on hand succeeded in destroying the Baali but not in time to prevent their targets summoning a monstrous sea serpent (see **Bygone Bestiary**, p. 55). The beast destroyed the castle down to its foundations and killed nearly all the inhabitants before returning to the depths. The ruins now stand alone and unattended, except perhaps for lone refugees who seek shelter there on their way to more hospitable climes.

The Other Houses

In addition to castles it controls and maintains directly, the order operates through a wide variety of other bases. In Greece and the Balkans, the order subsidizes several inns in convenient locations, with a provision that guests making the proper sign can use reserved backroom and downstairs meeting spaces. In Italy and Austria, the order has a similar understanding with certain monasteries and nunneries. And everywhere, the order arranges rentals — for a week or a year or even longer — of homes, inns, shops or whatever knights and their entourages need at the moment.

The order generally arranges for shelter suitable for knights and lords. Inappropriate poverty attracts as much attention as inappropriate wealth. Knights and entourages pretend to be in poorer straits only in special cases, like when evading pursuit.

The Castle in the Lake

In the ninth century, a demonic infestation blighted a Scottish valley, killing everyone in the area and creating a permanent drought. Twisted vegetation all around discouraged anyone from entering, and the valley stood desolate for two centuries. In 1057, a Gatherer discovered the valley and spent three years purifying it, years involving not just religious ceremony but physical and spiritual combat with the remaining demons. He won, despite near-fatal injuries. He then offered a simple prayer for rain to wash away the remaining stains. The heavens opened, and over the next month, the valley filled entirely with water.

The unnamed Gatherer recognized the potential in a now-sunken castle. He stored some of the relics he'd gathered there and, in return, visits installed waterproof doors and lanterns burning a thaumaturgical oil that doesn't require air. After the destruction of the Gatherers' Jordanian haven, the Castle in the Lake suited everyone as a good sanctuary. Restoration and expansion continues to this day.

Except on very special occasions, only Cainites ever enter the Castle in the Lake. Mortal servants of the order stay in concealed shelters on the lake's shore, when they must come that far; much of the time, mortals come no closer than order-sponsored inns in nearby towns. The order does not conceal the fact of the Castle in the Lake. It relies above all on the extremely harsh conditions to keep observers away and wraps the fact in a wide variety of contradictory folk tales and legends.

Gatherers skilled in Animalism have used the fish of the lake and beasts of the woods to help keep the castle safe. They have also made certain animals into ghouls to further the bond between the order and the surrounding wilds. Visitors to the castle or the surrounding area find wolves shadowing their steps, birds and bats

flying above and large fish swimming by them. These strangely silent and menacing animals help feed the rumors that perhaps not quite all the demons succumbed to banishment.

Paying For It All

It's not cheap to pay for havens, equipment and everything else the order requires. The order makes money primarily in four ways:

- Like the Knights Templar, the order provides loans to cash-poor knights who want to go on crusade. The order manages the knight's estate in Europe in exchange for a cut of the income. This also provides the order with constantly changing cover locales. The order also sometimes loans money at interest, although always through many intermediaries because such activities tend to cause anti-Semitic outbursts of violence ("proper Christians" assuming that all money-lenders are Jews and vice-versa).
- Members of the order sell their services as knights, craftsmen and so on. Members are forbidden to spend more than three months out of each year (or one full year out of every four) at such undertakings. Given the potential for improvement with more than a lifetime of practice, some of the order's members are masters indeed of their various arts and can command very substantial fees.
- The order sells loot taken from slain monsters. This ranges from simple weapons and armor on up to unique artifacts and masterpieces of art. The order keeps some valuable goods for later use and then converts most of what it seizes from monsters into cash or credit.

Personalities of the Order

The order attracts strong-willed men and women. This list provides examples; equally distinctive leaders, peers and subordinates surround all of the individuals listed here.

Gatherer Khentik-Khert

7th generation Brujah, childe of Mezekht

Nature: Gallant

Demeanor: Caretaker

Embrace: circa 1380 BCE

Apparent Age: mid-20s

Khentik-Khert was a young man when Akhenaton took the throne, and the Gatherers quickly accepted the new teachings of Aton as the sole god. His sire was a Brujah embittered by lifetimes of struggle in an ideological battle he never explained fully to Khentik-Khert. Khentik-Khert knows only that his Embrace was a sort of desperate move, a test to see whether he could retain his fundamental good cheer as a vampire. His sire said that he would continue to watch his childe and act to reward or destroy Khentik-Khert once the sire felt the issue of vampiric optimism had been settled. Khentik-Khert has never seen his sire since.

Khentik-Khert has been fascinated by Jewish thought ever since the Exodus and diligently studies developments in Christian theology; for him, the Sun remains fundamental, and he treats new insights as further clues to Aton's plans. Khentik-Khert believes he's retained his good cheer but worries that he may yet prove unsatisfactory to his sire. The order is in part a way of earning more merit in the eyes of that unseen watcher.

The Egyptian travels pilgrimage routes, talking with pilgrims about their motives for going to holy sites. He listens in particular for tales involving holy artifacts. In his guise as an earnest young man seeking signs of God's presence, he gathers information about where relics worth protecting now lie, then passes the necessary details on to relic-harvesting Grail Knights. Khentik-Khert was an early advocate of the idea of founding the order and gives it his enthusiastic support.

Count Humbert Dideaux, Seneschal of the Castle of the Holy Family

Background: Count Humbert maintains the first of the order's Provençal strongholds but was born a commoner. A Gatherer using the name Montferrat rescued Humbert from the wilds after a deranged Gangrel Embraced him shortly before the First Crusade. Montferrat had been studying the Dideaux family's collection of paintings of the saints, some of which contain symbolic clues to the saints' graves. The Gatherer helped Humbert understand his new condition and arranged a new identity for the young vam-

pire. The last of the Dideaux had died in a plague, and their name became Humbert's.

The order came into being not very much later, and Humbert volunteered his services to maintain his acquired castle. Humbert, raised on the estate, knew how to oversee renovation and maintenance. The Gatherers gladly accepted his offer and used their network to add to the pedigree of the Dideaux family, giving it a chain of false genealogies and other documentation running back to Charlemagne. They also circulated the tale of a terrible family curse: Only one of the male lineage may inhabit the castle at a time. When it becomes time to replace one identity with another, Humbert goes off and returns as his own heir.

Image: Humbert appears to be a man in his early 30s with a carefully trimmed beard. He favors a certain deadpan humor, which earns him a reputation as being perhaps not as serious as his public position warrants. That reputation, in turn, makes it easier for him to circulate among the lower ranks of knights and hear stories they might not tell lords who seemed more intimidating.

Roleplaying Hints: You behave as a gregarious, friendly lord, less concerned with station than with good relations with your fellows. You smile and listen carefully to your vassal's tales and joke with knights and fellow lords. All the while, you are suppressing the Beast within and the damned fur your rage made sprout on your back.

Destiny: As times become more desperate and the Albigensian Crusade leads to his castle going up in flames, Humbert flees to Scotland and takes the Grail Embrace. As a Grail Knight, he watches the rise of the Inquisition and finally surrenders to the Sun in the 14th century.

Clan: Gangrel
Sire: Unknown
Nature: Judge
Demeanor: Caretaker
Generation: 11th
Embrace: 1099
Apparent Age: early 30s
Physical: Strength 3, Dexterity 2, Stamina 3
Social: Charisma 4, Manipulation 4, Appearance 2
Mental: Perception 3, Intelligence 2, Wits 3
Talents: Alertness 2, Brawl 2, Dodge 2, Intimidation 2, Leadership 3, Subterfuge 2
Skills: Chivalry 2, Etiquette 3, Melee 3, Ride 3, Survival 2
Knowledges: Occult 2, Politics 3, Seneschal 3
Disciplines: Animalism 1, Fortitude 4, Potence 2, Presence 2, Protean 1
Backgrounds: Allies 3, Contacts 3, Generation 1, Influence 3, Resources 4, Retainers 4
Virtues: Conscience 3, Self-Control 2, Courage 4
Road: Humanity 6
Willpower: 6

Lady Seinia of Muscovy, Grail Knight

Background: In the 1150s, evil spirits ravaged estates in the less-tamed reaches of the Republic of Novgorod. Seinia, who had spent a century as the night mistress of a mortal fiefdom in the area, watched her herd perish, and she fled. She had cared for the little things, and their death wakened in her a surprisingly strong desire to see justice done for them. Two years after she left Russia, an entourage of the order on other business rescued her from brigands. Upon hearing her story, they decided to provide the help she sought. With her acting as their anchor, they destroyed the predatory spirits over the next year.

Seinia proved her courage and competence and asked to remain with the order. Her people were still dead, and working with the order had shown her a new way. After serving as first squire for several years, she became one of the few women to receive the Grail Embrace. Now she travels on behalf of the order, gathering information from the women of the Dark Medieval world, who might keep quiet about their secrets in the presence of men. She suspects that some powerful vampire may have been responsible for the destruction of her people and makes a special point of gathering leads about monsters in Russia.

Image: Seinia is a cold beauty, her blond hair and deep-blue eyes somehow adding to her austerity. She dresses in fine clothes and gladly wears custom-made armor when on assignment. In mortal company, she dresses

more traditionally, but comports herself with the regal bearing of a queen.

Roleplaying Hints: You have accepted the chance at salvation that the Grail and the order provide and have taken the protection of your native land as a sacred quest. Yet, you still feel the impulse to rule and treat your entourage as vassals and most mortals as serfs.

Destiny: Seinia sees the order through hard times and makes the hard compromises needed to survive. When the Inquisition rages, she first fights to preserve the ideals of the Grail but eventually falls to bartering relics for safe passage into Russia. These compromises cost her dearly, as the benefits of the Grail Embrace wane from her blood until she is but a childe of Ventrue once more. When the Sabbat rises, she sees in it a new way to add meaning to her inhumanity, trading in lofty religious chivalry for the emergent Path of Honorable Accord. Eventually, she flees to the Americas as an *antitribu* and survives into the modern era.

Clan: Ventrue
Sire: Piotr
Nature: Survivor
Demeanor: Autocrat
Generation: 10th
Embrace: 1042
Apparent Age: late 20s
Physical: Strength 2, Dexterity 3, Stamina 2
Social: Charisma 3 , Manipulation 3, Appearance 4
Mental: Perception 3 , Intelligence 3, Wits 2
Talents: Alertness 2, Brawl 2, Dodge 3, Franchise 3, Intimidation 3, Leadership 4, Subterfuge 1
Skills: Animal Ken 2, Crafts (Embroidery) 2, Etiquette 3, Melee 3, Ride 3
Knowledges: Hearth Wisdom 2, Linguistics 2, Politics 2
Disciplines: Dominate 3, Fortitude 3, Presence 4
Backgrounds: Generation 2, Resources 3, Retainers 3
Virtues: Conscience 4, Self-Control 2, Courage 4
Road: Chivalry 7
Willpower: 8

Playing Among Bitter Ashes

The Order of the Bitter Ashes is a small and largely self-contained group of Cainites who have only occasional dealings with other vampires. It is possible to play a scout or other envoy of the order within a standard coterie, but this will likely require a great deal of secrecy and can only last for so long. The simplest way to play members of the order is to portray the Cainite members of a Grail Knight's entourage.

The Grail Knight himself can serve as a patron and mentor, although he will expect his vassals to display initiative, be able to take care of their own problems and meet the objectives he sets for them without hand-holding (as befits characters in a storytelling game). The prospect of the Grail Embrace should serve as a possible reward, with the characters receiving the gift after a great deal of play. The chronicle can then enter a second phase in which the characters form a company of Grail Knights, each with their own entourage of retainers.

The first phase of the chronicle requires little explanation for a player. The standard character creation system from **Vampire: The Dark Ages**, along with the knightly permutations in Chapter Five of this book, are all you need. Assuming everyone wishes to play Cainites, players can create characters to fill the roles of first squire, second squire, one or more men-at-arms, loremaster and possibly scout or anchor (see pp. 81-82). Players can also choose to play mortals or ghouls, if they wish.

The precise workings of the Grail Embrace and its benefits do require some further explanation, however.

Earning the Embrace

To earn the Grail Embrace, a member of the Order of the Bitter Ashes must prove both her dedication to the cause and her skill at her chosen tasks. As a knightly brotherhood, the Order of the Bitter Ashes places great importance on martial skill and the virtues of chivalry (see Chapter One). The Gatherers are open minded, however, and will accept those who have distinguished themselves in other ways — especially erudite loremasters, for example. They insist on proof of bravery and dedication to the cause, however.

Practically, this means a character must have participated in several successful quests or operations and distinguished herself on at least two occasions. The blessing of the Grail Knight she serves is an absolute prerequisite — unless he has fallen in battle, of course.

The Gatherers call a viable candidate to Scotland in the spring and conduct a series of long interviews, backed by Auspex. The result of these discussions and the reports of the candidates fellows combine to give the Gatherers an idea of whether the Cainite is ready for the Grail Embrace.

In terms of Traits, Storytellers may require a player to meet the following preconditions: three dots in at least two Abilities connected to the character's duties (Melee and Ride for a traditional knight), 4 Conscience and Courage, 7 Road (of either Chivalry, Heaven or Humanity) and 7 Willpower.

Storytellers who wish to keep track of such things may also require players to accumulate experience points to pay for the Embrace. Saving up these points rather than raising Traits represents time spent in prayer and devotion rather than practice and exercise. If you use this option, the Embrace costs 30 points to attempt.

Drinking from the Grail

Candidates who pass muster return to Scotland in September to undergo the Grail Embrace. They go through the ritual described on page 80. This is a painful process during which the character's Beast emerges to wrestle for supremacy, as if it senses its ultimate defeat in the Grail Blood.

A series of resisted rolls represents this battle. The candidate's higher nature gets a dice pool equal to the total of Conscience, Courage and Road, while his Beast gets a dice pool equal to 10 + Generation Background (the Beast is stronger in those closer to Caine). Both sides have difficulty 6, and the Storyteller should roll for the Beast. Each roll represents one hour of internal struggle, which causes searing agony to the vampire and continues throughout the night. As such, the contest can continue for up to 13 rolls, with each side trying to accumulate 10 successes. Several possible outcomes exist:

- If the higher nature reaches 10 successes first, the Grail Embrace is successful, and the ritual ends with the sunrise. The character greets the now much less painful sun and seeks shelter with the Gatherers.
- If the Beast reaches 10 successes first, the Grail Embrace fails completely, and the vampire enters frenzy. The Gatherers may have no choice but to destroy him if he strikes at them, but the vampire may also escape. The precise effects once the frenzy wears off are up to the player and Storyteller, but the Gatherers will never again consider the vampire for the Grail Embrace.
- If neither side gets 10 successes by sunrise, the ritual ends unfulfilled. The searing pain of the Grail Blood causes two levels of aggravated damage, and the vampire must immediately check for Rötschreck as the rising sun begins to burn him. The Gatherers will provide shelter as fast as they can. The candidate may attempt the ritual again one or more years later, but in the meantime, he must further prove his worth.

Effects of the Grail

A successful Grail Embrace grants a series of unique benefits and a few restrictions to the new Grail Knight:

- He does not need to feed. His body replenishes its own vitae, at the rate of one-fifth his total blood pool per day of slumber.
- Inanimate sources of aggravated damage like sunlight and fire do lethal damage instead. Direct attacks like claws and fangs still do aggravated damage.
- The Grail Knight no longer suffers from Rötschreck.
- His skin takes on a snow-like pallor and glows with something like reflected moonlight, darkest in the full moon and brightest in the new moon. During the week around the full moon, the pale glow provides no advantage or drawbacks. In the week around the new moon, it's bright enough that attempts at Stealth fail automatically and those using ranged attacks on the vampire gain a -1 difficulty bonus. The rest of the time, it's bright enough to cancel out normal penalties for maneuvering in darkness but imposes a +1 difficulty penalty on Stealth rolls (assuming the watcher can see the Grail Knight).

The glow also affects social interaction. At its brightest, the glow gives the player an extra die to all efforts at persuasion and intimidation. Otherwise, the Storyteller may impose a difficulty bonus or penalty (+1 or -1) on Manipulation-related rolls if the vampire is dealing with someone prone to respond well or poorly to such pallor. Christian Europeans generally see this pigmentation as a sign of purity and holiness, while most others see it in the same negative light as the Cappadocian deathly pallor.

The knight can spend a point of Willpower or a blood point and suppress the glow for one hour. He may also wear a cloak to cover his skin.

- He can no longer drink Cainite vitae, and all existing blood oaths are broken. From now on, every ingested point of Cainite vitae causes a level of aggravated damage as it burns. The knight's blood causes the same effect in other Cainites. The knight can drink mortal blood and that of other Grail Knights, however.
- His blood can create especially powerful ghouls (see sidebar on page 81).
- He gains protection from the ravages of True Faith. Any True Faith-backed action taken against the Grail Knight (warding him with a cross, for example) suffers a +2 difficulty penalty, and the knight can automatically soak one level of damage from Faith (such as that caused by potent holy water). This protection only functions against explicitly Christian faith.

The Order and the Clans

The only clan or bloodline the order rejects out of hand is the Baali. Most members of the order come from the clans with the most involvement in chivalry (see p. 53), but there are exceptions. While the order principally recruits among knights, it also looks for individuals who show the right virtues, whatever their social classes. Sometimes the Gatherers arrange for a worthy candidate to become a squire or otherwise gain admission to chivalric society — two of the order's most valued infiltrators were peasants in life, one elevated to status as a swordsmith, the other as a chirurgeon. The Gatherers recognize that god might choose as a tool someone who isn't great in worldly terms precisely to make the point that divine power is not temporal power. Just as the order accepts the worthy of every social class, so it does with every clan, apart from the Baali.

The Gatherers sometimes wish for more Tzimisce recruits. (There have only been three so far, and all perished in monster hunts.) Vicissitude is very useful indeed for the order's purposes, and the Gatherers make some effort to see that members who know it instruct others. Some of the Gatherers hate or fear Chimerstry; some find it fascinating and wish they could recruit a Ravnos or other vampire who could teach it. So far, none of their attempts have succeeded, and it's not currently a high priority.

Storytelling with the Order

Despite having a very strong central mandate, the order does many things. A shift in emphasis can produce very different chronicles. Feel free to mix and match from this list of suggestions and to modify to suit the needs of your own chronicle.

The Order Among Its Own

Many members of the order spend little time in the world. They tend the relics stored within the Castle in the Lake and other havens, train younger members and consider what to do next in response to ever-changing mortal societies. Such an existence can be deathly dull, but it doesn't have to be; it's possible to run a chronicle heavy on intrigue and drama focused on characters who spend almost all of their time with the Gatherers and other members of the order.

The Gatherers are far more benign than other elders. This doesn't mean they altogether lack manipulative and secretive impulses. Every vampire who's survived millennia learns something of subterfuge and puts the younger vampires and mortals around her to use in ways they might well disapprove of if informed. So it's necessary, from the elder's point of view, to lie or, at least, misdirect. Players comfortable with elder power levels may play Gatherers themselves or focus on Grail Knights trying to establish a firmer place for themselves in the order's deliberations or play ghoul and mortal members of the order, who try to balance their human concerns with the driving faith of the order and Cainites' sundry obsessions.

Tending the relics sometimes involves more than just dusting them off. Raiders, both mortal and supernatural, attempt to steal objects of power. The relics' guardians must remain alert and ready to engage in combat at any time. Months or years may go by without a challenge, and then, several may come in short order. In addition, some relics bind spirits or other supernatural powers, which can escape if triggered properly. In some cases, handling or dropping releases anything inside, while in others, a particular phrase or the use of a particular Discipline in the relic's vicinity breaks bindings.

One mission of the order's scholars, therefore, is identifying latent traps and their origins, so as to take effective action against them. This is a difficult and slow process, involving a great deal of puzzling over incomplete sources. Players interested in a more scholarly chronicle may find this just to their taste. The lore their characters must cover ranges from this week's broadsides to the remains of records from the First City and the mystical works of other cultures.

The Order Among the World

Stories About Relics

The search for relics can go literally anywhere in the known world and beyond — wherever devout men and women gather, wherever they travel and rest, they may leave signs of possibly divine power. Christian missionaries, for instance, established substantial communities as far away as India in the first century after Jesus' ministry, and the Jewish Diaspora spans the known world. Relics wait for protectors in crowded cities and remote wilderness alike.

The order's relic hunters usually favor one of two strategies, though neither is compulsory and alternatives also often produce good results.

"Miners" focus on thoroughly mastering a limited area, like a single town. They take up residence and build cover identities to enable them to move through all social strata. They take years or even decades to become established. They harvest relics slowly, being careful not to create panics about crime waves, witches or other trouble that might lead to the hue and cry. At least one of the cover identities enjoys wealth or power, so as to provide appropriate cover for the space and security measures necessary to protect relics. The others must avoid resembling each other too closely and allow for as wide-ranging a movement as possible.

"Travelers" forsake the advantages of working in depth for the advantages of wide scope. They wander freely and generally specialize in investigation of certain types of potential relic hoards. Some master the art of studying and infiltrating castles, while others concentrate on extracting relics from unwitting guardians who don't appreciate what they have, and still others specialize in thefts from caravans and pilgrimages. Every recurring environment draws the attention of at least a few of the Grail Knights. In addition, some mortals who practiced deception for less pure reasons before joining the order now put their worldly skills to work in the service of a better cause.

Finding the relics takes time. Getting them takes more. Nor is the job done then: The order's members must get the relics to safekeeping. Particularly powerful or important relics go to the Castle in the Lake, others to the storehouses in the order's castles. Outsiders who do not appreciate the order's motives may well conclude that the members are mere thieves, and in any event, a well-planned cover story collapses if the knight simply departs suddenly right about the time a relic goes missing. The element of suspense can run very high here, in chronicles where that's a pleasure.

Cover stories determine what goes on in addition to the relic search itself. Order members who present themselves as knights can and should take part in the routine of chivalrous existence. The Storyteller should be careful not to let knights and entourages take their cover for granted: It works only as long as it's maintained and supported by genuine behavior that fits the story told.

Stories About Guiding

The mission of guidance offers very wide scope for chronicle emphases.

First of all, some order members must be skilled at mingling with all aspects of Cainite society. They must move from the heights of noble courts to the bizarre domains of non-European vampires to the depths of Furores anger and Caitiff confusion. The potential for enlightenment, after all, occurs everywhere. The order knows that rumors of its existence and purpose circulate, but so far, it's managed to keep almost all its secrets. The seekers of vampires ready for guidance are the ones most likely to reveal order secrets, intentionally or otherwise, and must be the most prepared to resist mundane and supernatural efforts at extracting information. A chronicle about this aspect of the process offers a constantly changing foreground and the potential for interaction with Cainites and mortals who also move through diverse social milieus. Players who cannot commit to long-term chronicles might enjoy such a game, as every few sessions can plausibly involve a new locale.

Once the order identifies vampires seeking enlightenment, the members on the scene must decide how best to offer advice without overwhelming the seeker's own judgment. No single answer applies to all cases. Direct approaches and indirect manipulations both carry risks (see pages 78-79 for the detailed discussion). Whatever approach the guides settle on, stealth and dissimulation are their main tools. The combination allows for action without necessarily a great deal of combat. In general, by the time fighting starts, things have gone very wrong; this still leaves room for feats of derring-do, suspenseful tight-timing maneuvers and the like.

A darker face of the order comes to the fore in cases where a candidate for guidance proves unworthy. It takes a lot to make the order abandon hope: Diablerie and similarly dramatic crimes alone suffice. The order must then decide whether to destroy the vampire who's turned away from enlightenment or to persist in further manipulation. In the latter case, the new manipulation lacks the sense of restraint that governs most guidance. The order's members do whatever they deem necessary to force a crisis of conscience that can lead to clear repentance or destruction. The temptations of such activity lead many Grail Knights into sins of their own, and the order does not allow members to engage in corrective guidance on a regular basis. Even the Gatherers worry about the threat to their souls when they undertake to shatter another's.

Stories About Releasing

The order's mission to help release vampiric souls offers subtle and intense roleplaying opportunities for those interested. It also requires substantial care and tact in presentation.

The process of release *is* a form of suicide, and some players are understandably uncomfortable with the topic in this context. Make sure that players are willing to deal with the issue *before* play begins, and keep checking to see if anyone's getting uncomfortable. Ask, don't just assume players will speak up.

Stories of release are extremely personal and rely heavily on character interaction instead of action. The characters spend almost all their time dealing with a single character, who is struggling with the decision to end her unlife. As long as this style suits the players, these stories work very well as a change of pace between demon-hunts or quests for relics. Entire chronicles on the subject are less auspicious, however, because they often lack variety.

Since the order as a whole holds no single view about what God wants, every decision to seek release comes with substantial uncertainty. Order members make an effort to establish that a vampire has a firm conviction and reasons for holding it before helping out in the process. Characters can take part in these arguments. If the Storyteller wants to have a discernible uniquely correct answer to questions like "What does God want?" the chronicle likely takes on a very different feel than games in which the questions remain answered (at best) only in part. Avoid the urge to turn the chronicle into a pulpit for preaching: Real-world truths are best communicated outside the game, leaving the game world free to be itself with its own postulates.

Stories About Smiting

A Storyteller and players who want clear-cut enemies and heroic motivations can certainly use the Order of the Bitter Ashes for it. Assign the characters to monster-hunting, pull up this week's adversary, and roll lots of dice. This can be a lot of fun, and the Drama Police won't drop by very often to demand players include more angst.

The nature of monsters smitten can and should range widely. Play up the demonic, and use loosed demons — medieval stories of the saints' lives sometimes suggest that demons lurked behind every door and in everyone's clothing. They didn't, not even in the Dark Medieval world, but it's entirely appropriate to have a town or county unusually demon-ridden, requiring the sustained attention of experienced demon-hunters. A chronicled focused on the hunt could easily branch out, if and when players want more context for the fight scenes, to include the ramifications of the demonic infestation. Who cooperates with the forces of Hell? Who tries to resist? How do officials accountable to larger institutions like the Church and the kingdom explain what's going on, or how do they try to conceal it?

Some demon-haunted locales make the demonic presence obvious: The landscape is withered (or rich with unwholesome, twisted life), and the people are haggard or twisted. The order's members must find what support they can and spend time healing broken souls, as well as smiting the demons themselves. In other areas, the demonic presence isn't at all obvious, and the monster-hunters may themselves seem suspicious in their pursuit of an unknown enemy. Experiment with various combinations to keep it from being the same thing over and over again.

Lupines make fine monsters, particularly the ones who belong to the tribes most hostile to humanity. (Lupines the order confronts may have nothing to do with "tribes" at all, of course, and simply be shapechanging menaces.) A careful pack of Lupines could easily seal off a remote town in the winter and start slaughtering its inhabitants at their leisure. Perhaps a single survivor escapes to find help and encounters the order or a member of the order on some other business altogether becomes trapped along with everyone else.

Can a single knight and his retinue effectively challenge what might be dozens of wolf-creatures who've been planning this attack for some time? If the order's representatives are there when the attack begins, should they conceal the presence of the monsters from the intended victims or flout the Sixth Tradition by explaining further? What sorts of plans can a knight and a handful of experienced assistants hope to implement, given a town's worth of random mortals who may or may not have any useful clues? Do the Lupines have a motive beside destruction — recovering a valued artifact or revenge for a past injury? Can it be satisfied so as to avoid the battle? Should it? A story of this sort benefits tremendously from a detailed map of the vicinity, as well as strong descriptions of the people around the players' characters.

The order's lack of emphasis on purely human evils means that it puts no effort into hunting magicians. A magician who becomes possessed or directly involved in releasing monsters would be a suitable target, but the Gatherers have no objection to magic as such. The order simply doesn't know anything about the fae, but would apply the same general criteria in making decisions about particular cases.

Two groups attract the order's enmity on a particularly frequent basic: Baali (and other infernalists) and the Cainite Heresy. The order bitterly hates all traffic with demons, who offer cheap gratification and eternal loss. The Heresy teaches the only doctrine all Gatherers believe definitely wrong: that Caine enjoyed God's favor. Everything the order does aims precisely to overcome the Curse, not to accept or glorify it. Since both of these groups infiltrate their way into human society, pursuit of them most often brings members of the order into contact with mortals. The order prefers to assign its most experienced hunters to the task. Circumstances don't always allow that, so all members of the order receive training in detecting and destroying infernalists and Heretics.

Chapter Five: Knightly Things

Our lives are rivers
which flow to the great sea
that is death.
There go the nobles
directly to the end
to be consumed and vanquished.
– Jorge Manrique
(trans. by Joseph Ricapito)

Character Creation: Becoming and Aftermath

Arnoul stood motionless before the narrow window, unflinching in the icy wind. Beneath him, in the great hall, he could hear roars of approval as servants shuffled through the rushes covering the stone floor, hoisting aloft heavy platters laden with roast pork. Faint strains of music penetrated the thick walls of the tower room.

For a moment, Arnoul was tempted to flee the darkness in favor of the bright firelight and even brighter raiment enlivening the hall. He'd begged off from the day's hunting expedition by pleading sickness, but surely his pallor and cool skin would convince the guests he'd really been ill. The idea of playing at eating seemed unbearably tiresome, though, and he disliked the wary aloofness he'd already experienced from the hounds who so eagerly snapped up scraps from others' hands.

Actually, he thought, were he to be honest with himself, he would have to concede that it was dread of another painful conversation with the seigneur of Lanvaux that kept him where he was.

"Arnoul," Guibert had said in shock and dismay, "you can't really mean to let me be overrun. I understand you can't send all the family knights. Come back with me yourself, and bring a few followers with you — even that would mean something. All this needs is a show of force. And after all I did for your father...."

But dark-eyed, perpetually smiling Hilduin had been present, and an all but imperceptible shake of his head left no room for Arnoul to maneuver. He could not go against the command of the seneschal who'd served his family for so long, the man he still couldn't quite bring himself to think of in new terms. Nor could he explain to de Lanvaux exactly why it was he could not travel with him the next morning or stand at his side in the battles to come.

Now, somewhere deep in Arnoul's mind, a formless wonderment arose that, having become so unbelievably strong, he could still find fear within himself. He would not go down into his family's hall this evening, he decided, but did not allow himself to finish the thought — and perhaps never would again.

Starting Out

Vampire: The Dark Ages covers character creation quite thoroughly, but the walking paradox of a chivalrous Cainite requires some special attention and considerations. Players should be aware up front that generating such a character will involve difficult choices, in that the achievements of a knight are wide-ranging enough to be nearly impossible to accumulate in their entirety with the points allotted for new characters.

It is certainly possible for a famously doughty warrior to get away with unpolished behavior or for an awkward stripling to silence objections with the dazzling wealth attached to his family name. Knightly characters who fail to display one or more of the generally accepted qualities of knighthood (see Chapter One), however, will appear unaccomplished or worse. As such, it is difficult to create a perfect Galahad or an established knight of many years' standing given the system's restrictions — instead, it is more likely that you will find yourself with an inexperienced character or one who needs to develop in particular areas. Your knight's need for more experience and more development can be the focus of much of the early stage of the chronicle.

Concept

The first step is to establish a basic concept for your character, a rough sketch of who you are and in what context you perform your everyday actions. This should include an assessment of both your true inner personality and the façade you present to the world around you. For example, the mocking, sarcastic young fop who seems to scoff at his responsibilities as a knight of the queen's guard may secretly be passionately devoted to her and willing to go to any extreme on her behalf; meanwhile, the gruff old warrior whom everyone thinks has taken one too many blows to the head may turn out to be an unbelievably subtle and skillful manipulator of the people and events around him. Even more so than mortals, Cainites thrive on such deceptions — and chivalrous Cainites are no exception.

At this point, you should choose a clan and a Road, although you may wish to consult with your Storyteller about having these revealed during or after the prelude. Your sire and

By the Numbers

The requirements for knighthood in the courts of Provence and Flanders differ greatly from those in the warring states of Italy, so creating hard and fast Trait minimums for these characters is inaccurate at best. Nevertheless, those who want to be sure that their characters will at least have the basics, should match the following Traits.

Attributes:

Strength ••, Dexterity ••, Stamina •••, Charisma ••

Abilities:

Chivalry •, Etiquette •, Franchise •, Leadership ••, Melee •••, Ride •••

Backgrounds:

Influence •, Resources •, Vassalage •

Other Traits:

Courage 3, Willpower 5

What *Else* Do Knights Need to Know?

Obviously, the time has not yet come when knights are expected to be Renaissance men. But the assumption is starting to spread that a knight will be reasonably able to amuse himself and others as need be by telling stories, playing chess, hunting with hounds and hawks or engaging in other appropriate pastimes; also, if he is under a certain age, he will be conversant to some degree in the art of courtly love.

the events around your Embrace are important elements to work into these aspects of your character.

For example, Arnoul (the young knight whose story begins above) is the model of a perfect courtier on the surface but a troubled, questioning philosopher at heart. Although he does not really yet comprehend how it affects his existence, Arnoul has recently been Embraced against his will by the Lasombra who has secretly influenced his family for many generations. His Road will become clearer to him as his story unfolds.

Why any question at all about the Road? Not all Cainite knights will walk the Road of Chivalry simply because they are knights. The "old school" of knighthood had very little to do with these newfangled concepts of courtesy and self-restraint. Also, some who were knighted before their Embraces become disillusioned afterward or acquire new perspectives on the nature of their world. Some who seek to be knighted after their Embraces do so for political gains, for expediency or for other reasons having nothing to do with genuine belief in the ideals of chivalry. Assess your character's real opinions regarding the recently emerged principles which make up this difficult Road before assuming that it will be her true path. Even Cainites who truly believe in the morals of chivalry may follow the Roads of Humanity or Heaven instead.

Attributes

The next step is to consider the relative importance of Attributes. The prime qualities of chivalry (prowess, loyalty, generosity, courtesy, frankness and honor) do not correspond directly to the little dots on your character sheet, but should rather guide and inspire your character creation.

Your character may not be ideally suited to the physically demanding life of the knight errant; perhaps he was forced to take up a position he had no taste for following the deaths of two older brothers. On the other hand, a tomboy who has spent her entire life wrestling with her older brothers (and stomping the tar out of them) will likely have a great deal of Strength and Stamina.

Physical prowess alone does not a knight make. Although knights of the 10th and 11th centuries were little more than glorified warriors, by 1197, more is expected of those who bear the title of knight. A small or physically weak knight may have so intimidating a demeanor that practically everyone backs down before him. Similarly, he may be so clever or so charming a speaker that his courteous words make up for his lack of musculature. Knights who plan on making a career of service to nobility or who wish to found militant orders had best be quick-witted and perceptive in order to survive.

Abilities

After you've set the character's Attributes in order, you must select Abilities. Keep in mind that there are certain basic activities that knights are routinely expected to perform and, conversely, certain others that they would seldom deign to attempt. For example, it is extremely unlikely that a knight would be unable to Ride, although possible that a moderately advanced squire had not yet mastered the skill. It is equally improbable that a knight would have much in the way of Larceny. All knights should have the Melee skill, although some knights specialize in one-on-one combat or jousting rather than in large battles.

You may choose to make your character's Disciplines interact smoothly with his (or her) chivalrous career or to use them to provide other opportunities. A Toreador knight may not have much use for her Auspex while tilting at rings, but the Soulsight power could serve her well should she need to untangle a complicated rivalry in her liege's court. A Ventrue knight might set out to achieve a high enough level of Fortitude to be able to make brief, well-armored appearances in combats on cloudy days. Then again, that same Ventrue might be far more concerned with using Dominate to convince the local sheriff that those mangled bodies found in the woods really aren't much to be worried about.

Pay special attention to Backgrounds. Contacts, Allies and Mentors need to be well developed in order to account for both your character's past (how he became a knight) and future (how he plans to maintain or adapt his status). This is an excellent opportunity for a player to elaborate on who has inspired — or forced — her character to undergo the arduous process of attaining a chivalric peerage. Is the character still connected to the person who taught her how to fight, and is

Playing the Lady

When creating a vampiric lady as a character, buy extra levels of Influence and either Status or Vassalage. In addition, be sure to buy dots in Seneschal as well as in Crafts, Etiquette, Herbalism, Medicine, Performance and Music, the more "ladylike" arts of the Dark Medieval world.

that person acquainted with her Cainite sire? Is there an accord among the three, or has she had to renounce an important relationship?

Resources can be tricky to handle. It takes a great deal of money to provide oneself with a halfway decent horse, a sword, a set of armor and a retainer or two. It also takes money to maintain the lifestyle of a noble, even though vampires can save on certain expenses like food and firewood. A player should establish whether that money is coming from a hereditary estate, from a generous patron or from some effort on the knight's part and whether the knight is bankrupting a genteel family of many generations' standing or incurring great debts in order to keep up appearances.

Other Issues

Training

Becoming a knight almost always requires martial training of some sort and sufficient resources to obtain a knight's basic equipment, with the latter requirement presuming that money will result from good breeding or at least the pretense thereof. Many knights spend years in service first as retainers, then as squires to older knights who can teach them not only how to swing a sword but also how to conduct themselves at a royal court.

Those of gentle birth become squires, usually through family connections, although sometimes a knight can be persuaded to take on an unknown of unusual talent. It also sometimes happens that one whose noble blood or position potentially qualifies him for knighthood lacks the opportunity or money to be formally squired and so must scrabble to receive any kind of guidance.

Being a squire is hardly glamorous — you get stuck doing the low-level jobs no one else wants to do, while being expected to pick up on the important things by watching other people handle them. However, squires are generally treated reasonably well, since everyone knows it may someday be their own son fostering in another's household.

Taking into account how the Storyteller will handle the prelude, players should decide how thorough their training as a squire was. If the Storyteller wishes to roleplay this portion of the character's life, the player will probably not have total control over what her character did or didn't learn during that time. The player, in contrast, may be accounting for the training on her own. In that case she and the Storyteller should work together to make sure that she has created a realistic curriculum and that, for example, she has not claimed to have mastered short sword, great sword and polearm within the span of three months.

The player should also establish the quality of his character's relationship with his knight. Has the knight been a careful and concerned trainer, teaching his squire everything he knows and inspiring great devotion in him? Perhaps he has been a brutal taskmaster, one the student is pleased to finally escape, or a skilled knight but a poor teacher. The bond between squire and knight will shape the squire's entire subsequent career.

Role Models

Thou were the meekest man and the gentlest that ever ate in hall among ladies. And thou were the sternest knight to thy mortal foe that ever put spear in the rest.

— Sir Thomas Malory, *Le Morte d'Arthur*.

Depending on how self-aware a character is, he may consciously model himself after a prominent knight, real or literary, and even proclaim that he is doing exactly that. Players may also choose to utilize legendary knights as templates for building characters. Chrétien de Troyes' *Lancelot* and *Perceval*; the numerous *chansons* and epics and various other period fictional works provide excellent sources for modern players and Dark Medieval would-be heroes alike.

A character may also be patterned after a significant figure in her life: an inspiringly feisty matriarch, a distant cousin with few opportunities but an indomitable will, a knight who consistently fights in the most beautiful apparel and with the most finely expressed chivalrous spirit. Record such modeling as part of your character concept.

Destiny or Choice

Eventually you will need to wrestle to some degree with the question of *why* your character ever wanted to be a knight in the first place. Fighting large battles (for mortals) is usually a tedious, draining affair characterized by standing around in the hot sun in heavy armor, waiting for commands which may be all but incomprehensible when they come, all underlain by the ever-present fear of death. Fighting in tournaments is less boring but can appear completely unproductive, depending on your perspective. The whole act requires large financial investments as well as the willingness to drop anything and everything that may be taking up your attention at home in order to obey the summons of your superior on the feudal ladder. And how *do* you know what your wife and your castellan are up to while you're gone? Add to this the many constraints the Curse imposes on attempts to partake in mortal chivalry, and the whole endeavor may sometimes appear pointless.

Additionally, Cainites may come to question their adherence to a mortal code of behavior. Players should establish the underpinnings of a commitment to chivalry early on, so that characters have real motivations and desires to guide them through future difficulties. If the Fates have conspired at every turn to force a character into knighthood, that character may have supreme confidence in the rightness of her path or a dismaying conviction that things could have been better otherwise. Or she may vacillate between the two extremes. Of course, characters who freely chose their positions may feel the same way.

Religion

Generally speaking the concept of knighthood is strongly linked to Christianity. While this means that pagans, Jews and Muslims are not likely to be dubbed knights, it does not mean that they cannot admire or exhibit chivalrous qualities.

The player should assess how strongly the character actually feels about his religion. Is he devout? Can he tolerate interactions with characters of differing religious backgrounds, or do such situations turn him into a frothing-at-the-mouth zealot? The strength and nature of the character's religious conviction may become of great importance if he travels about Europe or to the Holy Land or if he begins to question his place in God's creation after his Embrace.

Use of Inhuman Powers

Players intending their characters to follow the ideals of chivalry need to select carefully from among clans and Disciplines during character creation or else roleplay the conflict between intent and capability. Many actions technically possible for vampires fly in the face of the knightly qualities; using Dominate to program lords and vassals to make things go your way regardless of accomplishment or behavior is hardly chivalrous.

Of course, players can be very persuasive in justifying their characters' actions. Players and Storytellers should be clear on what constitutes yielding to the Beast.

What Happens After the Vigil?

There lies the stuff of high romance in the procedure of being knighted: the silent, solemn night-long vigil, the heady thrill of one's fair consort girding on one's belt and sword, the final glory of the *accolade* or blow ceremoniously received from a benevolent monarch.

The vigil represents the culmination of an often tedious and lengthy stint as a squire — or, in some cases, of a dizzyingly sudden ascent. Those who served many years as a knight's retainer trained in the ways of combat and chivalry may well resent individuals elevated capriciously, while the latter may find themselves floundering without the guidance of an influential knight. No matter how it happened, having achieved the prize, the new-made knight must still establish himself.

If not from a wealthy background, a young knight will probably either hire himself out to a noble family, try to make a marriage with a suitably dowered bride (this practice of consolidating might of arms and money was very common) or else go on crusade. Knights of independent means may choose, in effect, to do nothing — to stay home in their fiefs, possibly participating in the occasional armed conflict or tournament or attending revels held in other demesnes. Perhaps they become so passionately absorbed by the ideals of chivalry that they dedicate themselves to a quest or sit beneath a fair maiden's window singing songs of love for a year and a day.

Then again, some knights find themselves patrolling the same stretch of territory every day in order to intimidate potentially rebellious peasants or orbiting as anonymous satellites on the fringes of vast and powerful households. Others become trapped in meaningless ceremonial positions, like the hereditary post of wine selector held by generations of knights in one French castle. There is far more to knighthood than the gallant deeds sung of by minstrels, as many a would-be *miles* discovers to their regret.

Such banal and uneventful fates are not the lot for characters in a chronicle, of course. They are the exceptional few who find themselves in the center of things and experience great highs and lows — not the least of which is the Embrace itself. Players should be very clear about why their knightly character stands out from the mass of knights who perform no more than unremarkable services. A knight may have specific goals based on her past: A scrawny youth teased and tormented by older siblings may have fought long and hard to accomplish knighthood as a sort of revenge, or a victim of a violent family feud may desire a more tangible vengeance.

The Unanswered Blow

When a monarch strikes the knight he is in the process of dubbing, that blow is meant to represent the last physical assault a knight will allow to pass unreturned. The gesture is at once an assertion of authority and an acknowledgment that this authority will no longer extend as far as it used to over the warrior in question.

A character being dubbed a knight may find the person on the throne at the time completely irrelevant to her life. Then again, she may be undertaking the most awful and most permanent bond of fealty she will ever experience. If the character is of sufficiently high rank, she can offer her loyalty directly to the king. If she is not so highborn, she will probably take an oath of fealty to a baron who, in turn, swears his loyalty to the king.

Take some time to determine your character's opinion of the monarch directly or indirectly responsible for his knighting. Is he grateful for the honor, or does he feel resentful at its long-overdue timing? Did the ruler seem so indifferent to the ceremony that the knight now bears a grudge or so attentive that the character revised a previous bad opinion?

You will want to decide whether your character was knighted by a mortal or Cainite ruler and if a knightly order was designated at the time. This bears strongly on the character's status in the two different worlds: A man who considers himself a knight after being dubbed by an elder vampire may be challenged, ridiculed or even attacked if he asserts himself as such in a mortal court.

Establishing a strong mutual pact with a powerful regnant holds obvious benefits for characters, although the act may also entangle them in politics extending far beyond anything they had anticipated. Fealty goes both ways.

The Master's Lady

Knights can't always keep themselves busy with martial pursuits. You might wish to think about what entertains your character when he isn't out fighting, what personal interactions he enjoys beyond the company of his fellow knights.

One of the useful aspects of the newly developing culture of courtly love is that it provides ways of keeping potentially rowdy, trouble-making individuals in check. For instance, if the perfect knight is expected to have a noble and beautiful lady to whom he gives his chaste and unsullied adoration, that means he must actually find a married gentlewoman and somehow remain close to her.

Generally, what that entails is taking service in her lord's entourage — a useful arrangement for the lord, who thus acquires armed forces; for the knight, who thus fulfills both a practical and an impractical sense of purpose and for the lady, who thus gains a new and endlessly fascinating form of entertainment. Sometimes, of course, such relationships slip into unabashed adultery, which may or may not be beneficial to a knight's career, depending on his and his paramour's political resourcefulness.

Knights can also gain advancement by marrying above themselves, arranging matches with daughters of households in which they serve. In contrast, a knight who has lost his master's favor may be chastised by being paired with a bastard daughter or, worse, a household servant. A female knight might also face a forced marriage, an attempt to make her change her ways, but is unlikely to be a desirable candidate for a nobleman trying to marry his sons to greatest advantage.

To Be or Not To Be

Arnoul awoke, thoroughly disoriented, to find himself lying under a flea-infested pallet in a dirty, shabby room. He scrabbled free and tore the layers of fabric away from the small window, before he remembered having hung them there himself, and cursed softly as moonlight filled the tiny room. It had been difficult, very difficult, to convince the suspicious innkeeper to stable his horse and admit him at that unusual pre-dawn hour. Now he kicked himself for not having thought more carefully about exactly how he would travel.

Before leaving the room, he made sure to don his sword and spurs and to take anything remotely valuable with him. He looked carefully around the main room, pausing on the steps, before descending. He felt fairly sure that neither the surviving members of his family nor the seneschal and his ghouls would have yet realized he was gone but checked for familiar faces nonetheless. He actually had time to seat himself and call for the ale he would not drink before being surrounded by pale faces and blazing eyes.

The leader gazed appraisingly at him. "I am Sir Fulke. I do not care to know what you were formerly called, so do not fret yourself overmuch on that account. All that I need to know I have seen from your garb, your arms and... certain other aspects of your bearing. We will be pleased to have you among our company of knights."

Arnoul's glance flicked briefly to each ruthless face around him, then he adopted the easy mien and formal language he'd known since birth. "Your Excellency, you do me honor with your most gracious offer, but I am sworn to maintain the defense of my ancestral hall and must, with regret, decline your invitation."

Fulke grinned wolfishly. "I don't think so. You've run away from home and sire, and by God's beard, I don't believe you'd care to have it noised about. Never fear, childe, I'll not force you back to whence you came. If you behave yourself, I'll protect you from those who'll call you Caitiff or worse. But you're finished with that other life. You'll take a new name, and you'll fight with me and mine from now on."

One of the most important decisions to be made when creating a vampiric knight in the Dark Medieval world is whether the character was already knighted at the time of his Embrace or achieved that status as a vampire. The answer to that question will provide the basis for much of the character's background.

Relatively straightforward reasons for a character to have been knighted include having spent time as a squire, inheriting the position from a deceased father or uncle, being acknowledged by the king or queen for extraordinary service or having made so much money that he is, in effect, pressed into becoming a knight. Consider how much more complicated these paths may become if the character in question is already a vampire. What if the character is mortal but has unknowingly been training with or in service to a vampire? Or if a beloved family member suddenly turns out to have been hiding a very dark secret indeed?

A newly vampiric knight may have just embarked on her career and find herself deeply resentful of the new limitations on her chivalrous adventures. On the other hand, she may have served faithfully for years and grown weary enough not to miss her former pursuits.

Perhaps a struggling man-at-arms accepted the Embrace after the dubious promise that it would ease his path into knighthood and now must accept that his new talents come at a terrible price. Or an aging knight desperate to recapture the glory of his youth struck a bargain which restored his skill, yet made it nearly impossible for him to achieve renown in the mortal world. Characters Embraced by force (because they were potentially useful or just in the

wrong place at the wrong time) must come to terms with not having chosen their new conditions, yet at least have the consolation of not having deliberately given themselves to the Devil.

Think about the import of a knight becoming a vampire. He will no longer be able to fight in the vast majority of medieval battles, since nighttime melees are held only under unusual circumstances. He, therefore, finds himself unable to fulfill service which may be mandatory, depending on his location. Worse, he will no longer be able to rally his own followers, if he has any, in the manner to which they and he are probably accustomed. Nor will he be able to attend the most common social event of the period, Mass in the local chapel. Perhaps his followers — or his enemies — will conclude that God's grace has departed from him.

However it falls out, in the course of a prelude or later in game play, the player and Storyteller both should acknowledge the magnitude of such a change. A once-mortal knight cannot simply pick up the pieces of her life and go on from her Embrace as if nothing has happened, but must build herself a whole new structure, either imitating as best as possible her former existence or attempting to establish an alternative.

It is possible a character that may have had neither the inclination nor the means to become a knight in his mortal life will find himself in possession of both as a Cainite. Although some of the vampiric orders restrict their ranks to those who were knighted in their previous existences, others do not discriminate against vampires formerly of even the lowest castes. Those who join the Cainite orders will be admired in certain circles, scoffed at in others. Opinions differ widely on whether such efforts are shallow human inventions or glorious ideals. Opinions differ even more widely on whether such orders should participate in mortal causes or dedicate themselves to furthering Cainite goals. For more on the Cainite orders, see Chapters Three and Four.

Knights, both vampiric and mortal, are tied by tradition and obligation into a wide-reaching network of familial and feudal relationships. Squires and men-at-arms are fostered and trained by nobles who then expect some sort of reciprocal service, and those nobles are, in turn, expected to do their duty to their monarchs. Is a knightly character just starting to make these connections, or is she throwing them off in search of something else? Cainites will find it challenging to maintain their previous ties to the mortal world or to establish new ones, and many must struggle to carve out a role for themselves.

Setting out to become a knight when one is already a vampire is a daunting task. A good family name is crucial, yet may be compromised even when honestly possessed by something as simple as a casual remark from a noble surprised to find that one's decrepit old line yet has an extant scion. It becomes extremely difficult to make an impression on people with your fighting, no matter how valiant you are, when all but the merest handful of tournaments and battles take place in the light of day. Many obstacles can be surmounted with the clever and judicious use of Cainite Disciplines and others with simple skill. An ambitious count will not question a mysteriously reclusive knight overmuch if that knight defeats 10 of his rival's fighting men every night.

New Traits

The following Traits are useful for representing some of the unique aspects of chivalry. Storytellers always have final say on whether or not to allow these Traits. In a chronicle not centered on knightly affairs, the Storyteller may judge that the Abilities below are so specialized that their cost should be lower (half the regular price in freebie or experience points); in a chivalrous chronicle, they will be quite useful, however. (Some of the following Traits have appeared in previous products and appear here for convenience's sake.)

Talents

Franchise

No tutor could instill the quality of frankness or franchise into a baseborn churl, no book learning could bestow it upon a poverty-stricken scholar. The mien of a free and noble knight is his instinctive birthright, enhanced by, but not dependent on, good manners or elegant speech.

This Talent is not a mandatory purchase for a knightly character, but most characters of high birth carry themselves differently than serfs or villeins. Franchise quantifies that difference and may be used instead of Etiquette, Leadership or Intimidation at the Storyteller's discretion (in situations where inherent social superiority matters more than actual behavior).

• Novice: You still have a tendency to blush, duck your head or flinch at loud commands, but it's clear that you are no farmer.

•• Practiced: Save for when you are in the throes of depression, you carry your head high and your shoulders squared.

••• Competent: You drop your eyes before the gaze of no man or woman.

•••• Expert: You radiate a confident authority that seems to serve as a constant reinforcement of the current hierarchical status quo.

••••• Master: It is readily apparent to anyone with functioning eyes that you are a powerful noble.

•••••• Legend: *Jongleurs* compare Lancelot to you when they compose songs.

Possessed by: Knights, Nobles, Kings and Queens

Specialties: At Court, Battlefield, Challenges, Silent Bearing, Oration

Skills

Chivalry

Chivalry denotes knowledge of the growing chivalrous culture and the ability to live up to its expectations of behavior. A character with Chivalry knows what is expected of him (or her) in what situation and can discuss the merits of crusade and tourney, all while maintaining the bearing of his assumed station. Characters without actual rank can use this skill to fake it, and minor knights can inflate their position. This skill can also be used to draw the attention of a particular lord or lady.

• Novice: Familiar with the ideas of chivalry, you seldom put them into practice.

•• Practiced: You have a noticeable chivalrous bearing and recognize station at tourneys.

••• Competent: Passages of various troubadour songs come easily to mind.

•••• Expert: Your romantic and martial life appear as examples of knightly behavior.

••••• Master: The virtues of chivalry run deep in your blood, and you may exert your station with only a glance.

•••••• Legend: You know the troubadours songs extremely well because they often refer to you.

Possessed by: Knights, Squires, Nobles, Courtiers, Social Climbers, Charlatans, Poets

Specialties: Documentation, Individual Favor, Courtly Gossip, Tourneys

Knowledges

Heraldry

Although the formal rules of heraldry have not yet been finalized, you are familiar with the intricacies of blazoning. This knowledge enables you to identify knights and nobles by the coats of arms they bear. In addition, you can connect the blazon to the ancestry, often important when trying to keep track of political intrigues or to determine if the cute young thing you've just been introduced to is actually your third cousin twice removed.

• Dabbler: You know the difference between *vair* and *vert*.

•• Student: When you spy a line of armed men wending their way toward your keep, you can make an educated guess as to whether they are friends or foes based on their banners.

- ••• Learned: You have designed a pleasing and distinctive blazon for your own family's use.
- •••• Scholar: You can follow convoluted melees and large-scale battles and identify individual combatants.
- ••••• Savant: You recognize nearly all the coats of arms in general use in your kingdom and several neighboring countries and can accurately recite several generations' worth of genealogy for almost all of the devices you recognize.
- •••••• Visionary: Your input will go a long way toward shaping the lasting structure of heraldry and blazonry; your opinions are quoted as authoritative by prominent heralds.

Possessed by: Squires, Troubadours, Knights, Artists
Specialties: Specific Region, Noble Lineage

Backgrounds

Vassalage

You serve a lord of more than usual importance and get more opportunities to mingle with the high and mighty than most knights. You also get more scrutiny from troubadours looking for targets of satire, priests seeking evidence of sin in chivalry and ambitious commoners who'd like to take your prerogatives for themselves. You can substitute Vassalage for Intimidation or Leadership when acting on behalf of your lord or in an assigned official capacity.

- • You serve a lord with notable power in your area. He may occupy a castle in a contested border zone or, as bishop, organize campaigns against heretic enclaves. As his regular companion, you share in some of whatever glory or blame comes his way. When introduced to gatherings within a few days' travel, you can expect others to know who you are and what you've been doing lately.
- •• You serve a lord who holds substantial power through out your region, one of the principal players in several counties or active in directing several diocese. You feature in local homilies as an example of virtue or vice; if you're particularly good or bad at chivalric activities, your deeds attract local comment.
- ••• You serve a lord who plays a role in the affairs of your kingdom or the Church: a well-known count or bishop, most likely. You join your lord at important gatherings several times a year, and special assignments may take you far and wide.
- •••• You serve one of the most significant lords in your kingdom, a prominent duke or perhaps one of the cardinals with extensive holdings. Anyone who deals regularly with your lord knows who you are, as do many of those who serve your lord's other vassals.
- ••••• You serve one of the great lords of the Dark Medieval world, a king or one of the most powerful dukes or warlords. Your name appears in poems and tales about the exploits of your lord and his court.

Merits and Flaws

The following Merits and Flaws largely deal with matters of reputation and standing amongst fellow knights and lords. They can create real advantages and drawbacks in a chivalrous chronicle. However, they may be next to meaningless in chronicles that go further afield or deal mostly with Cainites who do not care about such things. Use these Traits only when appropriate.

Crusader (1pt. Merit)

It is known that you once donned the crusader's cross and successfully returned from the Holy Land, having done your duty to God. In all likelihood you joined the forces of Richard the Lion-Hearted and Philip Augustus in the Third Crusade and may even have seen Jerusalem (although not "freed" it). This accomplishment gives you special standing and repute among those knights, lords and ladies who never made the journey to Outremer. *Jongleurs* may request you share stories that they may turn into fanciful tales, and others may ask your opinion about events in the Latin Kingdoms or Iberia. You gain a -1 difficulty on social rolls in circumstances where a crusading background comes into play and on Knowledge rolls related to the region and events you experienced. Note that in some areas, the courts and tourneys may be bursting with former crusaders, making this Merit so common as to be meaningless.

Prestigious Order (1pt. Merit)

You are a member of one of the most prestigious of the knightly orders of the day, most likely the Templars or Hospitalers. By your membership, you stand as a paragon of Christian knighthood, a warrior monk. You gain a -1 difficulty on social rolls among knights not part of the order. This Merit does not define your status within the order (use Allies, Contacts and Influence to do so). Note also that Templars and Hospitalers generally cannot have the Resources Background, as they take a vow of poverty (although they might have land in holding while they serve with the order).

Celebrated Lineage (1-4pt. Merit)

Your mortal lineage brings you certain status, even if you may have fallen far from the tree. You get some preferential treatment at tourneys and at court, and troubadours will pay special attention to you. In circumstances where she judges it appropriate, the Storyteller may give you a -1 difficulty bonus on social rolls. This is a variable cost Merit, where cost indicates the repute of your lineage. A one-point version indicates that your family is relatively minor but said to descend from heroic stock (Charlemagne or Roland, perhaps). A four-point

version indicates that you are a recognized member of one of the prominent royal houses of Europe, such as those of Anjou or Aquitaine. Note that this Merit does not indicate your own reputation or power, only that of your relatives. You still need to purchase the Influence and Vassalage Backgrounds.

Exceptional Steed (2-3pt. Merit)

You own a warhorse of supreme quality, one with greater speed or courage than the norm. It also has a special bond with you, and you receive a -1 difficulty bonus on all Animal Ken rolls with it and on Ride rolls that involve stunts of one kind or another (simply chasing an opponent does not qualify, but jumping a hedge to do so does). The two-point version of this Merit indicates an exceptional but natural warhorse; the three-point version indicates a ghoul horse. Note that you must have Animal Ken • or Animalism to purchase the two-point version. You should develop a background for this steed. Where did you get it? Who trained it? If it is a ghoul, what dangerous qualities has it developed?

Infamous Lineage (1pt. Flaw)

You family name turns heads for all the wrong reasons. Your grandfather may have been an infernalist or your great uncle a traitor and scoundrel, but a pall of ill repute hangs over you because of it. You may still have station and substantial authority, but you play at a disadvantage in the spheres of courtly rumor and troubadour stories. You suffer a +1 difficulty penalty on social rolls in such circumstances. Note that this Flaw does not indicate a lack of feudal standing; you may still buy the Influence and Vassalage Backgrounds at high levels.

Sacred Oath (1-3pt. Flaw)

Many Cainites leading lives as mortal knights claim to have taken an oath not to see the sun for one reason or another. You may do so as well, but in addition, you have taken a true oath that limits you in another way. This oath must both be important to you and known to others in order to qualify. The limitations imposed on you by your pledge determine the Flaw's point cost. A one-point oath might be to honor a lady with a special gift on her marriage or birthday; a three-point oath might be to wear a hair shirt until Jerusalem is again in Christian hands. Violating an oath can have dire consequences. At the very least it will damage your reputation (gain the Virtueless Flaw). In a chronicle in which faith is real, potent and present, breaking an oath could result in heavenly repercussions (gain any of the supernatural Flaws in **Vampire: The Dark Ages**). Note that Storytellers can use this Flaw to represent a knightly oath of fealty in a mixed chronicle (2 points). In a purely chivalrous chronicle, everyone will have such an oath, so it is unnecessary to quantify it.

Horses by the Numbers

Game statistics for horses appear in the **Dark Ages Companion** and elsewhere, but the importance of a steed for any knightly character makes them worth repeating here. In the following section, a "horse" is a standard farm animal, a "warhorse" is the typical knight's steed, an "exceptional warhorse" is the quality represented by the two-point version of the Merit Exceptional Steed and a "ghoul warhorse" is represented by the three-point version.

Horse

Strength 4, Dexterity 2, Stamina 3

Willpower: 2, **Health Levels:** OK, OK, -1, -1, -2, -2, -5, Incapacitated

Attack: Trample or kick for six dice; bite for three

Abilities: Alertness 3, Athletics 2, Brawl 1

Blood Pool: 6

Warhorse

Strength 6, Dexterity 2, Stamina 5

Willpower: 4, **Health Levels:** OK, OK, -1, -1, -2, -2, -5, Incapacitated

Attack: Trample or kick for seven dice; bite for three

Abilities: Alertness 3, Athletics 2, Brawl 3, Empathy 2, Intimidation 2

Blood Pool: 8

Exceptional Warhorse

Strength 6, Dexterity 3, Stamina 6

Willpower: 5, **Health Levels:** OK, OK, -1, -1, -1, -2, -2, -5, Incapacitated

Attack: Trample or kick for eight dice; bite for three

Abilities: Alertness 3, Athletics 3, Brawl 3, Empathy 2, Intimidation 3

Blood Pool: 9

Ghoul Warhorse

Strength 6, Dexterity 3, Stamina 6

Willpower: 5, **Health Levels:** OK, OK, -1, -1, -1, -2, -2, -5, Incapacitated

Attack: Trample or kick for eight dice; bite for three

Abilities: Alertness 3, Athletics 3, Brawl 3, Intimidation 3

Disciplines: Potence 1, Fortitude or Celerity 1

Blood Pool: 9

Fraudulent Order (2pt. Flaw)

You claim to be a member of a distant knightly order but are no such thing. You may claim to belong to a true and recognized order such as the Templars or Hospitalers or to one of the spurious orders described on pages 67-68. This pretense gives you a combination of prestige without obligation that suits you just fine. It is a risky proposition, however, because you face very serious consequences if others discover your fraud. If exposed, you will be disgraced, probably banished from respectable company and may face the ire of other knights (and the order you claimed covenant with).

Landless (2pt. Flaw)

Through some reversal of fortune you have been stripped of the land that helped define you as a knight. Pagans, Moors or rival lords may have overrun your fief; plague or curse may have made it uninhabitable. Already having earned your spurs, you retain something of your status, but it is now only founded in service and action, not in wealth and position. You may not have high Resources, and high Influence or Vassalage are also difficult. You suffer a +1 difficulty penalty on social rolls in the company of landed knights. Note that some areas (such as Germany) have large numbers of these landless knights. Second or third sons who have become knights errant usually have this Flaw as well.

Rogue Knight (2pt. Flaw)

You are known as a rogue, a knight who has abandoned his holdings and responsibilities for life as a bandit or mercenary. There may well be extenuating circumstances to your position — not least of which is the Curse of Caine — but few people pay any attention to them. You suffer at least a +1 difficulty penalty on social rolls in the company of "respectable" knights and nobles, and they will likely assume you to be a liar, murderer and cur on principal. This Flaw is incompatible with significant ratings of Influence, Resources and Vassalage, unless those Backgrounds represent non-feudal standing and wealth.

Virtueless (2pt. Flaw)

Chivalrous culture places more and more importance on the observation of a pantheon of virtues. Knights must display *prouesse*, *loyauté*, largesse, *courtoisie*, franchise and *honeure* (see pp. 20-23). You have gained the unfortunate reputation for being lacking in one or more of these virtues. Perhaps you made inappropriate advances to the wrong lady, broke your word, consistently lose at tourney or even fled the field of battle. This black mark hangs around your neck, hampering your career. You suffer a +1 difficulty on all social rolls among knights and nobles. Eliminating this Flaw is a task both long and hard. You must prove that you were slandered or have made amends and that you are now a paragon of the virtue you supposedly lacked.

Woman in Disguise (4pt. Flaw)

You are one of those rare women who have decided to live the knight's life. The opinions of your fellows — both male and female — have forced you to assume the role of a man, changing your name and appearance as best you can. You live your life in a careful subterfuge, doing everything you can to avoid the discovery of your secret, while still appearing at tourney and at court. You likely have trusted aids (the Retainers background) who share your secret and help you keep it. If your secret were revealed, you would, in all likelihood, be utterly disgraced as a liar and a woman who doesn't know her place. This Flaw does not grant you the ability to maintain the disguise (you still need Subterfuge and other Traits).

Woman in Spurs (5pt. Flaw)

A Joan of Arc long before the day, you flout convention and publicly act as a knight without hiding your gender. This closes many doors to you, and most mortal knights will refuse to treat you as anything resembling an equal — most think you insane, evil or possessed, in fact. Only by proving yourself to each and every man you face will you gain even a modicum of respect. In Cainite circles, you are treated more fairly, but masquerading as a mortal is nearly impossible unless you shed your arms.

The Road of Chivalry Revisited

Chivalry is, by far, the newest set of ideals to provide the foundations for a vampiric Road. Any vampire on the Via Equitum commits himself to a path still in flux: He gambles that beliefs by no means extensively tested can help him resist the Beast. The Via Equitum exists because chivalry happened to impress some vampires looking for a fresh set of moral guidelines almost the moment ideas about Christian duty, the nobility of the profession of arms and the hierarchy of vassalage came together in the mortal world.

Followers of the Road of Chivalry commit themselves to the calling of battle, purity of spirit and honor in their dealings with both superiors and inferiors. This last element, service, distinguishes the Road of Chivalry from otherwise similar vampiric paths which emphasize absolute mastery. Chivalry tempers every hierarchy by imposing responsibilities on superiors as well as inferiors. Practitioners of this Road see themselves as the righteous anchors who secure everyone else in the midst of social chaos. They protect the weak, smite the wicked and enforce justice.

It's hard to be a good knight and a Cainite. The Curse constantly tempts the knight to sin. A knight who excels at the Via Equitum proves himself worthy indeed and may even hope for redemption of some sort. Whether mortals recognize it or not, the knight on the Road of Chivalry embodies chivalric ideals better than any human being can.

Cainites on the Road of Chivalry accept responsibilities to kine as well as to other Cainites. While mortals cannot be worth as much as Cainites, nonetheless, the noble knight honors and protects his inferiors. Vampires who make clan loyalty or other exclusively vampiric commitments fundamental find this confusing, if not actively offensive.

The Road of Chivalry teaches Conscience and Self-Control.

Revised Hierarchy of Sins

Road Rating	Minimum Wrongdoing for Conscience roll
10	Showing disrespect to a fellow knight.
9	Allowing injustice within your fief to go unpunished.
8	Allowing another knight to injure an innocent.
7	Failing to answer the Pope's call for holy war.
6	Failing to offer hospitality to anyone except a sworn enemy.
5	Showing disrespect to anyone with whom you've exchanged oaths of fealty.
4	Injuring an innocent (anyone who has not voluntarily entered battle).
3	Showing cowardice in battle.
2	Failing to discharge your sworn duties.
1	Breaking your oath.

A Road of Pre-Chivalry

The Road of Chivalry presented in **Vampire: The Dark Ages** represents a stage along the way in chivalry's evolution. It differs from the full-blown chivalry discussed in **Ashen Knight** in two key aspects. First, it does not include any obligation to subordinates except in general terms and very far along the Road. Second, it makes little mention of obligations to mortals, focusing almost entirely on the vampire's role in vampiric rather than human society. As a model for tyrants and absolute lords, it's very suitable for vampires ruling in areas where chivalry spreads late or not at all. Simply rename it the Road of Lordship or something of the sort.

Personalizing the Road

Chivalry doesn't have just one definition; it's a fluid and complex set of ideas. Once you understand what elements go into the chivalric ideal, you can adjust one or more steps of the Road of Chivalry to suit your particular character. The Road Rating 7 sin obviously doesn't apply to pre- or non-Christian characters, and you should replace it with some comparable obligation to fight chivalry's enemies, promote the well-being of those who cannot protect themselves or some other aspect of the ideal.

Women and Fighting

Arnoul had not yet been able to train himself to respond consistently to the demeaning cry of "Adkyn," and so he was startled to be abruptly spun around by a heavy hand on his left shoulder. He was even more startled to find himself facing a woman of nearly exactly his own height, armored in unmistakably high quality mail beneath a richly embroidered surcoat.

"You're the new one, Adkyn?" she asked in a rough but not unpleasant voice. He nodded. "Fulke calls me Judith. We work together sometimes. You'll be traveling with me for the next few days — I've been hired to escort a rich young bride, and I'm borrowing four of Fulke's men."

There was a loud shout behind her. "Judith!" called one of the young retainers, as he hurtled toward her. Arnoul was startled to see her eyes narrow slightly, and the boy thump abruptly to the ground as if he'd been struck by an unseen force. He got up and laughed, looking like a puppy who'd been wrestled down by a littermate, but Arnoul was disturbed by the woman's casual use of power. "That was not chivalrous," he said.

She shrugged off his criticism. "Don't think it means I don't know how to use my sword or my fists. I can tell you haven't been taught much, but if you're lucky, we'll have a boring trip, and there'll be time for me to show you a thing or two."

"I am not sure I care to learn such... tricks," Arnoul forced himself to say. "I wish to defeat my opponents cleanly, without deception or unfair advantage."

Her eyes met and held his. "While you are under my command, you will defeat your opponents with whatever means are available to you, however I tell you to do it. Maybe you'll learn something, and maybe you won't, but we'll all survive."

As she walked away from him, Arnoul considered how reluctant he'd been to practice his increased strength and speed against other knights, even those he knew to be of the Damned. He could indeed learn, he thought, if this woman and Fulke were willing to teach. But he was not at all certain he would make use of such skills only in worthy causes, and to do otherwise would violate the code he'd absorbed. Resolving to comprehend the mysteries of his powers but restrain himself at all times, he followed after the disconcerting Judith.

For a woman to take up arms is no small matter. In the Dark Medieval world, a girl's training — in almost all cases — teaches her not to hit. Not to fight back. Not to project authority or confidence. To use words as her weapons, but to apologize for exhibiting more skill or more cleverness than those around her. To take it for granted

that she will be protected by the nearest male, as well as be submissive to him.

Like it or not, our early socialization shapes us on the deepest and most subconscious levels, and to overcome it is a grueling task. Such an effort becomes even more difficult when the prevailing cultural wisdom is that what you are attempting to achieve exists only for mythical figures or even that your struggles against the status quo are signs of demonic possession. Fortunately, lady fighters are likely to find more acceptance and less open hostility among Cainites than among mortals.

A player taking up a female fighting character needs to think long and hard about how exactly she learned to fight. Issues which should be resolved include: Who taught her and why? Where did she get her first weapon? Against whom did she spar? And how did her family react to these bizarre activities? Most importantly of all, what does it mean to her to be a lady fighter in the Dark Medieval world? How has she managed to break out of the mold of ideal womanhood without losing her sense of self, and is she glad or sorry to have turned her back on traditional marriage and motherhood — or does she hope to combine a martial and a domestic life?

The player of a male character would also be wise to consider in advance the character's response to encountering a female fighter. A man's prejudices learned in life linger with him, no matter how open-minded he thinks he's become after death. Remember that for almost all mortals and many inhuman beings in the Dark Medieval world, a woman in armor is a novelty deserving of comment, not something to be quietly accepted, unless the observer is so worldly as to be positively jaded. Humans and those passing as human run the risk of being accused of encouraging heresy and deviant behavior if they seem tolerant of sword-wielding women in the presence of the wrong individuals.

Lamia as Lady Knights

The **Dark Ages Companion** discusses several obscure bloodlines still in existence during the Middle Ages, one of which lends itself nicely to the formation of female knights. The Lamia predominantly Embrace women who refuse to conform to societal expectations. These women, daughters of the Dark Mother Lilith, often serve as the strong right arms of the Cappadocians. They are widely feared and respected as bodyguards and warriors.

Lamia who actively take up fighting may have far fewer conflicted feelings about killing, given their worship of death personified as the Dark Mother. They also have the benefit of an established hierarchy that encourages and rewards physical exploits and examples of admirable woman fighters to emulate.

A Lamia character might well become frustrated in a limited role as sentinel for a skulking Graverobber and set out to be dubbed a knight. Alternatively, a recently Embraced Lamia might seek to overcome the general fear and distaste of her clan's weakness, the plague all Lamia carry, by becoming the epitome of chivalry. Or she might wish to avenge Lilith and all her sex by destroying men who rape or attack women.

An older woman not part of a larger household, widowed or estranged from her husband and grown children, might consider herself useless in medieval society. But age holds far less meaning for Cainites than for mortals, and a woman who thought herself finished in life might find herself a formidable foe in unlife.

Whose Breastplate Is This?

Armor and weaponry are most definitely not unisex items. Men carry weight reasonably effectively when it is distributed across their shoulders, while women carry it better across their hips, so a heavy mail hauberk that suits a man well may very nearly immobilize a woman of the same stature. Women's hands, wrists and shoulders are constructed slightly differently than men's, so a lady fighter will often find that hilts, grips and balance points of standard weapons must be altered for her.

These are not hard and fast rules — obviously, not all bodies are shaped alike. Women can and do compensate for gear that fits imperfectly, as must many men who cannot afford customized equipment. However, people looking for authentic detail when playing female fighters should keep in mind that there are very real physical issues involved. For instance, a lady fighter may have a constant bruise on her right wrist where the weighty hilt of her sword chafes against her gauntlet when she strikes a certain type of blow. She may have developed a habit of circling to the left when engaged in one-on-one combat, in order to compensate for the blind spot caused by her shield's being slightly too large.

If the fighter is openly female and has found people willing to equip her (or willing to take her money to do so), almost any problem can be solved through a little experimentation and research. If, on the other hand, she is in disguise or not wealthy enough to purchase new armor, various quirks or mannerisms may be the result of using armor and weaponry not designed for her. Male disguise entails a bevy of practical problems of its own. Constant concealment is troublesome in a society where solitude is considered an abnormal, undesirable state — people in noble keeps and humble cottages alike sleep, eat and bathe together, and someone who chooses not to do so may well be marked as an oddity.

There are some potential benefits to counteract the drawbacks of being a woman fighter. Many women find themselves more agile and faster on their feet than their male opponents. Because their hips rotate slightly differently than men's, they can sometimes generate a surprising amount of power from seemingly awkward positions. Women's centers of gravity tend to be lower than men's, making them difficult to unbalance or unhorse.

Lady fighters are not the equivalent of men scaled down and stuffed into smaller armor. It is not sexist simply to acknowledge that there are differences in the physical construction of bodies. Working with those differences can make for a highly realistic, detailed roleplaying experience.

In Mortal Company

Lamia and other Cainite women who take up arms may find some hard-won acceptance among other vampires. If the character wishes to fully pursue chivalry, however, she will find herself drawn to human courts where such ideals were born and are still developing. There, what little understanding she found among those of the blood will vanish like so much mist. A female knight will either have to be willing to "go public" and endure insults and attempts to strip her of her arms or take her mythic inspiration to another level.

That level is disguise. The romances popular with nobles and knights all over Europe are filled with mysterious knights of uncertain identity, knights who only reveal their names to opponents capable of defeating them in battle. The new, visored great helm keeps its wearer's face covered, and mail hauberks combine with quilted padding to keep figures largely uniform. Fully armored and prepared for battle, a female knight is indistinguishable from a male counterpart, at least to the eye.

Once a female knight has her disguise down pat, she needs to make sure of her support staff. Only the poorest of knights have to forego esquires and valets; would-be woman warriors must either let their retainers in on the secret or have a foolproof plan for keeping their true identities from the men who accompany them everywhere. Lord-vassal relations and oaths sworn over relics are a great help in the latter case. A secluded manor or keep helps as well, providing female knights with a place to train and practice their skills in private.

Court and campaign are another matter entirely. Even with the development of institutions like scutage (see page 24), almost every knight is still someone's vassal and is thus required to perform knightly service on her lord's behalf. Armor can't help a female knight when it comes to dining in the great hall or attending councils; nor is it worn during wartime except when attack is imminent. Abilities like Subterfuge can help in these contexts, but it is difficult for even the most skilled actress to fool a dedicated observer for too long. In the plus column of the ledger, medieval court fashion has not yet reached the extremes of exposure it will come to know in the 14th century (when tunics are cut so short as to leave nothing in the hose to the imagination). A male haircut, a loose-fitting tunic and a reclusive nature can all prove useful in maintaining one's disguise. So, too, can creative use of Disciplines such as Obfuscate. Still, most Cainites prefer to rely as little as possible on their supernatural abilities, as they are ever worried about the havoc a single moment's lapse could wreak.

Ensuring Silence

Female knights who are also Cainites almost inevitably resort to the blood oath to make certain their retainers remain loyal and silent. It is simply a matter of common sense. Every Cainite woman under arms fears the too-clever servant who sells his mistress' secrets — her gender, her nature or both — and thus seals her fate. As a result, the servants of a Cainite woman masquerading thus are extraordinarily hard to subvert.

Arms and Armor

All knights rely on their equipment. Most make do with the best they can get, represented by the normal mechanics in **Vampire: The Dark Ages**. Some knights manage to find, buy, commission or steal better arms and armor, and these require special rules. Others struggle with inferior gear. The state of a knight's possessions marks his status in the world and should matter in the course of play.

Maintenance

Dirty, fouled and otherwise neglected weapons don't do as much damage. Blades rust; edges dull; spikes become blunt; shafts weaken. A knight normally spends several hours each week cleaning his arms and armor. Contrary to some romantic images, knights do not carry around bare blades secured only by a stout leather thong. Any weapon worth carrying travels in a sheath to protect it against rain, extremes of heat and cold, mud and the other complications of the road. This applies to spears, bows and other wooden weapons as well as to swords, axes and the like. It takes time

The Ugly Truth

If functioning as an active female knight sounds insanely difficult, that's because it is. Joan of Arc will be a sensation in the 1400s precisely because her decision to publicly dress as a man while maintaining a female identity is so culturally unprecedented (and, in the end, her gender-bending helps to bring her to the stake). At the same time, there were numerous men willing to follow her to the death. Like Joan, the players' characters are an exceptional bunch: Should a female knight display sufficient prowess in public, she will no doubt have allies and defenders to turn to in times of difficulty.

and effort to shape wood, and it's subjected to precise tension for its intended task.

A knight should spend at least one hour per week maintaining each of his weapons and two hours per week on his armor. He must scrub off any lingering blood or gore from recent battles, sharpen cutting edges, check the weapon's balance, tighten all the screws and fastenings that hold the weapon together and keep it oiled for an extra layer of protection while traveling.

Each weapon or piece of armor that doesn't get this attention gradually starts wearing out. The player rolls Wits + Melee, with a difficulty of the weapon's difficulty number for combat plus one for each week with skipped maintenance. If the roll fails, the weapon's damage rating drops by one. Armor has no damage rating; instead, at the player's discretion (and with Storyteller approval), reduce the protection rating by one or add one to the Dexterity or Perception adjustment penalties. It takes a week of twice normal cleaning time to repair a point of damage rating, protection or adjustment penalty lost to neglect.

Weapons that do no damage and armor that can stop no damage are extremely fragile. At the Storyteller's discretion, any strike at them that deals damage shatters them altogether.

Badly maintained gear reflects poorly on the knight who carries it. In situations where other knights can see neglected weapons, each point of impairment created by neglect subtracts one from the player's dice pool for social tasks. Exceptions do apply: If the knight can persuade other knights that the neglect could not have been avoided, then they grant him a temporary reprieve. The player rolls Wits + Etiquette, with a difficulty of the highest temporary Willpower of the knights present plus one for each point of visible impairment. Each success suspends the social penalty for one night. If the knight takes the time to repair a point of damage within that period of time and engages in repair each week thereafter, the penalty does not apply.

Purchase

The vast majority of weapons and armor sold to knights (or acquired through trade, barter and other means that may not strictly be "sale") are of average quality. They perform like most others. Knights can seek out better or worse gear, however.

Refer to **Vampire: The Dark Ages** for the standard costs of knights' equipment.

Knights can purchase inferior gear. Each point of reduction in damage rating reduces the Resource cost of a weapon by one. Each point of reduction in protection rating or increase in Dexterity or Perception penalty reduces the Resource cost of armor by one. A knight cannot choose to buy weapons that do no damage or armor that offers no protection. If he's really bent on useless equipment, let him make his own.

Knights can also try to purchase superior equipment. Each added dot of Resource cost improves a weapon's damage rating by one. Each added dot of Resource cost does one of the following, at the knight's discretion: increase protection rating by one, reduce Dexterity penalty by one or reduce Perception penalty by one (this will never lead to bonuses, eliminating the penalties is the best that can be done). Each added dot also increases the weapon's rarity by one level. Players should note that the "knight's armor" described in **Vampire: The Dark Ages** is already very rare and requires 5 Resources. Gaining a better version of that armor is left to the Storyteller's discretion.

Society by the Numbers

Don't reduce the social aspects of maintaining equipment to dice rolls if you and your players are comfortable roleplaying the situation. Disdainful looks and lack of confidence in a knight's competence should matter. Lords do not place great trust in vassals who neglect basic responsibilities; vassals come to lose respect for lords who let the defining tools of their profession suffer. Dice pool penalties shouldn't substitute for roleplaying, merely back it up. If players deal with the game world with a sufficient sense of responsibility, then don't drag the dice in just because there's a roll that could be made.

The Consequences of Excellence

Superior arms mark superior status. A knight who carries equipment above his rank had better have an explanation, or he risks sanction for inappropriate ambition.

A knight may carry equipment that costs in Resource dots as many or fewer than the dots in his Status or Vassalage rating, whichever is higher. A knight whose equipment costs as many Resource dots as his Status or Vassalage looks good: He carries the best that's readily available to him. Properly maintained, it reflects well on his attention to his duties.

Carrying equipment that costs more than the knight's Status or Vassalage arouses questions. How could he afford it? Is he becoming improperly proud? Did he steal it? Each extra dots, of Resource cost of the knight's most expensive gear imposes a +1 difficulty penalty to the knight's social tasks when dealing with other knights.

It's possible to avoid this penalty through proper explanation. For instance, a lord may give his vassal superior equipment as reward for services well performed. The lord announces his gift, and the story circulates. A knight may take the equipment of another knight defeated in battle or tournament as ransom; once the defeated knight or appropriate authorities confirm the victory, the taken gear is the victor's property. A knight may also inherit superior equipment from a more prosperous relative.

If the knight is in the area where he made his acquisition, most likely other inhabitants of the area know the story. More than a few days' travel away, accounts become unreliable. The knight must succeed in presenting his claim. The player makes an Intelligence + Melee roll, difficulty 7, laying out his story and demonstrating the proper respect for his possessions. If the roll succeeds, the knight earns the respect of all in the area, and the social penalty no longer applies. If the roll fails, the penalty continues to apply, though the knight may make another attempt each week until he overcomes the skepticism of his peers.

The Limits of Force

Vampires with mastery of social Abilities and Disciplines may feel that they can simply command others to hand over whatever they want and arrange a suitable cover story. Chivalric society doesn't always oblige.

The story is the common currency of knightly reputation. Knights talk to each other about what they've done and seen. Discrepancies in stories make it difficult to sustain deceptions unless *everyone* is deceived. A vampire who, for instance, commands his lord to give an overly valuable gift in the implanted belief that the vampiric vassal deserves it isn't done once the lord complies. The circumstances in which the lord believes need to seem plausible, or other knights start to question the lord's judgment as well as the vassal's honesty. Supporting details must be present, or knights begin to suspect duplicity or collusion.

It's actually easier in the long run to earn gifts than to try to take them dishonestly.

Appendix: Ill-Made Knights

You cannot have a proud and chivalrous spirit if your conduct is mean and paltry; for whatever a man's actions are, such must be his spirit.

— Demosthenes, c. 384 - 322 BCE

Bitter Ash Paragon

Quote: *No true knight would cower in the face of these odds. Look at them. They are rabble. We shall prevail once again, no matter how many they are.*

Prelude: You grew up in a prosperous commoner family, your father one of the most successful merchants in Genoa. Not long after you reached manhood, your father bought himself a knighthood and excitedly rode into battle as if it were a game. He died in a minor skirmish against Bolognese knights two weeks later, a sacrifice to his ignorance and hero-worship.

For years, you raged against the evils of knighthood to anyone who would listen. One evening, a stranger listened carefully and started arguing back. The debate lasted all through the night, ending only with his need to retire before sunrise (a rare illness, he explained). He was, he said, a traveling scholar, and could spend only a few weeks every year or two in Genoa. You came to look forward to his visits as a high point in your existence. Over the years, your views changed, and you realized that it wasn't the institution of knighthood that failed, but knights themselves. They needed to follow good examples of righteous endeavors, just like the people in every other stratum of society.

More than 20 years after the great conversation began, your sire-to-be told you the truth of his condition and Embraced you. He trained you in the use of your new powers and exposed you to the ultimate quest: to serve as a guardian of the Grail and other holy relics. During a long journey to Scotland two years after your Embrace, he told you of the Order of the Bitter Ashes and its sacred duties. When you arrived at the Castle in the Lake, you gladly took a position as second squire for one of the blessed Grail Knights.

Your travels with the order have often brought you back to the troubled Italian peninsula. There you seek out mortal knights and try to demonstrate through your courage and honor that nobility comes from the heart, not one's ancestry. Some knights resent your arrogance, others respect you. It's sometimes a difficult existence, but if you can warm the frozen hearts of your fellow knights, perhaps you can save other men from the fate that consumed your father.

Concept: You come to chivalry as an outsider, aware of its failings: how it lures men into extravagant displays, foolish risks and moral callousness. Precisely because of your hard-earned appreciation of the drawbacks, you now appreciate chivalry's strengths even more. You don't take them for granted, and you strive to make other knights aware of their opportunities and responsibilities. Now a first squire in the order, you seek both to follow your duties as a holy warrior of the Grail and to inspire mortals around you. It can be a hard road — especially when the order demands secrecy — but it is yours to travel.

Roleplaying Hints: Others see you as humorless and driven. You agree at least about the "driven" part. There are so *many* errors to remedy. You give thanks each night for the gift of immortality that allows you all the time you need to instruct each wayward soul, through teaching and deed.

Equipment: Horse, armor, weapons, well-worn Bible

The Ashen Knight

Name:	Nature: Fanatic	Generation: 11th
Player:	Demeanor: Defender	Haven:
Chronicle:	Clan: Brujah	Concept: Bitter Ash Paragon

Attributes

Physical		Social		Mental	
Strength	2	Charisma	3	Perception	2
Dexterity	4	Manipulation	2	Intelligence	2
Stamina	4	Appearance	3	Wits	2

Abilities

Talents		Skills		Knowledges	
Acting	0	Animal Ken	1	Academics	1
Alertness	3	Achery	1	Hearth Wisdom	0
Athletics	2	Crafts	0	Investigation	0
Brawl	2	Etiquette	3	Law	0
Dodge	0	Herbalism	0	Linguistics	0
Empathy	0	Melee	3	Medicine	1
Intimidation	0	Music	0	Occult	1
Larceny	0	Ride	2	Politics	0
Leadership	3	Stealth	0	Science	0
Subterfuge	0	Survival	2	Seneschal	2

Advantages

Disciplines		Backgrounds		Virtues	
Celerity	1	Contacts	2	Conscience	4
Potence	2	Generation	1	Self-Control	3
Presence	2	Mentor	2	Courage	4
		Resources	2		

Other Traits

Chivalry 1

Road

Chivalry: 7

Willpower

6

Blood Pool

Health

Bruised		☐
Hurt	-1	☐
Injured	-1	☐
Wounded	-2	☐
Mauled	-2	☐
Crippled	-5	☐
Incapacitated		☐

Weakness

The Countess

Quote: *I happen to know that Sir Ottavio is very fond of hunt scenes. If you were to add his image to this painting, I believe that he would gladly buy it and commission more work from you, young sir.*

Prelude: You grew up on the fringes of French nobility, one of several not-particularly-wanted daughters raised by a baron who dreamed of grander things. He married you off young to the first knight who suited his sense of propriety, and he never bothered about you again. The early years of your marriage suggested that your life would pass in the sort of nondescript haze of routine that lay over your mother's life.

Then something interesting happened. While off on pilgrimage to Santiago de Compostela, your husband received a vision of grander things in store for him. He returned with newfound ambition. It took time, but he worked his way up through the ranks, distinguishing himself on the battlefield and in court alike. You supported him, not really understanding what drove him but pleased at the prospect of change. By the time you and he were middle-aged, he'd earned himself a position in the court of the King of France (a minor position, admittedly, but significant), and your children could look forward to entering society as nobles of standing.

It was at court that you met the mysterious lady who spoke so knowingly to you. She described your husband's vision as an experiment she conducted — but not to test him, to test *you*. She wanted to see how a woman given fresh opportunities would respond. She professed herself not entirely pleased with the outcome and felt that you needed some further incentive to change. Then she Embraced you.

Cut off as you now are from so much of life, you seek to live through the success of others. You patronize young knights and artists, offering them the financing and encouragement they need. You act as peacemaker in court disputes and sometimes even take part in hunts for bandits or heretics. You wonder just what you'll do when it becomes necessary to leave the existence you have now, when it's no longer possible to hide as a mortal. In the meantime, you hope that God looks with favor on your efforts to help others.

Concept: You're a vampire who wants nothing to do with vampire society. If someone offered you the chance to become mortal again, you'd take it at nearly any price. In the absence of such a gift, you seek to enhance the lives of others.

Roleplaying Hints: Beneath it all, you hate your condition. But you know that people don't like to be around the dour and despairing, so you make a calculated effort to be of good cheer. You try to understand what others are doing, so that you can discuss it with them knowledgeably.

Equipment: Fine clothing, handicrafts

The Ashen Knight

Name:	Nature: Autocrat	Generation: 10th
Player:	Demeanor: Caretaker	Haven:
Chronicle:	Clan: Toreador	Concept: Countess

Attributes

Physical		Social		Mental	
Strength	●●○○○○○○○	Charisma	●●●●○○○○○	Perception	●●○○○○○○○
Dexterity	●●●○○○○○○	Manipulation	●●●●○○○○○	Intelligence	●●○○○○○○○
Stamina	●●●○○○○○○	Appearance	●●○○○○○○○	Wits	●●○○○○○○○

Abilities

Talents		Skills		Knowledges	
Acting	○○○○○○○○○	Animal Ken	●○○○○○○○○	Academics	●●○○○○○○○
Alertness	●●○○○○○○○	Achery	○○○○○○○○○	Hearth Wisdom	●●○○○○○○○
Athletics	○○○○○○○○○	Crafts	●●○○○○○○○	Investigation	●●●○○○○○○
Brawl	○○○○○○○○○	Etiquette	●●○○○○○○○	Law	○○○○○○○○○
Dodge	●○○○○○○○○	Herbalism	○○○○○○○○○	Linguistics	●●○○○○○○○
Empathy	●●○○○○○○○	Melee	○○○○○○○○○	Medicine	●●○○○○○○○
Intimidation	○○○○○○○○○	Music	●●○○○○○○○	Occult	○○○○○○○○○
Larceny	○○○○○○○○○	Ride	○○○○○○○○○	Politics	○○○○○○○○○
Leadership	●○○○○○○○○	Stealth	○○○○○○○○○	Science	○○○○○○○○○
Subterfuge	●●○○○○○○○	Survival	○○○○○○○○○	Seneschal	●●○○○○○○○

Advantages

Disciplines		Backgrounds		Virtues	
Auspex	●●○○○○○○○	Allies	●●○○○○○○○	Conscience	●●●●○
Presence	●●○○○○○○○	Generation	●●○○○○○○○		
	○○○○○○○○○	Influence	●●○○○○○○○	Self-Control	●●●●○
	○○○○○○○○○	Status	●○○○○○○○○		
	○○○○○○○○○		○○○○○○○○○	Courage	●●○○○

Other Traits

Franchise	●●○○○○○○○
Chivalry	●●○○○○○○○
	○○○○○○○○○
	○○○○○○○○○
	○○○○○○○○○
	○○○○○○○○○
	○○○○○○○○○
	○○○○○○○○○
	○○○○○○○○○
	○○○○○○○○○
	○○○○○○○○○
	○○○○○○○○○

Road

Humanity

●●●●●●●●○○

Willpower

●●●●●●○○○○

□□□□□□□□□□

Blood Pool

□□□□□□□□□□

□□□□□□□□□□

Health

Bruised		□
Hurt	-1	□
Injured	-1	□
Wounded	-2	□
Mauled	-2	□
Crippled	-5	□
Incapacitated		□

Weakness

The Lost Knight

Quote: *There is nothing in the world so precious as your soul, my fellow knight. What accounting can you give of how you've used God's gift?*

Prelude: As the fifth son of a fairly poor noble, you knew from childhood that you'd be expected to enter the priesthood. It wasn't very exciting, but it would be secure employment and keep you from being a burden on your family. Manhood arrived, and off you went.

You weren't a very good priest, and you never liked it. After more than a decade of bouncing from one out-of-the-way post to another, you realized that you simply never would become an asset to the clerical hierarchy. Your heart lay with the warriors you'd grown up knowing. Your family made it clear that they wouldn't accept you back, so you faked your own death and disappeared to go errant as a man of mystery.

You donned a cowl and explained that you'd taken an oath not to reveal your face until you expiated the sins unnamed relatives had committed. It sounded plausible. From a certain point of view, it was even true. In any event, the story sufficed to let you spend 20 happy years roaming the war zones of Italy and the Byzantine frontier.

Unfortunately for you, your genuine courage and interest in learning more about the world attracted the attention of a deranged vampire hermit. He arranged for you to suffer an ambush and then Embraced you while tending your wounds. He explained cheerfully that he would use you as a sort of steed for himself, displacing your soul but retaining your knowledge so that he could have the adventures his own weaknesses made difficult.

You slew him in a moment when his attention wavered. You're sure you stopped him before he could force his soul into yours.

Nearly sure.

Concept: All you really want to do is live the chivalric existence, smiting the wicked and protecting those who cannot protect themselves. Even though the priesthood didn't work out, you love God in your own way and seek to make the world a better place. That mad vampire complicated everything. Now you don't know if God will ever regard you with favor, and you're not quite sure you can trust yourself. You compensate by renewed enthusiasm for chivalry, hoping to demonstrate to yourself your virtue through superior deeds.

Roleplaying Hints: The doubts you feel about the integrity of your soul must never show. Instead, you strive at every moment to embody courage, humility and zeal for justice. When other knights discuss what the chivalric virtues are all about, you're the one they point to.

Equipment: Armor, weapons, two books of notes taken from your sire which you somehow can't bring yourself to throw away

ASHEN KNIGHT

The Ashen Knight

Name:	Nature: Penitent	Generation: 10th
Player:	Demeanor: Judge	Haven:
Chronicle:	Clan: Cappadocian	Concept: Lost Knight

Attributes

Physical		Social		Mental	
Strength	●●●●○○○○	Charisma	●●○○○○○○	Perception	●●●○○○○○
Dexterity	●●●○○○○○	Manipulation	●●○○○○○○	Intelligence	●●○○○○○○
Stamina	●●●○○○○○	Appearance	●●○○○○○○	Wits	●●●○○○○○

Abilities

Talents		Skills		Knowledges	
Acting	○○○○○○○○	Animal Ken	●○○○○○○○	Academics	●●○○○○○○
Alertness	●●●○○○○○	Achery	●○○○○○○○	Hearth Wisdom	○○○○○○○○
Athletics	●●○○○○○○	Crafts	○○○○○○○○	Investigation	●●○○○○○○
Brawl	○○○○○○○○	Etiquette	●○○○○○○○	Law	●●○○○○○○
Dodge	●●●○○○○○	Herbalism	●●○○○○○○	Linguistics	●○○○○○○○
Empathy	○○○○○○○○	Melee	●●●○○○○○	Medicine	●●○○○○○○
Intimidation	○○○○○○○○	Music	○○○○○○○○	Occult	●●○○○○○○
Larceny	○○○○○○○○	Ride	●●●○○○○○	Politics	●●○○○○○○
Leadership	○○○○○○○○	Stealth	●●○○○○○○	Science	○○○○○○○○
Subterfuge	○○○○○○○○	Survival	○○○○○○○○	Seneschal	○○○○○○○○

Advantages

Disciplines		Backgrounds		Virtues	
Auspex	●●○○○○○○	Contacts	●●●○○○○○	Conscience	●●○○○
Fortitude	●●○○○○○○	Generation	●●○○○○○○		
	○○○○○○○○		○○○○○○○○	Self-Control	●●●●○
	○○○○○○○○		○○○○○○○○		
	○○○○○○○○		○○○○○○○○	Courage	●●●●○

Other Traits

Chivalry	●○○○○○○○
	○○○○○○○○
	○○○○○○○○
	○○○○○○○○
	○○○○○○○○
	○○○○○○○○
	○○○○○○○○
	○○○○○○○○
	○○○○○○○○
	○○○○○○○○
	○○○○○○○○
	○○○○○○○○

Road

Humanity

●●●●●●●●○○

Willpower

●●●●●●●○○○

□□□□□□□□□□

Blood Pool

□□□□□□□□□□

□□□□□□□□□□

Health

Bruised		□
Hurt	-1	□
Injured	-1	□
Wounded	-2	□
Mauled	-2	□
Crippled	-5	□
Incapacitated		□

Weakness

Warrior of the Ages

Quote: *This kingdom is a blank book in which I shall write the true history of my lineage. All kine will one day speak the story I tell them this night.*

Prelude: A hundred years ago, you rode off to help free the Holy Sepulcher. It seemed like an adventure, those years of maneuver and epic battle and dramatic enterprise. You even earned a commendation from the Duke of Normandy for your valor in one skirmish. Then the First Crusade ended, and you returned home to stagnation, struggling to make ends meet and find some way to secure a better life for yourself.

Ten years after your return, you had what seemed like a chance encounter with a count you'd met while in Tyre waiting for the ship home. He was an odd one, cursed (so he said) so that the sun would burn him. He told you the story, about how he drove out a family of witches from a lair on the road to Jerusalem and how one struck back at him before he could kill her. You didn't know what he was doing so far from his new estate in the Holy Land, but his familiar face was a welcome change of pace. At least, at first.

Then he explained what he really was and why he'd come for you. He explained to you about the Curse of Caine and about the endless struggle between lineages of vampires. You would, he said, become his secret weapon, a blade that would slowly work its way close to the heart of his enemies. At first you wanted nothing to do with it, but when he described the wonders that you'd see and do as his childe, you yielded.

He met Final Death half a century ago, one more casualty in the War of Ages, but you remain true to the agenda he presented. Through cover after cover, you've earned the respect of the mortals around you. You went from knight errant to minor fief-holder to trusted retainer. With every passing decade, you gain an understanding of the weak points in the society around you. In time, you'll be able to take a position of major power; become one of the great dukes, perhaps. Then your sire's memory will receive the honor it is due, as your clan becomes the preeminent shaper of chivalric society.

Concept: Chivalry is your path to power. You do believe in its ideals, but you give primary loyalty to your Cainite nature. You're prepared to take as many lifetimes as seems necessary to master the skills chivalric society values, so as to become indispensable.

Roleplaying Hints: You speak and move with elegance and refinement. When it's time to fight, you waste no time in flourishes, preferring to close quickly and defeat your foe at once. While not exceptionally intelligent, you carry with you a century of insight into what knights expect and want, and you give it to them. You enjoy a great deal of popularity, partly because you genuinely enjoy the people around you. It's just that you know they need your leadership more than they yet realize.

Equipment: Mail, horse, sword and shield, feudal holdings

The Ashen Knight

Name:	Nature: Autocrat	Generation: 12th
Player:	Demeanor: Defender	Haven:
Chronicle:	Clan: Ventrue	Concept: Warrior of the Ages

Attributes

Physical		Social		Mental	
Strength	●●●○○○○○	Charisma	●●○○○○○○	Perception	●●○○○○○○
Dexterity	●●●○○○○○	Manipulation	●●●●○○○○	Intelligence	●●○○○○○○
Stamina	●●●●○○○○	Appearance	●●○○○○○○	Wits	●●○○○○○○

Abilities

Talents		Skills		Knowledges	
Acting	○○○○○○○○	Animal Ken	●●○○○○○○	Academics	○○○○○○○○
Alertness	●●○○○○○○	Achery	●●○○○○○○	Hearth Wisdom	○○○○○○○○
Athletics	●●○○○○○○	Crafts	○○○○○○○○	Investigation	○○○○○○○○
Brawl	●●○○○○○○	Etiquette	●●○○○○○○	Law	○○○○○○○○
Dodge	●●○○○○○○	Herbalism	○○○○○○○○	Linguistics	●●○○○○○○
Empathy	○○○○○○○○	Melee	●●●○○○○○	Medicine	○○○○○○○○
Intimidation	○○○○○○○○	Music	○○○○○○○○	Occult	○○○○○○○○
Larceny	○○○○○○○○	Ride	●●○○○○○○	Politics	○○○○○○○○
Leadership	●○○○○○○○	Stealth	○○○○○○○○	Science	○○○○○○○○
Subterfuge	○○○○○○○○	Survival	●○○○○○○○	Seneschal	●●●○○○○○

Advantages

Disciplines		Backgrounds		Virtues	
Dominate	●●○○○○○○	Influence	●●○○○○○○	Conscience	●●●○○
Fortitude	●○○○○○○○	Resources	●●○○○○○○	Self-Control	●●●○○
Presence	●●○○○○○○	Status	●●●○○○○○	Courage	●●●●○
	○○○○○○○○		○○○○○○○○		
	○○○○○○○○		○○○○○○○○		

Other Traits

Chivalry	●○○○○○○○
Franchise	●○○○○○○○
	○○○○○○○○
	○○○○○○○○
	○○○○○○○○
	○○○○○○○○
	○○○○○○○○
	○○○○○○○○
	○○○○○○○○
	○○○○○○○○
	○○○○○○○○
	○○○○○○○○

Road

Chivalry

●●●●●●○○○○

Willpower

●●●●●●○○○○

□□□□□□□□□□

Blood Pool

□□□□□□□□□□

□□□□□□□□□□

Health

Bruised		□
Hurt	-1	□
Injured	-1	□
Wounded	-2	□
Mauled	-2	□
Crippled	-5	□
Incapacitated		□

Weakness

Knights Famous and Infamous

Fame is a dangerous proposition for a Cainite knight. On one hand, if he performs in accordance with knightly ideals — or even the demands of basic knightly existence — he will sooner or later garner victories, notable exploits and notoriety. To shun the limelight is to shun the deeds that make him a knight.

On the other hand, too great a reputation can also be quite the hindrance for a Cainite who has earned his spurs. Sooner or later, fame presses upon him demands that his cursed condition cannot allow him to fulfill, and he is left with the choice of exposing his true nature or subjecting himself to shame and disgrace. Thus, most Cainite knights tread a careful path of moderation, ever wary of the dual threats of obscurity and celebrity.

Savaric, The Knight of the Doleful Countenance

A son of the nobility of Poitiers, Savaric sought to mix his twin callings a century before the Poor Knights of the Temple were born. A noble born and bred, he nevertheless felt the call of the Church keenly. Devout beyond words, he took to mortifying his flesh with whips and rods to purge sins real and imagined, especially those committed in the pursuit of his secular duties. Still, no flagellation seemed enough to cleanse the stains he saw as besmirching the very fabric of his soul. In an agony of religious doubt, he gave himself up to despair.

There, in the blackest pit of self-loathing, he conceived a plan both sublime and monstrous. In his works for the Church, he had heard more than once of creatures called "nosferas," who were punished with devilish countenances by God for their wickedness, yet who still maintained an air of sanctity about their defiled bodies. This seemed the perfect solution to Savaric, an ultimate sacrifice of the flesh for the sake of the spirit. Thus, he sought out the Nosferatu across France, never ceasing from his quest until by dint of faith and persistence, he cornered one of that foul breed in a barn.

"Grant unto me your curse, and I shall free you. Deny me this, and I will destroy you," he said. The Nosferatu, being no fool, offered his willing victim the Curse of Caine and then bound the knight to his service through the powers of the blood. Three years he kept Savaric as his apprentice in matters vampiric, and three years he trained the knight in the ways of the blood. Compelled as he was by the power of the blood oath, Savaric was studious, but he felt keenly the absence of sanctity in his new existence. The stories, it seemed, had only been half- true. While he might indeed be cursed of God, and doubly cursed with powers that could only have come from the Devil, Savaric had gained neither enlightenment nor grace.

After three years, Savaric's sire released him, albeit with the knowledge that the knight was no longer master of his own destiny or soul. Thus it was that Savaric returned home, humbled and cursed, and bitterly ruing the choices he had made. He still serves God as best he may, with humility and devotion, but he serves his sire first.

Savaric rarely goes out in public save with his head covered. It is widely known that he wears a hair shirt beneath his mail and that he has sworn an oath not to remove his helm in the presence of any Christian until such time as the last infidel presence has been cleansed from the Holy Land. Savaric's armor is black, a sign of the disdain in which he holds himself, and his shield bears no device.

Profile

Clan: Nosferatu

Generation: 12th

Nature: Penitent

Demeanor: Penitent

Attributes: Strength 3, Dexterity 3, Stamina 3, Charisma 3, Manipulation 3, Appearance 0, Perception 4, Intelligence 3, Wits 3

Abilities: Academics 3, Alertness 3, Animal Ken 2, Brawl 2, Chivalry 2, Dodge 3, Empathy 2, Etiquette 3, Investigation 3,

Ashen Knight

Leadership 1, Linguistics 2, Melee 4, Occult 2, Ride 3, Seneschal 2, Stealth 2 , Subterfuge 3, Survival 2

Disciplines: Animalism 2, Auspex 1, Celerity 1, Fortitude 1, Obfuscate 4, Potence 4

Backgrounds: Allies 2, Contacts 2, Influence 1, Resources 2, Vassalage 3

Road: Heaven 8

Conscience: 5, **Self-Control:** 3, **Courage:** 4, **Willpower:** 7

Talbot Fitzwilliam, The Ghoul of Flanders

Young Talbot is not yet a score of years in age, yet he has already made something of a name for himself among the Cainites who haunt the lists at Flanders. It seems, according to all accounts, that Squire Fitzwilliam arrived from England some six months previous, all full of vim and vigor to see for himself the famous tourneys that Flanders offered. It seems that his ambition there, in addition to beholding some of the finest knightly spectacle, was to make a place for himself with one noble or another, so as to further himself along the road to knighthood.

With his carriage and noble bearing, he caught the eye of a dozen knights, each eager to have such a young man as his squire. But young Fitzwilliam knew that to accept the offer of one knight was to spurn and gravely insult the others, and rather than give insult, he has chosen to make his own way for the time being, praying for guidance and honoring all his would-be patrons.

Or so the story goes, if one listens to the court gossips and troubadours of Flanders. The truth is somewhat different. Fitzwilliam did indeed arrive from London, intent on making his future at the Flanders lists, and he did indeed make a remarkably seemly appearance for one of his station. Among the knights whose heads the lad turned, however, was one Guy du Berry, a bastard of that noble house dead and under the fang some three decades. Guy had been searching for just such a mortal agent as this to extend his influence in Flanders and wasted no time in binding the promising boy to him through the blood oath. He needn't have worried, however. Talbot is as ambitious as he is pleasant and no doubt would have found his way to Guy's service in any case.

Now Fitzwilliam haunts the lists doing Guy's bidding and making something of a mock-epic figure of himself. A pleasant enough fop in appearance, he is rapidly becoming a skilled and vicious courtier under his unliving master's tutelage and serves as a willing blade in du Berry's hand.

Talbot is a tall man and a slender one. His hair is brown and straight, and his eyes are clear and blue. His garb is rich, but not ostentatious, and it displays no favor toward any knight or nation. The lad never seems to have a cruel word for any, though his eye for the niceties of the lists is one of the sharpest in Flanders. Of late, many younger squires have begun flocking to him for advice and leadership, and the whole arrangement is laughingly referred to as "Talbot's Court" by the wags and wits of the area. Some of the knights whose squires prefer Fitzwilliam's company are less than pleased with this state of affairs, but it must be said that the late du Berry finds it very praiseworthy indeed.

Profile

Nature: Survivor

Demeanor: Gallant

Master: Guy du Berry

Clan Affiliation: Ventrue

Attributes: Strength 2, Dexterity 2, Stamina 2, Charisma 3, Manipulation 3, Appearance 3, Perception 3, Intelligence 2, Wits 2

Abilities: Academics 1, Alertness 2, Brawl 1, Chivalry 3, Dodge 2, Etiquette 3, Heraldry 3, Linguistics 2, Melee 3, Music 2, Politics 2, Ride 3, Seneschal 2, Subterfuge 3

Disciplines: Potence 1, Presence 1

Backgrounds: Contacts 5, Influence 3, Mentor 3, Resources 3, Retainers 1, Vassalage 2

Road: Humanity 5

Conscience: 2, **Self-Control:** 2, **Courage:** 3, **Willpower:** 4

Iulus, Immortal Sword Maker

Iulus is no knight, nor has he ever had any intention of becoming one. A relic from the hoary days of Caracalla's reign, he is a refugee from empire. He looks about himself at the Dark Medieval world and spits in disgust. None of this, he feels, can compare to the glory that was Rome. Still, in his own way, he does his best to elevate the sad state of affairs and to try to restore lost glory.

In his living days, Iulus Rufus Naso was a sword maker of no small reputation. While there were many weapon makers in the empire, most of whom had been mustered out of the legions, Iulus was able to survive by creating blades for the wealthy and privileged. His craftsmanship was impeccable and his reputation was spotless; a blade marked with Iulus' mark was considered a marvel.

Alas, then, that some of those who held Iulus' blades were of weaker stuff than their swords. "Politics" does not do justice to the murderous intrigues of Caracalla's Rome, and when a sword of Iulus' was used to murder a member of the Praetorian Guard, the swordsmith himself faced punishment rather than the murderer. After all, the logic ran, had he not created so fine a blade, the victim would have been able to fend off his attacker.

Iulus was to die in the gladiatorial arena, armed with one of his own blades. And so, armed with his craftsmanship, Iulus fought — and triumphed. He became a favorite of the crowd and of several of Rome's Cainites in particular. After a particularly valiant performance, several of them simply abducted the object of their admiration from his quarters, and one of them granted him the Curse of Caine.

It is many centuries since that fateful night, when the Toreador took a humbled swordsmith into their ranks. In those intervening years, Iulus has made a towering name for himself amongst the childer of Caine. It is he that many turn to for instruction in the arts of the sword, the trident and the spear. It is he that they turn to for blades of surpassing keenness and balance. And it is he that the very wise ones turn to when they seek the knowledge of how to survive the centuries.

So now Iulus dwells, perhaps foolishly, in his native Ostia. His forge glows from dusk until dawn, and from far and wide, the petitioners come to see him. "Make me a sword," they say, "Make me a dagger." And he honors each request in turn, taking his payment in gold, silver or blood.

Iulus has noticed the rise of this mortal chivalry and watched the evolution of the Via Equitum among his fellow Cainites with some amusement. Neonates on this road spend hours pontificating about the honor and truth in their chosen path, but when their blood boils, it's the sharpness of their blade they seem to care the most about.

Iulus is a short man, with the broad shoulders and massive arms of one who has spent a lifetime at the forge. His hair is close-cropped and white, and his nose is truly remarkable in its prominence. He dresses as a smith of the era does, so as to avoid suspicion, but every so often, the local priest comes to Iulus for some help with a particularly difficult Latin passage. Old habits, it would seem, die hard.

Tercio Bravo, Hero of the *Reconquista*

The last surviving member of El Cid's war band, Tercio is a man of faith who has not let death hinder either his sword or his convictions. The only one of the great war leader's compatriots to have been Embraced, Bravo has been an itinerant warrior for the *Reconquista* since the time of his Embrace. He has fought for one Taifa against another in hopes of weakening both, for a handful of Christian kings against the Almohads and Almoravids and, most importantly, for the Christian Cainites of Iberia against those vampires who stand for the cause of al-Andalus.

The details surrounding Bravo's Embrace are something of a mystery. He himself will not speak of them, but those who know him say that his sire is of Greek lineage, perhaps born of Athens itself. What is known is that

Elieser de Polanco, The Subtle Shadow

Elieser is the other side of Tercio Bravo's coin. Whereas Bravo is angry, aggressive and single-minded, de Polanco is quiet, dignified and subtle. A Lasombra of notable lineage, de Polanco is also a major player in the Shadow *Reconquista*. His devotion and blood are beyond reproach, his manners and talents are impeccable. And of course, he despises the low-born, ill-mannered, clumsy Bravo (for that is how de Polanco perceives Bravo) as a personification of everything about the *Reconquista* that must be forestalled. When Bravo sought to purge from Toledo all Cainites who were seen as sympathetic to the Moorish cause, it was de Polanco who intervened and demonstrated how that purge would fatally weaken the Cainite court of that noble city. Acts such as this earned de Polanco Bravo's undying enmity, and it is an enmity the Lasombra gladly returns.

Unlike his rival, Elieser is a noble born and bred, and he was raised to command man and beast. Little did he know that he was also groomed for life as one of Lasombra's childer, the latest in a long line from his family to be taken thus. Still, when the offer was made and the demonstration of how he might better serve Christendom as a monster was given, Elieser leapt at the chance.

Bravo came under the Curse of Caine two years before El Cid himself died and has since made it something of a holy crusade to carry on his warleader's work until such time as not a single Muslim draws breath — or drinks blood — on Iberian soil.

At the moment, Bravo works more among immortals than mortals. His role as advisor and general to the prince of Toledo grants him a long reach in the so-called Shadow *Reconquista*, and he uses that strength with angry abandon. Fortunately for Bravo, his master shares his near-fanaticism and beliefs and so tolerates the brazenly aggressive tack Bravo takes on the battlefield. While an excellent tactician, Bravo seems wedded to a strategy of attack, attack, attack, and this limitation does not serve him well in all cases. His record in the field over the past decade has been increasingly spotty, perhaps because his surviving enemies have gotten better at goading him into battles he cannot win. By the same token, Bravo has many foes on his own side, ones who see him as ineffective, barbaric or savage.

Tercio is average in height, with dark skin for a Cainite and a broad, honest face. He was a self-made man under El Cid, and he is a self-made Cainite now. His sword, like his garb, is plain, but the man himself has an air of power and authority that serves him well at court.

With many years and many nights, de Polanco's fanaticism has faded. He has grown to appreciate the art and music of the Moors, to marvel at what they keep in their libraries and to covet their science. On the other hand, his conscience tells him that it is unseemly for such marvels to remain in the hands of unbelievers, and so he pursues the cause of the *Reconquista* in his own dogged way. His beliefs often bring him into conflict with his putative allies, like Bravo, who are suspicious of his relatively forgiving stance, while those of his clan on the other side of the conflict see him as the worst sort of enemy. But, with infinite care, de Polanco rides out to battle as often as he may, as much to curb the excesses of his allies as to lay low his enemies.

Of course, there is another side to this noble, selfless scion of the shadows. He is keenly aware of the power the Moors' knowledge represents and has well-laid plans for putting that knowledge to use. De Polanco's ultimate ambition is no less than to rule all of Iberia from the shadows, lord of Cainite and kine alike. Others glimpse his naked thirst for power only dimly, and those who cry alarm at it — like Bravo — are dismissed as jealous or foolish. But should Elieser continue to garner praise and admiration on the battlefield and should the keeping of the great Taifa libraries fall into his hands and should no one of sufficient power recognize his ambitions before it is too late, then Elieser de Polanco could become a very powerful Cainite indeed.

A resident of Toledo, Elieser de Polanco appears older than most of his Cainite compatriots. His ringleted hair is iron-gray, and there are lines of worry and care in his face. He is still remarkably handsome, however, and while his hands may have a swordsman's calluses, his voice recalls the long-dead poets of al-Andalus.

Enguerrand, Serpent of the Family Tree

A Ventrue of several centuries' vintage, Enguerrand is the daemon riding his mortal descendants' shoulder. A Cainite for centuries, he has spent those years following two paths: seeking out bloody constraint wherever he might find it, and watching over the fortunes of his mortal family. For centuries, then, a vampiric guardian angel has stood over one mortal family, advancing its fortunes, laying low its enemies and gathering unto it riches and favor. All that he asks in return — though his wards know it not — is that that they share his joy in battle and that he taste their precious blood.

For it is upon his own descendants that Enguerrand must feed and upon them alone. He has no choice, then, but to ensure that they prosper and multiply. After all, the day his line becomes extinct, so too does Enguerrand.

Enguerrand and his scions dwell in Normandy, where they have dwelt since their illustrious ancestor's living days. Enguerrand himself has begun taking longer and longer trips away from the family seat, in part to debate with his fellow Ventrue. The trend of bringing merchants into the fold instead of warriors and nobles is one that Enguerrand likes not at all, and he takes every opportunity to argue against it with his peers. Alas for him, however, the changes are irrevocable. As Philip Augustus has changed France, so, too, have the times changed the Ventrue. Enguerrand's time has gone, though he knows it not, and all that is left to him is to try to hold back the tide of history with his sword.

A dark man with close-cropped black hair and a perpetual sneer, Enguerrand has a savage temper and a clear sense of his own superiority. The two traits often combine bloodily, and the Ventrue has had to make reparations for the loss of a favorite ghoul more than once. Still, he does not give up his position without a fight, and the best weapon in his arsenal is his mortal family. At the moment, Enguerrand is debating the risks of Embracing a number of his descendants. Should they share his weakness of the blood, he has doomed them all, but the prospect of allies in this struggle is a tempting one indeed.

Name:
Player:
Chronicle:
Nature:
Demeanor:
Clan:
Generation:
Haven:
Concept:

Attributes

Physical
Strength______●OOOOOOOO
Dexterity______●OOOOOOOO
Stamina______●OOOOOOOO

Social
Charisma______●OOOOOOOO
Manipulation__●OOOOOOOO
Appearance___●OOOOOOOO

Mental
Perception____●OOOOOOOO
Intelligence___●OOOOOOOO
Wits________●OOOOOOOO

Abilities

Talents
Acting_______OOOOOOOOO
Alertness_____OOOOOOOOO
Athletics_____OOOOOOOOO
Brawl________OOOOOOOOO
Dodge_______OOOOOOOOO
Empathy_____OOOOOOOOO
Intimidation__OOOOOOOOO
Larceny______OOOOOOOOO
Leadership____OOOOOOOOO
Subterfuge____OOOOOOOOO

Skills
Animal Ken__OOOOOOOOO
Archery_____OOOOOOOOO
Crafts______OOOOOOOOO
Etiquette____OOOOOOOOO
Herbalism___OOOOOOOOO
Melee______OOOOOOOOO
Music______OOOOOOOOO
Ride_______OOOOOOOOO
Stealth_____OOOOOOOOO
Survival____OOOOOOOOO

Knowledges
Academics_____OOOOOOOOO
Hearth Wisdom_OOOOOOOOO
Investigation___OOOOOOOOO
Law__________OOOOOOOOO
Linguistics_____OOOOOOOOO
Medicine______OOOOOOOOO
Occult________OOOOOOOOO
Politics_______OOOOOOOOO
Science_______OOOOOOOOO
Seneschal______OOOOOOOOO

Advantages

Disciplines
____________OOOOOOOOO
____________OOOOOOOOO
____________OOOOOOOOO
____________OOOOOOOOO
____________OOOOOOOOO

Backgrounds
____________OOOOOOOOO
____________OOOOOOOOO
____________OOOOOOOOO
____________OOOOOOOOO
____________OOOOOOOOO

Virtues
Conscience__________OOOOO
Self-Control________OOOOO
Courage___________OOOOO

Other Traits
Chivalry_____OOOOOOOOO
Franchise____OOOOOOOOO
Heraldry_____OOOOOOOOO
____________OOOOOOOOO
____________OOOOOOOOO
____________OOOOOOOOO
____________OOOOOOOOO
____________OOOOOOOOO
____________OOOOOOOOO
____________OOOOOOOOO
____________OOOOOOOOO
____________OOOOOOOOO

Road
____
O O O O O O O O O O

Willpower
O O O O O O O O O O
☐☐☐☐☐☐☐☐☐☐

Blood Pool
☐☐☐☐☐☐☐☐☐☐
☐☐☐☐☐☐☐☐☐☐

Health
Bruised		☐
Hurt	-1	☐
Injured	-1	☐
Wounded	-2	☐
Mauled	-2	☐
Crippled	-5	☐
Incapacitated		☐

Weakness

The Ashen Knight

Merits & Flaws

MERIT	TYPE	COST	FLAW	TYPE	BONUS

Experience

Total:

GAINED FROM:

Total Spent:

SPENT ON:

Derangements

NAME

Derangements

NAME

Combat

Weapon	Difficulty	Damage	Conceal	Range	Rate	Strength	Quality

BRAWLING TABLE

Maneuver	Accuracy	Damage
Bite	5	Strength +1
Punch	6	Strength
Grapple	6	Strength
Claw	6	Strength+2
Kick	7	Strength +1
Body Slam	7	Special; see Options

ARMOR: ____________

The Ashen Knight

Expanded Background

Allies

Mentor

Clan Prestige

Resources

Contacts

Retainers

Herd

Status

Influence

Vassalage

Possessions

Gear & Equipment

Steed

Strength:______Dexterity:______Stamina:______

Willpower:_____Health Levels:______________

Atacks:______________________________

Abilities:______________________________

Disciplines:____________________________

Blood Pool:____________________________

Distinguishing Marks:____________________

Feeding Grounds

Havens & Holdings

Location	Description

The Ashen Knight

History

Prelude

TITLE

SIGNIFICANT ACCOMPLISHMENTS

Appearance

Age

Apparent Age

Date of Birth

RIP

Hair

Eyes

Race

Nationality

Height

Weight

Sex

Visuals

Blazon

Character Sketch